# JACKPOT!

*To my friend
God bless you!*

*Rick Boyne*

*Matt 6:33*

## Rick Boyne

*Jackpot!*
ISBN: Softcover 978-1-955581-84-4
Copyright © 2022 by Rick Boyne

All rights reserved. No part of this book may be reproduced or transmitted in any form or by any means, electronic or mechanical, including photocopying, recording, or by any information storage and retrieval system, without permission in writing from the publisher.

Scripture quotations taken from the (NASB®) New American Standard Bible®, Copyright © 1995 by The Lockman Foundation. Used with permission. All rights reserved. www.lockman.org"

**Cover Credit: Brent Hale**

**Parson's Porch Books** is an imprint of Parson's Porch *&* Company (PP*&*C) in Cleveland, Tennessee. PP*&*C is an innovative organization which raises money by publishing books of noted authors, representing all genres. Its face and voice is **David Russell Tullock** (dtullock@parsonsporch.com).

Parson's Porch *&* Company *turns books into bread & milk* by sharing its profits with the poor.

www.*parsonsporch*.com

# JACKPOT!

For Audrey and Emily

Rick Boyne

# Acknowledgements

I want to thank the host of family and friends who have been a great source of encouragement. To my loving wife, Sally, who endured years of hearing about the book and continued to encourage me. To my friend, Dave Scott who graciously edited for content and grammar. To my friend, Brent Hale who created a wonderful book cover for me. And to my best friend, Martin Whipple, whose escapades with me over the past 50 years have given me enough to write 100 books! And in the end, all glory goes to my Heavenly Father.

Chapter One

# Growing Up in Oklahoma

"A simple man with simple needs." That's how I used to describe myself. My name is Owen Rigsby, and the lottery profoundly changed my life, but probably not in the way you are thinking.

Growing up in the 1980's in small town Oklahoma is simple and wonderful, for the most part. Before Wal-Mart came to town, Norton's Department Store carried anything anyone would ever need and had since the 1940's. My grandparents bought their clothes, shoes, gifts, and even some furniture there since the 1940's. Our town sported an old-fashioned band stand in the backyard of the courthouse. I heard that there used to be a concert every Saturday night, but the large white gazebo had long since fallen into disrepair.

Life revolved around church and high school football. McDonald's came to town in 1980, but Bar-B-Que was the cuisine of choice. We did have a few locally owned pizza places and several hamburger joints. Our first Sunshine Donut Shop came to town in 1970. I went to a small school with kindergarten through eighth grade under the same roof, where the principal drove a bus and coached boys' basketball. When I was in seventh grade, I was shocked to look out of the window and see two of my classmates, Randy Barnes and Scotty Henderson, smoking cigarettes in the back of the school. That was my first introduction to delinquent behavior.

Everyone thought of me as a good boy. I started going to church nine months before my birth. I knew everyone at church, and everyone knew me. I responded to Rev. Chapman at the end of church one Sunday and was baptized at eleven years of age, but never really knew God. My folks were good parents, but daddy died when I was thirteen. A drunk driver hit the church bus when he was driving the older kids to church camp.

The drunk driver was John Leroy Painter. I think it is strange how criminals come to be known by three names; it's like when you are in trouble by your mother and she hollers out the door, "Owen Robert Rigsby! You get yourself in here right now!" I'll never forget and never forgive John Leroy Painter for killing my dad. He actually got jail time for his drunk driving. Even judges and juries get mad at someone who's been convicted six times for DUI and hits a church bus full of kids, killing three. He received fifty years to life in "Big Mac," the State Correction Facility in McAlister, OK. I want him to rot in that prison and then rot in hell.

Momma did the best she could, and we never went hungry. She wanted to make sure that she raised my two sisters, Lizzy and Shelly, and me right, so we continued to go to church. I attended because it was "the right thing to do," and after all, that's what matters most in rural Oklahoma.

I muddled my way through junior high and high school. It was pretty tough going from my comfortable K – 8 school where I was a big fish in a little pond, to the city high school, where I was relatively unknown; a very small fish in, what seemed to me, a very large pond. The older kids picked on all of us from the rural school. I like to think they were jealous of us, but, in retrospect, I realize we were simply the new kids.

The city school had city kids. They weren't like us country kids. Most of us weren't farm kids, but we weren't raised "in town," either. We knew how to make our own fun. For example, my next-door neighbor, Johnny Upton, and I always took walks in the woods, looking for arrowheads. We found lots of curious rocks, but not one arrowhead. We explored every square inch of the big hill behind our rural housing addition and made-up stories about cowboys and Indians, cops and robbers, and other things that come from little boys' imaginations. The city kids were more interested in something we knew nothing about: hanging out.

When the time came for us to start driving, it finally dawned on us that we wanted to hang out, too. My best friend, Marty Westbrook, and I spent hours upon hours doing nothing down at the TG&Y parking lot. We drove our old cars up and down Main Street, with the turnarounds, like any other small town, at Sonic and another big parking lot. Some of the kids raced, but my car was too slow and couldn't compete with the other kids' newer rides.

During my sophomore year, I met Karen. She was the prettiest girl I had ever seen. Her long brunette curls framed her gorgeous green eyes that looked like a pair of twinkling emeralds. I dreamed about dating her, kissing her and spending all my time with her. I made plays for her attention, but she wasn't interested in me. She said I was a nice guy, but I wasn't taking life seriously enough. I understand now what she meant, but it just made me mad back then.

Karen faithfully attended her church and youth activities. As a high school senior, she participated in a mission trip to Southern Texas. I thought about going with the group to be close to her, but I knew we didn't have the money. To be brutally honest, I didn't understand the need to go to Texas. As I had heard many church people say, "we have plenty of poor people right here in Oklahoma." The thought of Karen always attracted me to her. She remained the girl of my dreams, even later when I enjoyed the company of other women.

I didn't go to a lot of parties in high school mostly because I didn't like being around kids that drank. The one or two parties that I did go to, someone offered me a joint. I never smoked one, but I tried to breathe in heavily whenever I was around potheads. After graduation, Travis Johnson invited me to a party out at his grandpa's farm pond. I was in the mood to stretch my wings and I did drink a little that night. Someone brought a bottle of champagne, and I took several swigs, right from the bottle. Someone's dad showed up with enough Budweiser for everyone to have one or two. I only had one. Marty and I ended up driving people home who were too drunk to make it on their own.

A carful of kids who were at the party got hit by a train that night and all five of them died. Randy Barnes, one of the smokers from seventh grade, was one of them. The sheriff said that he blamed the wreck on underage drinking. I was never really close to Randy and the others, and it surprised me that I cried the next day when I found out. Marty and I drove out by the crossing where they got hit. The repair crew was there replacing the crossing arm that the kids drove right through. Shattered glass and car pieces littered the ground, along with beer cans. Several other friends also drove by the crossing. Why is there some sort of universal need to see where people died? I wish I hadn't driven out to the crash site. It didn't do me any good and the image has haunted me for years.

The dad that had brought all the beer denied that he was to blame for their accident. The father of one of the girls that died tracked him down, beat him up and nearly killed him. Ironically, the father of the dead girl was charged with "assault with intention of bodily harm," but didn't do any jail time.

I graduated high school. Something to be proud of, I guess. At least that's what everyone wrote in their congratulations cards. I was still sharing one bathroom with my Momma and one sister. Driving a fourteen-year-old car was humiliating. All of my clothes came from Wal-Mart. I wanted something more.

I worked all through high school. Momma needed help with the bills because of some kind of trouble with dad's life insurance. She said that he had a half-million-dollar policy, but that the premium hadn't been paid for a year before his death, so we didn't get anything. Momma never worked while Daddy was alive, but she became the attendant at the dry cleaners within a month or so of his funeral. I didn't like seeing Momma stand in that drive through window taking in other people's dirty laundry. She deserved better than that.

My sister, Lizzy, was a year older than me and married some guy from the next town the day after her high school graduation. He joined the army and all of a sudden, my sister moved off to some military base in California. Momma cried and cried. She flew out to see them when my nephew was born. I was really happy to be an uncle. It made me proud, inside, somehow.

My little sister, Shelly, was a handful. She was extremely rebellious and never really did get over Daddy's death. She seemed sad. And bitter. She didn't like to talk about it. In fact, she didn't like to talk about anything. She always liked the boys a little too much and I had run-ins with several of her no-account boyfriends. It would have broken Momma's heart to know some of the things I knew about Shelly.

When Shelly was sixteen, she told Momma that she wanted to spend the night with her friend, Linda. Instead, she went to a boy's house whose parents were out of town for the weekend. Shelly got pregnant and the boy drove her to Tulsa for an abortion. Momma never found out.

My high school job was sacking groceries at Safeway. I quit about a month after graduation. The manager acted like a jerk, at least in my estimation. He made inappropriate remarks about my Momma and my sister; spending too much time in his lustful stares. He insinuated that he could make Momma happy in a way that a son doesn't want to talk about. He always scheduled me for the evening shift, even when I requested the day shift. While I was free for the summer to work full time, he would only give me part time hours. I wanted more.

On the day I quit, I had an epiphany. Although I had never planned to go to college, I realized that bagging groceries wouldn't make me rich or successful. I decided to enroll in junior college.

The admissions person said that while my high school grades lacked luster, they weren't too bad either. She asked me what I wanted to major in. No one in my family ever attended college before; I didn't even know what "major" meant. I told her "I don't know" to keep from being embarrassed and she put me down as "undecided." Come to find out, most college freshmen gave the same answer, so I didn't look so stupid after all.

Then the bottom fell out. She told me how much tuition cost. I never even thought about that! Evidently most freshmen never think about it either, because she handed me a list of places where I could beg or borrow the money for classes and books. I began to grasp that my sharing the one small bathroom with Momma and Shelly would continue, at least for a little bit longer.

It only took me two semesters to realize that I wasn't a college guy. The twenty-two-mile drive from our house to the campus took their toll on me and my wallet. I scheduled my classes too far apart and I wasted a lot of time just sitting around. It never dawned on me that I ought to study between classes. By the time I formally withdrew, I earned one "B"; the rest were "C's" and "D's" except for my beginning science elective, which I failed.

My dream of being a college graduate only lasted a short time, but I knew that I had to have the degree to make any kind of real money. I disliked being poor. Well, OK, I wasn't actually "poor," but I certainly wasn't rich either. I knew I could succeed in anything I put my mind to; at least that's what my grandmother always told me.

My grandmother, Hazel Rigsby, grew up during hard times. Her father's company laid him off from the oil patch in Oklahoma during the Great Depression. She said that they were poor, but so was everyone else, so it didn't hurt so badly. We all call my grandmother Granny. Granny always looks at the glass as half-full. She lives simply and loves extravagantly. She, without exception, is the most generous person I have ever met. There really is something different about Granny; an inner peace that always eluded me.

Granny never stopped loving me and my sisters. Even though Daddy died, it didn't diminish our relationship at all. Momma made sure of that. Granny never missed a Sunday at her church and faithfully gave her money. When she saw negative changes in me, she always told me, "Owen, God loves you and so do I." She flat out told me several times that I was headed in the wrong direction, but, well, I'm kind of hard-headed and I wanted to do what I wanted to do.

I continue to find it interesting that Granny gives so much money to her church and to charities and does without for herself. She always made a big deal out of mission offerings and food and clothing drives for the poor. She even gave money for Karen to go to Texas. She has given me a lot, too. Not necessarily money but love and support. She has always been a pillar of strength for me. She tells me she is praying for me every chance she gets.

Telling Granny that I quit college was too hard to do. So, I lied to her. I told her that I decided to put my college career on "pause" for a little while to earn some money. I blamed every failure, every downfall and every disappointment in my entire life on the lack of money. It seemed like it would work now, too. I didn't realize it then, but she saw right through my lie.

Granny was supportive but not judgmental. She told me she thought everything would work out alright. She suggested that I join the army to help me to grow up. That offended me and hurt my pride.

Rick Boyne

At nearly twenty years old, I was already grown up. I might have been angry, but I couldn't stay that way long, not at Granny. She realized that she upset me and apologized. She asked if she could pray for me to find my way. I told her "sure" expecting her to pray later. But she grabbed my arm and began to pray, "Heavenly Father, I pray for my grandson, Owen. I ask you to guide him and show him what to do. I pray that you would keep him safe from this world and let him find his peace and his satisfaction in You alone." I thanked her for praying for me. I thought it was an odd prayer, mostly because I didn't understand what she meant, but you don't question Granny! She promised to pray for me every day.

But now what?

CHAPTER TWO

# Hard Knocks

I was all out of epiphanies. In fact, I didn't know what to, so I moved out. I told Momma that I needed to go find myself. I rented an apartment in Tulsa. Did I say apartment? It was actually a converted motel room. But I could pay by the week, and I found a job at the washing machine assembly plant. Not too bad of a job, but it bored me. I just sat there all-day taking Mexican made parts out of the boxes to be assembled here in America. I could only stand ten months of that.

I happened to find a better job driving a delivery truck for a food distribution company. It paid well and I wasn't stuck in a factory all day long. I hung out there for three and half years. I found a better apartment situation and rented a one-bedroom, second-floor place on South Lewis Avenue. It beat my first-place hands down. Each individual building included a separate swimming pool and laundry room. During this time, I met Joann. We dated for a while, but she told me right up front she wasn't the marrying kind. So we enjoyed each other's carnal pleasures for a season, and then, one day, she disconnected her phone and moved away. That was a very strange time in my life. I loved the "fun," but I wanted more than just a good time.

I kept a good driving record, and the Sunshine Donut Company recruited me to deliver donut-making supplies to Southwest Missouri and Northwest Arkansas. I really liked getting out and making those drives. Most weeks, I drove nearly fifteen hundred miles. I didn't like driving in the infamous Oklahoma ice storms, though. That was about the only time that I prayed regularly.

I considered myself a pretty good man. I only drank a little and enjoyed the occasional casual fling, but I didn't take drugs and I'm proud of that. I saw how some of my friends from school messed up their lives with cocaine, heroin and crack. Adult bookstores line the highway coming in and out of Missouri. One day I decided to stop.

I never knew such debauchery existed in the world like what I saw in that shop, but I was still attracted to it. Something just took over and I spent a lot of time in there and bought several porn video. I'd watched dirty movies before, but not like these. I loved to watch them but felt so rotten afterwards. A beer or two usually helped me get over that feeling. However, as time passed, I searched out more and more dirty videos. That went on for four of the six years that I worked for the donut company.

During that time, I met a number of girls. They never seemed to want to do the kinds of things that I saw on those tapes though, and it made me realize that it was just empty fantasy. I quit cold turkey one day and never bought another tape and threw away all that I accumulated.

Sandra was my main girl and she moved in with me. I never told Granny, though. Momma, Lizzy and Shelly knew it. Momma hated that situation but all she could do was voice her disapproval. Shelly didn't care. She had been living with a number of guys off and on for a long time, ever since she dropped out of high school. Sandra understood me more than any other woman. She knew that I was restless and dissatisfied with my life. She recognized that I *needed* more.

She gave. And gave. And gave. Me- not so much. I took. After all, I needed to have, not to give. That is what finally broke Sandra and she moved out. That hurt. I thought she loved me. I think I might have loved her. But she was gone. She even took my good stereo, too.

Then Gina stole my heart, along with most of my paychecks. It didn't take me long to realize she abused drugs. Debbie moved in with me not long after Gina and I broke up. I really liked Debbie. She made me laugh. She really loved life. And booze. She died in a car crash coming home drunk from a party. No matter who I hooked up with, it never went right. They didn't have my interests in mind at all. In fact, most of them were really selfish.

At thirty years old, I was lost. Empty. Wanting more. I had lived with three women, slept with many more, but never married. I had no children and my life just seemed to be going nowhere. I didn't realize at the time how much better my life was than my younger sister's, Shelly. Momma called and said they found her dead. Her live-in boyfriend beat her and stabbed her in a drunken, drug-filled frenzy. He was passed out in the kitchen when the police arrived.

We held Shelly's funeral at Granny's church, a medium-sized congregation with another new pastor. Several years had passed since I stepped foot inside a church building; it gave me a strangely comforting, yet awkward feeling. Momma cried. A few other cousins and assorted family members tried to comfort her. Lizzy didn't come. We hadn't seen her in several years. I didn't ask Momma why she didn't even bother coming to her own sister's funeral. I was empty inside. I didn't cry, but I grieved, but somehow there were no tears.

We gathered at the family room away from the sanctuary. They told us to walk down the aisle to the front few rows of pews after everyone else had been seated. I remember the people there watching us file in. Why did it feel like they were judging me? Granny's new pastor got up and read Shelly's eulogy. It wasn't very long and certainly not very impressive. They played a tape of some country singer's rendition of *Amazing Grace*. Not bad, I guess. The preacher got up again and opened the Bible and began to read. He talked about Jesus preparing a place for us and taking us with Him.

To be honest, I wasn't listening much. I thought about Daddy and his funeral seventeen years before. I remember his dark brown casket adorned with big brass handles. He looked so strange laying there in his suit but not wearing his glasses. I miss Daddy. His death changed everything. My life echoes with thoughts of "what if?" and "if only" and "why". I can't help imagining that if he hadn't died that day, we wouldn't have to sit at my little sister's funeral. Of course I don't blame him, but I do blame John Leroy Painter.

The preacher told us all to bow our heads and he prayed for us. Momma just kept weeping. I had a sick feeling in the pit of my stomach; almost like a hole. The funeral director took the flowers off Shelly's casket and opened it up for everyone to gawk at her one last time. One last time to say what a pity it was she died so young. One last time to pass judgment on her for a wasted life. One last time to say "goodbye." People passed by and tried to comfort Momma. Some of them shook my hand, too.

After everyone paid their respects, it was the family's turn to say goodbye. I held Momma's hand as we went up to the powder blue casket. The mortician used heavy makeup to cover the bruises on her face, neck, and hands. She didn't look like my baby sister. It was surreal for me, as if it wasn't really her in that box. I placed a little memento into the casket; a key ring from Bell's Amusement Park that Shelly gave me for one birthday once when we were kids. Just then, her death became real to me.

I wanted to cry, but a couple of deep breaths kept me from it. My eyes began to water, and my nose began to run. I heard myself let out a little noise, from somewhere deep down inside. Momma held on tight and gave me a hug. I felt a hand on my shoulder. One of Granny's brothers was trying to comfort me. For the first time in a very long time, I felt a part of a family. I'm just sorry that it had to be under those circumstances.

We all loaded up in the funeral home Cadillac for the two-mile ride to the cemetery. Rigsbys from four generations would now be buried there. The ride to the cemetery was interesting, to say the least. Granny rode with Momma and me, along with Momma's younger brother, Allen, and his wife, Marge. Uncle Allen was an alcoholic and I hadn't seen him since the last family reunion I attended, some thirteen or so years before. Aunt Marge was also a lush and always made me uncomfortable. She hugged a little too tight and a little too long for a relative. It just goes to show you can't pick your family. I certainly would have left those two out.

Granny didn't say much in the limo. Momma tried chit-chatting with Uncle Allen, but it was an uneasy ride. What are you supposed to say, anyway? We arrived at the cemetery, and I realized that Shelly would be buried next to Daddy. I hadn't really thought about it, but it seemed strange. Momma bought five plots when Daddy died. At least he wouldn't be alone out here anymore.

As we stood around under the burgundy funeral home tent, Granny's preacher got up to speak. About 20 or so other people made it from the church. He read from the Bible again, and this time I paid attention. He said:

> *"But I would not have you to be ignorant, brethren, concerning them which are asleep, that ye sorrow not, even as others which have no hope. For if we believe that Jesus died and rose again, even so them also which sleep in Jesus will God bring with him. For this we say unto you by the word of the Lord, that we which are alive and remain unto the coming of the Lord shall not prevent them which are asleep. For the Lord himself shall descend from heaven with a shout, with the voice of the archangel, and with the trump of God: and the dead in Christ shall rise first: Then we which are alive and remain shall be caught up together with them in the clouds to meet the Lord in the air: and so shall we ever be with the Lord. Wherefore comfort one another with these words* (1 Thessalonians 4:13-18 KJV) *."*

Then the preacher asked a question. "If you were to die right now, would you go to Heaven?" That startled me. I didn't like the thought of ME dying. He went on to say that the only way to Heaven was to put all your trust in Jesus.

*Now hold on right there, preacher! You don't have to tell me about Jesus!* I grew up in Sunday School. I knew who Jesus was. At one time, I even had all the books of the Bible memorized, along with the twenty-third Psalm and John 3:16. He didn't have to worry about me! I knew full well who Jesus was. My grandmother was one of the finest Christian women around! I figured that even though I did some things wrong, I never killed anyone or robbed a bank. That ought to count for something! That whole graveside service shook me to my core. I hadn't thought about those spiritual things in a really long time, if at all.

We piled back into the limo and headed to Granny's church for some fried chicken, fried okra and pecan pie. One thing about Granny's church is they know how to eat! The ride back was less tense. We started talking about the old days. Granny told about the time when they brought Shelly home from the hospital for the first time. The doorbell rang and Momma opened the door to some church ladies bringing food. As they were setting the dishes on the kitchen cabinet, one of the ladies cried out. They all turned around to see me, at three years old, carrying Shelly down the hall with my little arms fully wrapped around her head. I just wanted to show off my new baby sister! Then Momma told about the time when Daddy was playing with baby Shelly in the living room, and she threw up all over his head and down his back when he held her up high. I told about the time when we went fishing at Grand Lake and Daddy accidentally dropped the whole picnic basket in the water. We all laughed. Those old stories made us feel better - feel connected.

As everyone left, Granny asked me to stay a few minutes. I dearly love my grandmother. I'd do anything for her. Except what she asked me to do next. She wanted me to come to church with her the next Sunday. I will admit, I kind of liked being in the church building again but going to church wasn't really my thing. I made some excuses, which she accepted. We hugged and she kissed me on the cheek. She told me "God loves you and so do I; don't ever forget that." I promised her I wouldn't. But I would leave that funeral a changed man.

I decided right then and there that I was wasting my life and I didn't want people to say "poor Owen" over my open casket one day. I decided that I needed to make something out of myself. I decided I needed to assert myself. I decided that I needed to make some "real" money in order to be somebody. The same old problem surfaced: I didn't know how to do it or where to begin.

# Chapter Three

# Marty's Revelation

I started playing the lottery as a truck driver. It wasn't available in Oklahoma at that time, so I bought my tickets out of state. Sherry Long, the dispatcher at the donut company, gave me about twenty bucks a week to buy her lottery tickets from Missouri. She always wanted me to go in half with her and then split our pots. I didn't go for that at all. If I won, I wanted to keep all of it. Sherry played a very specific set of numbers each time and won maybe close to a thousand dollars over the past six years or so. I played random numbers, except for one set; a combination of birthdays and the number seventeen. I always liked the number seventeen and thought it was lucky for me.

I spent about ten dollars a week and won around six hundred dollars over the past six years. Certainly nothing to get excited about. I came really close a few times, that is, my numbers were only one or two off. Seventeen wasn't drawn very much, but I wasn't going to let that bother me. Like clockwork, I pulled into the Phillips 66 truck stop just outside of Joplin. I bought my regular amount and hoped that I'd be a winner. Mr. Murray, the owner of the donut company, kept teasing me and telling me the best way to walk away with a dollar from the lottery was to put it right back into my pocket without buying a ticket. I always responded that "you can't win if you don't play". He pointed out that it had taken me three thousand dollars to win just six hundred dollars. I didn't see it that way. I saw it as my potential ticket to financial independence.

Mr. Murray was a super boss. He cared about his company and about his employees. He was a man of faith, driven not by profits, but by bringing glory to God. He held a Bible study on company time every Thursday morning at 8:00. Thankfully, my delivery route always required me to be driving by that time. He forbade alcohol at the company Christmas party, but always made it a "merry" Christmas for all of his employees, even when the company struggled through tough economic times. I never once heard him cuss at an employee. Come to mention it, I never heard him even say a bad word. He was a wealthy man, but he didn't flaunt it. Despite the fact he was a man of means, he didn't appear to put much stock in it. Generous to a fault, the profits from his donuts sponsored dozens of Little League Baseball teams and Boy Scout and Girl Scout causes. Whenever a school band needed instruments or a choir needed transportation to a contest, Mr. Murray's donuts paid the way. I respected him greatly and looked to him as a father figure. While he never meddled in my personal life, he made me feel that he genuinely cared for me.

My best friend, Marty Westbrook, and I stayed close. He married a pretty petite redhead, Tracy, and they enjoyed raising two boys. She fit the stereotype redheaded temper, but she really was a sweetheart. Marty attended college right out of high school and studied finance. He worked his way up to junior vice-president for one of the big banks in Tulsa. Out of my league, socially, but not as friends. We went fishing once in a while. On one of those fishing trips, he said, "Owen, something's happened in my life."

"Oh, yeah? Did you get another promotion?"

"No. It's bigger than that, but I feel kind of awkward telling you about it."

"Just spit it out."

"Owen, I got saved last week at church."

"Marty, you were baptized by Rev. Chapman when we were kids."

"Yeah, I know, but I just did it because you went down the week before and I was jealous. I didn't really know what I was doing."

While this made sense to me, I continued to press in on the past.

"Marty, why would you need to get saved again? Didn't the first one take?"

"I don't think you understand…all I got that first time was baptized. I didn't get saved."

I just sat there fishing, trying to understand what in the world he was talking about. He and I had both been baptized. Now, he's saying he wasn't saved? Why was he bringing this up at all?

"Why are you telling me this, Marty? Are you saying I'm not saved?"

"All I'm saying is that when I was a kid, I got baptized because my friend got baptized and I wanted to be baptized, too. I'm telling you this because I want to tell you what Jesus has done for me."

"Oh no! Are you gonna be one of those 'Jesus Freaks' now? You haven't been a bad guy. In fact, you are one of the nicest guys I know."

"Being nice doesn't get you to Heaven, Owen."

"Oh yeah? What does, then?"

"The Bible says.."

I cut him off.

"I know what the Bible says, Marty. I used to have the 23rd Psalm and John 3:16 memorized!"

"I did, too, Owen. But this is different. I've been attending church with Tracy. We go to a Bible study on Tuesday evenings. We've been looking at something they call the Roman's Road. It goes like this:

'Everybody sins and falls short of God's expectations of you.'

'Because you sin you have to die. But God can give you eternal life.'

"God shows us how much He loves us because even when we were sinners, He sent Jesus to die for us.'

'If you say out loud "Jesus is Lord" and believe in your heart that God brought him back from the dead, God will save you.' All this is found in the book of Romans."

"What? You memorized all of that?" I asked.

"Yep, I did," Marty replied.

"Why?"

"So that I can make sure I get it right when I tell people about getting saved."

"But why did you tell *me* all of that?"

"Because Tracy's pastor, my pastor, told me to tell five people that I care about and I wanted to tell you."

Frankly, I didn't know what to say. Marty memorized way more than just John 3:16. It all rang true, but I simply didn't understand all this about him recently being saved. I needed to think about this for a while. In the meantime, I thought I better change the subject before this got too uncomfortable for both of us, but just then my cork going under. I had a nice crappie on the hook; which got me off the hook, at least for now.

Marty had a pretty good little fishing boat. I had one, too, but his was a little bigger and had a bigger engine. Still, his was about 6 years old. We had been fishing many times; however this was the most awkward conversation I had ever had with my best friend. But, as men, we can ignore the elephant in the room, change subjects, and go on as if nothing else had ever been said. I thought we had successfully negotiated the change in conversation when Marty invited me to go to the Bible study with him next Tuesday. I just flat out told him that I didn't want to go.

"Bible studies aren't my thing," I said. "Maybe another time."

*Jackpot!*

I never looked up, but I could tell something was bothering him. Thankfully, he let it go and our conversation soon switched to lake levels, water temperatures and the best lure for catching bass.

I had a real knack for avoiding discussions about spiritual matters. Why do people want to keep talking about it? Can't they just shut up already? Why can't they just let people believe what they want to believe? Aren't we all going to get to Heaven eventually? I didn't understand that I was running from God. I didn't understand that I was lost in more ways than one. It was as if I had been inoculated against Christianity like a child receiving a polio vaccine. I had been exposed to it just enough to build up an immunity to God.

I honestly didn't give spiritual matters much thought. I didn't sit around thinking about Bible stories or singing little songs. I didn't even say "God bless you" when someone sneezed. I wore no crosses, but I had a Bible. It was the one that Rev. Chapman gave me when I got baptized. I don't think I had opened it since then, but I found it when I got back home from fishing and began to think about some of the stuff Marty had told me. I opened the Bible to see if I could find some of those verses he quoted. I remembered they were in Romans, but I couldn't find them. I looked in the back and found the maps, then remembered that the table of contents was in the front. I turned to the book of Romans and read a little, but I didn't find the verses he told me about. I did find a couple that seemed to slap me in the face. They were Romans 14:7-8, "For not one of us lives for himself and not one dies for himself; for if we live, we live for the Lord, or if we die, we die for the Lord; therefore whether we live or die, we are the Lord's."

As I sat in my comfortable recliner in my apartment living room, I thought about that for a moment. I finally came to the conclusion that, no, I was actually living for myself and if I died, it would be for me. The Bible was wrong about this.

So, I decided to look up John 3:16. I was able to find it without consulting the table of contents, mainly because I remember that the first books of the New Testament were Matthew, Mark, Luke and John. I read those familiar, but long forgotten words again. They were comforting and troubling at the same time. I consoled myself with "I believe Jesus existed." There! I believe in Jesus! What more could they want?

I was about to look up the 23rd Psalm when the phone rang. It was Sherry Long, the dispatcher at Sunshine Donuts.

"Is it really true? Please tell me you played your numbers!" she shouted.

"What are you talking about?"

Rick Boyne

"Owen! Your lottery numbers! Did you play the same numbers this week?"

"Yes, I bought the tickets. I played my regular set plus four other sets. Why?"

"Owen. I think you just won the jackpot!"

## Chapter Four

# Jackpot!

I had been so busy looking up those silly Bible verses that I completely forgot to watch the Lottery drawing. I slammed the phone down on Sherry and called the Phillips 66 station in Joplin, as I had done many times before, to find out the winning numbers. I repeated them back to the clerk as she read off 2-11-17-23-24-31 and Lucky Number 5.

I couldn't believe it! I think I just won the Lottery! I cautiously asked her what the jackpot was. I nearly passed out when she said, "One hundred, forty-two million dollars." I threw the phone down and shouted so loud I thought my neighbors might call the police!

"I'm a millionaire! I'm a millionaire!" I kept shouting to myself. I was so overwhelmed I had no idea what to do, or even what I did do for a short time. The very first thing I did was call Momma.

"Momma?"

"Owen, is that you?"

"Momma, are you sitting down?"

"Why, Owen? Is something wrong?"

"Yes, Momma. I mean no. Not at all. Nothing is wrong. In fact, everything is going to be right from today on. Momma, I think I just won the jackpot in the lottery. Momma, I think I just won one hundred and forty-two million dollars!"

"Oh Owen! Don't kid me like this!"

"Momma, I'm not kidding. I've never been so serious in my whole life! You can quit that job of yours. I'm gonna take care of you. I won't have you taking in dirty laundry anymore. You are now the mother of America's newest millionaire!"

"Owen, tell me you're just pulling my leg!"

"No Momma. It's the truth! I'm richer than I ever imagined!"

I didn't have to look up what to do to claim the money. I had been dreaming of this day for years! I just didn't expect it to actually arrive. As I hung up the phone with my mother, emotions overwhelmed me. First and foremost, I thought of Daddy. I always thought of my father when I got emotional about anything. I thought of Shelly. Then, I started to think about me and what the money could buy. What was I going to buy first? A new car? A new truck? A new boat? A new house? Why not all of these things? I can now afford to buy anything and everything I ever wanted! WOW! This was going to be great!

I contacted the lottery people and made arrangements to collect my prize. This was my first time to fly on an airplane and they flew me there first class. I hadn't ever travelled anywhere special before. When I was young, we went to Texas a few times and made trips to Branson, Missouri, and Eureka Springs, Arkansas, but that was just about the extent of my travels. I had a feeling that was about to change, too.

A stretch limo met me at John F. Kennedy International Airport. It wasn't like the funeral home limos that I had been in before. These had the regular back seat, then one long bench seat that went the length of the limo and curved around the front. It had a television and a bar. I noticed that the bar was stocked, so I fixed myself a little drink to enjoy while driving into Manhattan. As I sat in that limo all by myself, I marveled at the sights of New York City. The buildings were so tall. So many people out walking around. Where did they all come from and where were they going? I had seen it on TV and in magazines, but I had no idea how BIG New York really was. And now, I could buy anything I wanted in that big, beautiful city.

The limo took me to the Plaza Hotel, which they say is one of the finest, if not THE finest hotel in New York City. I could get used to this kind of luxury. Nothing but the best for Owen Rigsby from now on! The finest hotels. The fastest cars. And the prettiest women!

I ate dinner at Tavern on the Green, some fancy place that I had never heard of before then. All the people at the hotel told me it was one of the best restaurants in New York. If it was the finest, then it was good enough for me. My dinner and drinks came to over $270. Evidently, I have good taste in champagne and didn't know it! I must say that it was the best steak I had ever had in my whole life. I'll be spending the rest of my life trying to outdo this first night as a millionaire.

Technically, I wasn't a millionaire yet. The award ceremony would take place the next morning at 10 at the national lottery headquarters on Park Avenue. The limo arrived promptly at 8:30 A.M. and I nervously left my hotel room for the last time as a poor man. Never again would I want for anything. Finally, I had all I ever wanted, all I ever dreamed. Today would be the day that changed my life forever.

The ceremony wasn't nearly as big as I thought it would be. Oh, there were cameras and champagne and that huge, oversized check for the photo-ops. But all in all, it was almost a disappointment, except for the fact that I took home nearly eighty million dollars. I chose a lump sum amount. The missing sixty-two million dollars went to Uncle Sam. I don't understand why lottery winners have to pay taxes, but I'll take what I can get.

After all the photos were taken and the two reporters asked me the obligatory questions of what I plan to do with the money, I was ready to get out of there and have some FUN! I was just about to leave, after all the paperwork had been completed and they wired my money to Marty's bank, when I heard someone say, "Mr. Rigsby, may I have a word with you?"

No one ever calls me "Mr. Rigsby." Even the lottery people called me Owen. That was OK because that's my name. This man, however, indicated that he had something very pressing to talk with me about and asked if he could ride back to the hotel with me in my limo. Well, I thought that sounded rather devious, so I told him "no." He very quickly whispered that he represented the Las Vegas Peninsula Hotel and Casino Resort. He said that he was prepared to offer me a line of credit in the amount of one million dollars and he promised me that I would "want for nothing." I figured I owed myself a little vacation, so I decided to let him ride back with me to the Plaza.

Once in the limo, he told me that they had a special program for lottery winners, such as myself, and that they would treat me with every courtesy afforded the big rollers. He said they would give me a VIP luxury suite with a valet, exclusive use of a limousine and private gaming rooms, if I so desired; all complimentary, of course. He said they would even fly me to Las Vegas on a private jet, reserved exclusively for big rollers. It sounded too good to be true and I told him as much. He pulled out a letter from Richard Cole, the president and CEO of Peninsula Resorts verifying everything he had just said.

I told him that I'd like to think about it and that I needed to go back to Tulsa before I did anything and take care of a few things for my mother. He assured me that I could take all the time I wanted. He handed me his card. I chuckled to myself when I realized his name was "Vince." He already looked like a mobster; now he even sounded like one.

After arriving back in Tulsa, I went to see Momma and tell her about all that had happened in New York. I had insisted she come with me, but she was afraid to fly. I asked if I could take her out to lunch. It was a con for my real plan. We did go out to lunch. It wasn't anything fancy, but it wasn't the type of place that we were used to eating. It was actually a lot of fun. Then, after lunch, I said, "Momma, I think it's time you had a new car."

"What? Oh Owen. Now don't go spending a lot of money on me. It's your money. You won it; you spend it on yourself!"

"Don't worry about me, Momma. I've got plenty to spend on myself. I want to make sure you have everything you need, too."

With that, I pulled into Tulsa Cadillac with the intention of buying my Momma the most expensive model they had. The news about my winning the lottery made it to the Tulsa news and in the paper, too. Everyone in Oklahoma knew the name Owen Rigsby. The salesman couldn't contain a huge grin when we all introduced ourselves.

"Excuse me, sir" he started. "Are you the Owen Rigsby that recently won the Lottery?"

"One and the same," I said. "I'd like to buy my mother a Cadillac."

They had a nice selection from which to choose, and Momma decided she wanted a blue one. This car was incredible! It had electronic everything and even heated seats! The salesman told me the front windshield was heated. Just because I had won the lottery, I wasn't going to pay too much for a new car. We dickered over the price for a while then settled on something we could both live with. I thought the salesman was going to faint when I pulled the sixty-four thousand dollars out of my backpack in one-hundred-dollar bills. I had already been by Marty's bank and made a little withdrawal. I had one hundred and twenty-five thousand dollars in cash in my backpack. I didn't have any idea how much a new Cadillac would be, but I wanted to make sure I had the cash to buy one for Momma. I figured I'd buy myself a new car when I got back from Vegas. However, I needed to go see my boss, Mr. Murray, first.

Mr. Murray appeared genuinely happy to see me when I walked in his office. Before I could say anything, he said, "Well, my boy, I guess this is it!" That really took me by surprise and kind of disarmed me. I wasn't planning to go into his office and tell him to take that job and shove it, but I planned out what I wanted to say. I ended up saying, "Yea, I don't really need to work anymore."

"Nonsense," he said. "Everyone needs to work somewhere. You'd get bored otherwise".

"That may well be," I said, "but I'd like to find out on my own."

"Owen, would you mind if I gave you a little free advice?"

"Sure, Mr. Murray. You've always been very nice to me. You've treated me like family. I just wanted you to know that I appreciate that about you."

"Well, thank you, Owen. That really means a lot to me."

He continued, "I just want to warn you about your money. Don't let it become your master and you its slave. Money can corrupt a person just as quickly as power. And you have a lot of money; be sure to put it to good use. After all, you can't take it with you. You are going to have everyone and their dog asking for you to give them money. You are now a very wealthy man. Most will be trying to swindle it out of you by hook or crook. Just be on guard. Don't let this wealth make you a poor man."

"Thanks, Mr. Murray. I intend to enjoy this money. I've been living the life of a church mouse for so long that I want to live it up before I'm too old to do anything. In fact, I'm leaving for Las Vegas the day after tomorrow. The Peninsula Hotel has arranged to take very good care of me for several days. I intend to let them."

"Owen. You have millions of dollars. Why would you want to go to Las Vegas to gamble it away? It sounds like they are trying to take advantage of you."

"No way, Mr. Murray. They are going to fly me out in a private jet and give me a big VIP suite. They are even giving me a million-dollar line of credit. That's like they are giving me a million dollars, don't you see?"

"Just be sure to remember that the odds are always stacked in favor of the house. They aren't doing this to be nice to you; they are doing it to make money."

"In any case, I'm headed out to Vegas to have some fun. I really do appreciate you giving me a job for these past several years. I enjoyed working for you."

"God bless you, Owen. I'll continue to pray for you."

"OK, you too, Mr. Murray," I said, whatever that was supposed to mean.

CHAPTER FIVE

# Travel Arrangements

Vince asked that I give him four hours' notice for the private jet to Vegas. No problem. I wasn't in any hurry to do anything but have some fun. I gave the rest of the money in the backpack to Momma. I told her to go quit her job and buy some new clothes. I told her that when I got back from Vegas, I'd buy her a new house, too. She protested, but I could see that she was very excited about the prospect of having a ridiculously wealthy son.

Since beginning to work for Mr. Murray, I'd improved my personal economic position greatly, compared to where I was when I first moved out of my mother's house and into that motel apartment. I lived in a comfortable two-bedroom apartment on South Memorial Drive, not too far from Hooters. I enjoyed the feeling of being in a better kind of place than an ordinary bar. The girls were super-friendly and super-beautiful; I'll bet they'll have something to do with me now that I'm filthy rich!

I drove my truck out to the private part of Tulsa International Airport. Vince said they would arrive at hangar J-7 to pick me up. This was certainly not the fancy part of the airport! Barbed wire fencing and electronic gates served as the security. A disembodied voice on the other end of a speaker buzzed me into the secure area. I parked my truck in the passenger parking area of hangar J-7 and went in to look for the waiting lounge, as I was about an hour early. Hangar J-7, and apparently all of the hangars in the private section of the airport were actually working airplane hangars! Each one had an office with a waiting room of sorts attached. The furniture in this waiting room looked like it was there back in the heydays of Tulsa aviation, when Tulsa had more flights than London or Paris. There were no food or drinks provided or offered. It looked as if the waiting room was there for just that: waiting.

While waiting for my private jet, I reflected on my current, well, previous situation. I was making payments on a new truck. I guess I could pay it off when I got back from my celebration vacation in Las Vegas. I was making payments on some decent furniture, too. No more payments of any kind for Owen Rigsby! I could pay cash for everything from now on. Sunshine Donuts had a 401-K plan for its employees, and I contributed little since working there. I don't suppose retirement is something very many people take seriously before they're beginning to think about it, but it sure didn't look like I'd ever have to worry about it. In a manner of speaking, I could consider myself "retired" right now!

About 30 minutes before I expected the private jet to arrive, a pleasantly plump woman emerged from the hangar office. "Mr. Rigsby?" she said, expecting it to be me. "Your plane is about 10 or 15 minutes away. It will pull up to the hangar where you may board. Would you mind leaving your car keys with us so that we could move your vehicle in case of an emergency?" I took the Ford key off my key ring and handed it to her. "I have your contact information in Las Vegas if there is a problem."

Reality was beginning to blur again. People were offering to take care of me. People knew where I could be contacted. People were being nice to me. Or were they simply being nice to the money? By the time I thought of that, I saw the beautiful private jet taxiing toward the hangar.

My only experience with private jets is what I'd seen on TV and in the movies. I specifically remember the jet in the movie *Goldfinger*, where James Bond sprays shaving cream on the mirror to keep from being watched. I suppose that's what I expected when the jet pulled up. The door opened and the little ladder/steps where unfolded. Just like the movie. A man in a uniform emerged and introduced himself as the pilot. He asked to stow my luggage. It was just then that I realized that I hadn't packed a thing! I didn't bring so much as a toothbrush, and I was headed out to Las Vegas for an extended stay. It wasn't as if I couldn't afford to buy whatever I wanted and I decided that I'd do a little shopping out there, since I needed to anyway.

As I boarded the plane, I noticed how small the cabin was. It held six very nice leather chairs, a small table, and a couch-like bench in the rear. It was absolutely beautiful, but it was so small! It looked like real wood paneling throughout the cabin. There were no overhead bins like a commercial airplane, but a big screen TV hung at the front of the plane. I also noticed that there was a small galley and toilet just behind the cockpit. However, the most striking object in the entire plane was the stewardess. She introduced herself as Cindi, with two "i's."

I remember Vince asking if I'd be traveling alone. I told him that I was between girlfriends, and I wanted to spend this time on myself. Cindi seemed to be there to make sure I was completely comfortable and that I didn't get lonely. Once we were airborne, she offered to make me a drink. I vaguely remember asking for some drink or another. As she brought it to me, she put her hand on my arm and sat down next to me. She began to rub my arm, then touch my chest. I cannot exactly say that I was turned off by the advances of this stunningly beautiful woman. She took my hand and led me to the rear of the plane where she pushed a button which turned the little couch-like bench into a bed. This trip began better than I ever could've imagined!

By the time we landed at McCarran International, we made ourselves respectable again, that is, fully dressed. Cindi asked me if I would like for her to accompany me for my stay in Las Vegas. As I stammered around with an answer, she handed me her card and said that she was available to me anytime, day or night, that all I needed to do was call. She kissed me passionately on the lips and gave me a look that could have melted solid rock.

The captain opened the door and Vince appeared on board. He was all smiles and asked me how I enjoyed my flight. My smile was enough to tell him that I liked what he arranged. He asked me to sit down at the table in the rear of the aircraft so that we could take care of a little bit of paperwork before we continued the fun. He explained the offer of the million-dollar line of credit and that it had to be reconciled before I returned to Tulsa. He made me sign a document to that effect and handed me a copy. He explained that all of the expenses related to my hotel stay were complimentary. I could order as much room service, liquor, limos, laundry and meals as I wanted and there wouldn't be a charge for them. He also indicated, to my disbelief, that he would provide a "companion" for me while in Vegas. He said that I could call him at any time to change companions, but if I wanted the company of more than one woman at a time, I'd need to make sure that I "tipped" appropriately, to the tune of one thousand dollars per day. We finished a few other little details and went out to get in my limo.

As we descended the ladder, Vince could tell he made the wrong choice of limos. Waiting before me was a 30 passenger Hummer limousine.

"Is everything all right, Mr. Rigsby? You look disappointed."

"Well, Vince, to be perfectly honest, this doesn't look like the limo of a multi-millionaire. It looks like something from a redneck wedding back in Tulsa."

"No problem, sir." Vince quickly replied. "I can have a different one here in ten minutes or less. He made a quick phone call and within eight minutes, an elegant 1950's Daimler arrived to collect me. "This is more like it," I said to no one in particular.

CHAPTER 6

# Vince

Vince didn't care about Owen or any other of his clients. Vince was only concerned about himself.

He had worked in Las Vegas for the past 16 years, the first three, rising from a blackjack dealer to pit boss, which is unheard of, even in Vegas. Born in Detroit to a drug-addicted prostitute, he never had a chance to turn out good.

His mother, at least the woman who gave birth to him, abandoned him in a trash can behind the bar where he was born. He was found by a garbage collector an hour later and rushed to the county hospital.

He was in and out of foster care, abused by some of those who were charged with his care, and by some of the older children in the same homes. He ran away when he was 13 years old to a life even more dangerous and frightening than foster care.

Having been sexually abused as a child, it comes as no surprise that he has been promiscuous throughout his life.

One of the many negative defining moments in his life came when he saw how gullible people were easily conned out of their money. He was surprised and delighted to find so many naive people. His malevolent nature was encouraged when he discovered that greed accentuated this gullibility.

He spent most of his teen-aged years growing up on the streets of Detroit. He became an expert at petty larceny and never got caught. At one point, he had squirreled away nearly a thousand dollars, but someone must have seen him hide it or simply stumbled upon it, because one day, he discovered it missing.

He knew he had to make a change, so he hitch-hiked to St. Louis. There, just shy of his 18th birthday, he became a courier for a drug dealer. His capacity to understand money and the greed behind it allowed him to move from courier to dealer to distributor by the time he was 20. That came to an end when a group of men from a gang came to his house to put an end to the competition. If not for the surveillance cameras and other security measures he owned, he would not have made it out alive.

Six men with automatic weapons arrived at two in the morning. The motion sensors activated an internal alarm. Vince barely made it into his secret safe room when the men burst in, guns blazing. For an hour and a half, he watched them on closed circuit TV from his private sanctuary as they ransacked the house. They finally left after finding his safe with just over a million dollars in it and nearly as much in cocaine. They set the house on fire and sped away. Vince escaped with minor burns and minimal smoke inhalation. He decided that while the money was good, the stakes were too high.

The gunmen took everything from him that night. He was broke. He had $320 to his name. While he knew how to make the money, he didn't have the smarts to hold on to it. He now had experience; it was an expensive lesson.

The rival distributor, who had ordered the gang to kill him, wouldn't be satisfied until they brought back proof that Vince was dead. Fearing for his life, he left St. Louis in a hurry. The gunmen destroyed his Escalade in their rampage. He found himself at the bus station, so he bought a ticket to Cincinnati. He could start over there.

He came upon what can only be described as a "flop house" on Reading Road, not too far from the Greyhound Depot. He checked in for $25 per week. The bed bugs ate him alive the first night.

Next door to the flop house was a mission for transients. He didn't consider himself to be a transient, but he needed to get established and get an angle. While having lunch at the mission, Reverend Wilbur Cooper arrived.

Rev. Cooper was a traveling charlatan; a "faith-healer" who was more concerned with his saving account than saving souls. He preached a message of something or other but got Vince's attention when he said he needed some assistance at the healing crusade he was conducting that week. Vince approached Rev. Cooper and talked him into giving him a job. Constantly amazed at the number of people flocking to the Rev. Cooper for healing, he assisted the "ministry" by catching people as they fell down after being overcome by their emotional experience. Rev. Cooper called it being "healed," or "slain in the spirit." More than once, he saw supernatural things take place, but it was unholy supernatural activity; not the kind from Heaven.

One woman, who wanted to be healed, fell backwards into Vince's arms when Rev. Cooper touched her on the forehead. As he gently brought her down to the floor, she opened her eyes and looked straight at Vince and said in a deep, growling voice, "the kingdom of darkness is with you."

Another time, a cohort in the show, while pretending to be healed and praising God for it, had a massive stroke or heart attack and died on the spot. And many, many times, he watched Rev. Cooper's Bible slam shut while it was lying on the pulpit, with no one around. It was some really spooky stuff.

Never once did he ever see anyone get healed. In fact, he often played the part of someone coming for healing. He pretended to have cancer, or to be lame or blind. He would be helped onto the stage, usually as one of the first people to come forward and pretend to be healed. Rev. Cooper explained that sometimes people needed to be persuaded to step out in faith. Vince was amazed to see that Rev. Cooper never exposed his real self to his staff. He always presented himself as a true healer. More than once, many times in fact, Vince saw Rev. Cooper having sex with some young woman from the crowd. He realized Rev. Cooper was maintaining the illusion of being a man of God while really caring only for himself. This appealed to his corruption.

He decided that if it was good enough for the reverend, it was good enough for him. Not one night went by without Vince picking out a young woman, or sometimes a young man, from the audience to satisfy his voracious sexual appetite. He would pre-select them during the show and usually make some sort of intentional advance towards them during the healing time. He favorite line was "God has chosen you." Sometimes, someone other than his target would approach him. Either way was fine with him. All he wanted was sex; he didn't care how he got it.

He watched and learned from Rev. Cooper for a season but was uncomfortable in the "religious" environment. He knew there were bigger fish in the sea. He left the itinerate ministry while they were in South Florida, fleeing the small towns ripe with the geriatric faithful.

Vince learned that greed and sex are powerful forces in peoples' nature. He was a deviously intelligent young man, but had to learn from experience, as he didn't have much common sense.

In South Florida, Vince found his niche as a male escort to older rich women. He didn't have movie-star good looks, but he wasn't ugly, either. He learned that many older women were prime targets for financial exploitation by sexual means. Generally, younger men pay no attention to older women and older women begin feeling unattractive, generally in midlife. Vince was a smooth talker and word spread among the lonely, rich women that a man in his early thirties could make them feel young and pretty again. They were willing to pay any price for living out this lie.

This suited Vince fine. He had money, a nice place to live, a nice car to drive and all the sex he wanted. Some women would take him on cruises, where he wouldn't limit his sexual activity to his mark, but work the lounges, shops and top deck, sometimes having up to 8 different partners per day. He was a sex machine.

He was also a regular customer at the South Biscayne Health Clinic. There is no way of telling how many senior citizens suffered from syphilis because of Vince. He has no idea how many children he has fathered. He has no idea of how many lives he has ruined. He doesn't care to know; it wouldn't bother him, anyway.

Vince was practically dead on the inside, devoid of all good emotion. He felt lust, greed and hate. He repressed his bitterness years before because it got in the way of the greed. All he cared about was his next sexual encounter and the next dollar.

He was good at feigning emotion; most good con men are. He could look a 50, 60, or even 75-year-old woman right in the eyes and tell her he loved her. They always believed him. They would shower him with money, gifts and other favors.

As a teenager on the streets of Detroit, he was often drunk or high. It was a good escape from the living hell of his life. Once he started conning people, he laid off the drugs; no one trusts a junkie. As an adult, he had an incredible capacity and tolerance for alcohol. This worked to his advantage. More than once, concerned adult children of his senior citizen harem tried to get him drunk to get him out of their mothers' homes. It never happened.

He had only been arrested twice, but never convicted. The elderly women were reluctant to press charges because of the publicity and negative attention it would ultimately bring them.

Vince didn't buy property or invest in stocks or mutual funds. He kept cash and spent it on himself. He wore only expensive Italian shoes and clothes, and preferred Swiss watches. He rented a ridiculously overpriced condo with a view of the ocean. He leased his furniture. His kitchen had brand new dishes and utensils, but they had never been used. He never ate at home. He only drank there, usually very expensive scotch.

He never took time for self-examination. He wouldn't have been bothered by what he saw, anyway. When he wasn't having sex, he was watching it on video. The only downside to his clients of being a gigolo was insisting that the encounter include porn. The women tolerated it because they were getting the attention they desired.

He changed coastal communities several times, milking as many old women of their fortunes as he could. He often traveled with his marks, escorting them to Broadway shows in New York City, vacations to Atlantic City, cruises to the Caribbean and Hawaii and twice, to Europe. The women would give him huge sums of money in advance so he could pay for everything. It aided their delusion of an authentic relationship rather than a business arrangement.

A few times he played gigolo to some elderly men, but they weren't nearly as generous as the women, so he limited those occasions to times when he thought he would be able to pull off a huge bounty. The homosexual aspect didn't bother him. He had long since blocked out the abuse from a foster father and foster brothers. Not to mention the male case worker who raped him after "rescuing" him from an abusive foster home environment. His sense of right and wrong had been skewed at an early age.

A 68-year-old woman, Mary Jacobsohn, originally from New Jersey, but who had moved to South Florida when she was widowed at 63, asked Vince to accompany her to Las Vegas. He had traveled many places, but this was his first trip to Sin City.

Mary wanted to see the shows, the sights and gamble a little bit. Vince had escorted her several times and she was enamored with his charms. After checking in at Caesar's Palace, she handed him an envelope with $40,000 to take care of her. She excused herself to powder her nose and that was the last she ever saw of Vince.

Vince took her money in a taxi to a small motel on the outskirts of town. He waited there a full two weeks before venturing back to the Strip. He simply abandoned everything he owned back in Florida. It was mainly clothes anyway. He dreamed of relocating to Las Vegas, the city of greed and sex.

He took a while to study the city, the hotels and the clientele. He decided rather than rush headlong into some scam, he'd get a job in a casino to be able to learn how things work there. He went to a school to become a dealer and was quickly certified. He was hired at the Flamingo Hilton where worked the morning shift. He gained the favor of management and was moved to the graveyard shift, where the real action takes place. He exposed a skimming racket that was going on by other dealers and received a reward from the president of the company.

The whole while, unknown to the casino, he was also skimming to the tune of several hundred dollars a day. His charismatic personality endeared him to waitresses and guests, and he was never without a sexual partner. His natural ability with money and people won him the distinction of being one of the youngest pit bosses in the Flamingo's history. For him, it was just a step toward more money.

He worked as a successful pit boss for three years when he jumped on the opportunity to become a whale hunter. Talk about big fish! The whale hunter finds a potential gambler with lots of money and much less sense. He convinces him to come to the hotel where he is working and arranges all kinds of things, from prostitutes to show tickets, and gets a piece of the casino's action. If he is good enough, he is even able to talk the mark into a rather large tip.

His first whale, a state senator from the East Coast, was hauled in by sheer luck. Vince was in the lobby of another casino and the senator asked him about finding some female companionship. They started talking and Vince took care of everything. The senator wanted complete anonymity and some really kinky sex. Vince delivered. The senator was satisfied sexually and relieved of $250,000. Vince was rewarded with a tip of $2,000. The senator spoke to Richard Cole, the owner of the hotel to complement him on Vince. He had no idea who Vince was and asked hotel security to find him.

Vince relished the opportunity to talk with Cole and tell him about what he did for his Casino, the Peninsula. Cole saw something special in Vince and hired him on the spot. He told him if he had been working for his hotel when he hauled in the senator, his cut would have been $12,000. Vince was excited at the prospect of big money.

Cole started calling Vince "Captain Ahab" because of his relentless pursuit of whales. Vince had the idea to go after lottery winners. They tried it several times but didn't have much luck getting to them after they returned to their homes. Usually, they were already inundated with charity requests, relatives and other people wanting some of their money. Cole suggested that he try to be the very first one to approach them, before the relatives came out of the woodwork looking for handouts.

Vince had a few false starts and near misses, but finally landed his first lottery winner, a certain Billy Howard from Wausau, Wisconsin. He won $66 million dollars. Vince, and Billy's own greed, convinced him to part with four hundred thousand dollars in just over a week. Billy was married and brought his wife along. Unknown to her, Vince arranged for two different prostitutes for Billy while they were there that week.

Vince and Cole had it down to a science. Vince would fly to New York City to be at the presentation ceremony and would approach the potential whale before they got back into the limo. More often than not, the offer of a free vacation with a million-dollar line of credit usually did the trick.

There were few complaints. The goal was to keep the booze and sex flowing toward the whale and the money flowing out. They would act as if they weren't intruding or making the whale do anything they didn't want to do, but they were under constant surveillance and continual urging toward high stakes gambling.

One man complained that the prostitute Vince arranged wouldn't do certain sex acts. He apologized for the inconvenience and arranged another woman. He took the reluctant prostitute to his own room and started by slapping her almost unconscious. He brutally raped her, forcing her to repeat the act she had previously refused, over and over. He beat her and continued to rape her for several hours. When he was finished, he kicked her out of his room as if nothing happened.

After that, he never secured another prostitute without first checking her out himself. He made them start with the most deviant acts. If they were unwilling to do it, he wouldn't use them for his whales. He and Cole decided to start calling the women "companions" for the sake of discretion.

For Vince, it was a dream job. Sex and money, with no end in sight. Vince was good at what he did. He used the skills he developed as a conman to persuade new lottery winners to part with some of their winnings. It was a lucrative arrangement for the hotel and for Vince.

CHAPTER SEVEN

# VIP Treatment

My first trip to Las Vegas turned out to be more than I could have ever imagined. Sex with a stewardess on a plane and now a ride in the most luxurious automobile I had ever seen in my life! As I sat in the back of this old beauty, looking at the desert giving way to the artificial glitter that is Las Vegas, strange emotions suddenly filled my heart and head. Oh! How I'd love Daddy to be here to see me like this. At the same time, I was a little embarrassed by my escapades on the airplane with a perfect stranger. As thoughts like these kept creeping into my consciousness, I kept drinking. I can't remember when I finally realized that Vince was playing the role of a pimp by getting me the girls that week.

Limos, Ferraris, Mercedes, Jaguars, Cadillacs, Rolls Royces and other exotic and luxury makes, and models of all descriptions lined the avenues of Las Vegas. People of all sorts walked along "the strip." We passed the Bellagio, Caesar's Palace, the MGM Grand and all of the other famous and infamous casinos. While New York City was impressive with enormity, Las Vegas seemed to twinkle, even in the daylight! About 4:00 P.M. we pulled into the grand entrance of the Peninsula Hotel. The doorman's outfit resembled a British Beefeater's uniform. "Mr. Rigsby! We've been expecting you!" he said as he opened my door. "Welcome to the Peninsula Hotel and Casino Resort!" "Impressive," I said to myself.

The driver or Vince must have called ahead because no one asked to gather my luggage. Vince and I already took care of hotel check-in in the back of the plane. I had my key, and since I really needed to go to the bathroom, I asked to see my room. As we entered the main entryway, a cacophony of slot machine bells, chimes, musical tones and other sounds assaulted my ears. It was bright and it was loud! In the middle of the afternoon, people milled everywhere! They lined up at the roulette tables, the crap tables and the blackjack tables. Even the Keno parlor was nearly full! There seemed to be an air of excitement; electricity filled the room.

Vince had explained that my room key was my access to everything in the hotel. He showed me the bank of elevators with exclusive access to the VIP suites. The elevator doors slid open once I inserted my room card into the slot. Once inside, I re-inserted my room card and it identified me on a little TV screen as Rigsby, Owen R., Suite 3749. The elevator voice said, "Have a nice afternoon, Mr. Rigsby."

*Jackpot!*

Vince accompanied me to my room and waited while I used the restroom. Upon rejoining Vince, he showed me the amenities of the suite and introduced me to Karl, the valet. Karl was a mousy looking guy, and, judging by his accent, from somewhere in Eastern Europe. Vince assured me that Karl would look after me and obtain anything I wanted, related to the room. He told me back in the plane that I needed to contact him directly for any "companion" issues. Vince told me that I could practically ignore Karl and to realize that he practiced complete confidentiality on all matters related to our VIP guests. I wasn't really sure what all that meant, but at least I had someone who could get me something to eat when I wanted it.

The room was nice. It was well appointed with fine woods, granite countertops, chandeliers and a big, beautiful Steinway grand piano. The furniture in the "salon" looked comfortable and the bedroom was exquisite! While we were technically on the 37th floor, there were about three stories of unnumbered service floors above the main casino, so I was actually about 40 stories up. The room afforded a breathtaking view of Las Vegas. The top floors of some of the other hotels blocked part of my view, but otherwise, I could see the whole city, the desert and even the mountains. This view was available from the salon and from the magnificent Jacuzzi in the master bathroom. My entire apartment back in Tulsa could fit in the master bedroom. I felt like I finally made the "big time."

Vince said, "Well, Owen, what do you want to do first?" I thought about asking about companions, but I said, "I didn't really have lunch; I'm getting kind of hungry."

"No problem. Would you like French, Italian, Sushi, Mexican, Middle Eastern, Caribbean…"

"Hold on!" I interjected. "How about a nice thick steak?" I said, thinking of the one I had in New York and remembering my goal to find one better.

"Excellent choice. We have one of the finest grills west of the Mississippi. And we do offer twelve different cuisines in fourteen different restaurants on our property. Now," he said, "why don't we do a little shopping before we have supper? We have six different clothing stores on our property, or I'd be happy to take you somewhere else."

"Well, we can start here in your stores, Vince. That'll be fine".

"Very good. I'm sure you'll want to get cleaned up after you get your new clothes before you meet your companion."

At the word "companion" I couldn't help but to smile, the response he was waiting on.

41

"I hope Cindi met your expectations."

"Since I wasn't expecting her, she more than met my expectations." I said.

"She is one of our quality companions that I can offer throughout your stay here. Let me ask you this," he paused as if framing his question first, "do you anticipate a 'constant companion' or perhaps a different one each day?" This was more than I could have ever imagined. I honestly didn't know what to say, so I asked him if he had any suggestions. "If it were me," he said, "I'd enjoy the company of as many as possible." "Sounds like a good plan," I said.

I had only been a multi-millionaire for a few days when I hit Las Vegas. I was still living with a pauper's mentality. I rarely bought my clothes anywhere but Wal-Mart or occasionally Target. I had never shopped in, let alone been in, an upscale clothing store before. I thought I was going to have a heart attack when I saw the prices of the clothes in the hotel boutique. Three hundred and fifty dollars for a shirt? Five hundred dollars for a pair of slacks? Where was the Wal-Mart in Las Vegas? I struggled with my first real wealth related dilemma. Would I really spend this exorbitant amount on clothing and act as if it were no big deal or would I refuse to pay what is clearly an absurd chump price for overpriced rags? I'm sad to say that I caved into the pressure to act like a big shot. I ended up buying shirts, shoes, pants, underwear, belts, socks, and even a sport coat and spent nearly twelve thousand dollars on several days' worth of new clothes. I simply swiped my room card and charged it all to suite 3749.

It was getting on toward six thirty by this time and my stomach started to growl. I decided that I better go back, get cleaned up and changed so that I could meet my first companion. Opening the door to my room, I was met by a vision of complete loveliness. She introduced herself as Simone. I couldn't believe my luck! She was as pretty as the stewardess, but much sexier somehow. She said she prepared my bath and if I didn't want the water to get cold, I better get in right away. I wasted no time and wasn't surprised when she joined me. I guess my tummy could growl a little while longer.

Simone was exquisite. She smelled like strawberries and looked like a movie star. She was quiet, but aggressive; sweet, but rough. To put it bluntly, she entranced me like a lion intent on a gazelle. She anticipated my every desire. She was the epitome of feminine beauty and sensuality. When the bathing and other activities ceased and we were getting dressed, I was unpleasantly surprised to find Karl in the dressing room with a new set of clothes already laid out and all my other ones neatly hung in the closet. Had Karl been here the entire time I was with Simone? That was a little creepy if you asked me.

Karl seemed to act as if nothing was amiss and wanted to help me get dressed.

"Karl, I'm a grown man; I don't need any help getting dressed."

"Very good, sir. May I suggest your new sport coat this evening?"

I didn't know how long I would be able to tolerate Karl. But I had seen movies and TV shows where rich people had servants that did stuff like this. Maybe I would just have to get used to this kind of thing as a burden of being filthy rich! I was still new at having all I ever wanted; in fact, I'm not really sure what I DID want. "I took the liberty of procuring some toiletries for you, sir" Karl said. Sure enough, there was a toothbrush, a tube of toothpaste, deodorant, razor, and even a leather bag in which to keep my new goodies. Maybe I'd hang on to Karl a little longer to see how it was going to pan out.

It was almost eight o'clock before Simone and I arrived at the steak restaurant called The Peninsula Grill. They decorated it to make you think of old money back East somewhere. Dark walnut paneling covered the walls, and all of the seats were upholstered in dark green leather. In fact, the whole place was dark. The wonderful fragrance of charring meat emanated from the kitchen. For me, there is no better smell in the whole world. A line of at least an hour stood waiting to get in the restaurant. When they saw me coming, the maître d' stepped out from his post and greeted me by name and said that my table was available immediately. We walked past all of the other guests and were seated in a quiet corner where we could still hear the light jazz ensemble playing from the lounge. I ordered some wine, taking the suggestion of the wine steward since I know exactly nothing about wine. I ordered some fancy stuff that I had heard about, but never tried. In my mind I know that escargots are snails, but when the waiter set them down in front of me, I nearly lost it. I asked for a beer, and he handed me a menu of imported and domestic beer that had no less than one hundred selections from which to choose. Maybe I was getting in over my head here. Maybe I should just stick with Golden Corral and Miller Light.

Simone sensed my problem and she put her hand on my hand. She looked me right in the eye and said, "Everything will be all right." I couldn't help but believe her. She was just so beautiful that, well, we guys are dumb like that for a pretty face. She smiled at me, and I calmed down a bit. Our waiter, Bill, brought our salads and some bread, and once I began to get something in my stomach, my nerves settled down. This really was going to be alright.

Simone didn't say much, but she hardly ever broke eye contact with me. It was unsettling and it started to get a little irritating at the same time. I ordered the best steak in the house, but in the end, it wasn't nearly as good as the one in New York City. By the time we finished our desserts and drinks, it was 10:30. As we left the restaurant, Vince met us at the door.

"What would you like to do now? Would you like for me to explain how the gaming tables and private gaming rooms work?"

"Sure! That'd be great," I said.

"Please know that at any time, if I am crowding you too much, just let me know and I'll give you some more space. That goes for your companion, too," he said, glancing toward Simone. "You are not obligated to do anything you do not want to do or to go anywhere you do not wish to go. We are here for you."

"Thanks, Vince. I appreciate that. Let's gamble!"

"As a VIP, you have the ability to use your room card to get cash or chips, keeping in mind that it goes against your line of credit. Whenever you need cash or chips, simply step forward to the cashier and swipe your room card and use the four-digit room number as your password. The cashier will then provide you with the resources to meet your needs."

"That's pretty slick! It is just like an ATM card, huh?"

"Yes sir. Please notify me or any member of our security team if you lose or misplace your card. We wouldn't want anyone running up your tab."

"No, we wouldn't want that at all, Vince."

"Do you want instructions on any of our gaming tables before you play?"

I mentioned that I remembered watching James Bond play baccarat. He eagerly provided me with the rules of play, but frankly, it was a little too complicated for me at this time of night. I told him that I might just play a little roulette and some blackjack tonight to get my feet wet, then I'd really give them a chance to win my money tomorrow. Vince seemed well-pleased with that prospect.

Simone and I went over to the cashier's booth where I charged $10,000 to my line of credit. The cashier handed me ten $1000 chips. I handed them right back and told her that I'd much prefer to have one-hundred-dollar chips, at least to begin. Without comment, she exchanged the chips and gave me one hundred $100 chips in a little tray. I felt very conspicuous carrying the little tray everywhere I went, so I went back and traded about half of the chips for five-hundred-dollar chips. We headed straight for a roulette table where I lost most of my chips within 30 minutes. However, twice within that time span, a waitress had been by to bring me two complimentary drinks. I tipped her a hundred-dollar chip, because that was all I had. Simone and I headed back over to the cashier's booth, where I chalked up another $50,000, and I gave Simone about five thousand dollars to play. She immediately went back and converted some of the chips into cash and smaller denomination chips, explaining that sometimes she prefers to play with cash instead of chips.

I played some blackjack and some more roulette. I tried my hand at craps, but really didn't understand that one. I'd have to talk to Vince about that tomorrow, too. I found that I could swipe my room card directly into a slot machine and never had to put coins or tokens in. At about three o'clock in the morning, I blew all my money and was ready for some shuteye. I kept looking for a clock, but casinos kept them away from their guests. I also realized that I breezed through over $70,000 since landing in Las Vegas and I never once held a dollar or a coin in my hand. I spent more in eleven hours of shopping and gambling in Las Vegas than I earned in the past three years working full time as a donut delivery driver. That was exciting and distressing at the same time. But I shouldn't worry about those sorts of things; I'm on vacation and I want to live it up a little!

CHAPTER EIGHT

# The Unfortunate Incident

My first morning in Las Vegas found me awake just before noon. Simone was gone. I found a delightful breakfast of coffee, a blend of orange and pineapple juice, and something I had never eaten before; eggs Benedict. I left a breakfast order with Karl the night before. I'd noticed it on the IHOP menu back in Tulsa, but at nearly nine dollars, it just seemed like too much money to spend on breakfast. But, since I could now afford anything I wanted anytime I wanted it, I took my first bite of eggs Benedict.

I discovered that my palate was better suited for biscuits and sausage gravy than haute cuisine. This millionaire lifestyle would take some getting used to. I needed to acquire a taste for these highfalutin groceries. That was okay by me, because I'd eaten enough burgers and drank enough cheap beer to last anyone a lifetime; I was sure I could develop a taste for the finer things in life. It would just take some time to re-educate this Okie's taste.

About the time I sat down to eat breakfast, Karl appeared to inquire about my needs for the day.

He conveyed Vince's apologies for Simone's disappearance but gave no explanation. He told me that Vince said I'd have another companion as soon as I wanted one and asked if I had any preferences. To be honest, I was still so exhausted by last evening's gambling and frolicking, I told Karl to let me think about it for a little while. I told him to give me an hour or so to let me eat breakfast and muse over some things. He was most obliging and left immediately.

I sat in front of the big windows in the living room, er, salon and looked out over the cityscape of Las Vegas. From my penthouse suite, I could see the pyramid of the Luxor, the Eiffel Tower at the Paris Las Vegas, the replica Empire State Building at New York-New York, and of course, the beautiful mountains. I drank coffee as I pondered my new life situation and smiled to myself at my good fortune. What *was* I going to do? Did I really need a plan? Did I really *have* to do anything at all? My thoughts drifted back to the present and to the two lovely ladies I had been with the past two days. How many times had they been other men's companions? As I considered the entire state of affairs, I realized that these girls were really nothing more than prostitutes. Vince veiled it by calling them companions. As a matter of fact, whenever I mentioned the word "gambling" he would answer me and use the word "gaming" instead. He simply dressed up virtue-less things to make them less distasteful. There was something nagging me in the back of my mind that just didn't add up, but I was drunk with wealth and couldn't keep properly focused to figure it all out on my own.

Wrapped in my plush, royal-blue Peninsula Hotel bath robe, sipping my exceptionally good cup of coffee, my thoughts went back to where they always did when I was idle; back to Daddy. Hardly a day passed that I didn't think of him somehow. Finally, after all these years without him, I had finally made something of myself. I was rich. I was in a position to take care of Momma for the first time in our lives. The house she lived in, the house I grew up in, was not in good shape. It needed many repairs and the neighborhood turned bad in the past 20 years. Well, not bad, maybe, but not good enough for my Momma. I decided to call her. She didn't pick up at home, but she answered the phone at the dry cleaners.

"Momma, I thought I told you to quit your job!"

"Owen, I can't just up and quit. That wouldn't be right."

"But Momma, you don't need to work anymore. I'm going to take care of you. In fact, that's why I called."

"Are you having a good time in Las Vegas?" she asked, successfully changing the subject.

"Oh my word! Yes!" I exclaimed. "They gave me a private jet (I didn't dare tell Momma about Cindi) and I have a huge penthouse suite in the hotel (I sure didn't tell her about Simone). There's this guy, Vince, who has arranged to take care of my every need. I even walked right past a long line of people waiting to get in a fancy restaurant last night because of Vince."

"Oh! Owen! That sounds like so much fun!" Momma said. "Don't let them take advantage of your money," she added.

"Don't worry, Momma. I'm in the driver's seat." I said. "Listen, the reason I called is because I just had a great idea! I'm going to buy you a big, new house."

"Now listen, Owen, I know you want to take care of me and I'm still thinking about all that. But I really don't need a new house. In fact, I really don't want a new house. Your father and I picked this one out and it has a lot of special memories for me."

Well, that did it for me. If Momma didn't want to move because of the house being special to Daddy, then she wasn't going to move. "Well, I'll tell you what I'm gonna do then," I said. "Let me fix it up for you real nice. I know it needs a new roof. It could probably use a new heating and air conditioning unit. And I know for sure the bathrooms and kitchen need remodeling. It could stand for some new carpet, too."

"To be honest with you, son, I could really use those things. That would mean a lot to me. Thank you, Owen" she said, starting to choke up a little bit, which made me teary-eyed, too.

"Momma, I love you. I want you to be happy. I'll be home in a few days. Go down and pick you out some new carpet and tile for the whole house. Don't look at or even ask about the price. Get what you want. We'll arrange the rest of it when I get home."

"Thank you, Owen. I love you, honey."

"I love you too, Momma."

As I got off the phone, it occurred to me that my apartment back in Tulsa wasn't going to cut it anymore. I would need a place of residence that reflected my newfound wealth. What could say "money" in Tulsa any more than the old oil mansions near downtown? Back in the first half of the 1900's, Tulsa's oil boom made millionaires of many in a world where a million dollars was a boatload of money. Consequently, near downtown Tulsa, which was way out in the country back then, there are many beautiful mansions built with revenues from black gold. I've driven along 21st and 31st Streets between Harvard and Peoria Avenues and drooled at those grand old houses. Now one of those would become the Rigsby Estate. I might need to cut my time in Las Vegas short just to go back to T-Town and buy myself a mansion!

About that time, Karl reappeared. From where, I do not know, because he didn't come in through the only door I knew about. I hadn't realized I had been sitting there so long and it was now a little after two. However, all the thought about the oil mansion made my mind flow with self-indulgent greed and I immediately gave him an "order" for a new companion. I also told him I wanted to get out of the hotel for a little while and take a drive. Refusing his offer of a limo, I told him I wanted a red convertible Ferrari. He thanked me for my requests. I told him I was going to take a shower and would be ready to leave the hotel in about an hour.

When I got out of the shower, Vince was sitting in my salon waiting for me. He apologized and told me that the hotel didn't own a red Ferrari but could arrange for me to rent one from a local business. He actually had the paperwork for me to sign and said he'd be back in a half an hour with my new companion and my red Ferrari. Perhaps my oil mansion could wait.

I boarded the elevator and that disturbing female voice greeted me again by name. As I looked at my reflection in the door of the elevator I couldn't

*Jackpot!*

help but notice the silly grin on my face. That made me smile even more. As I exited the elevator and was told to have a good afternoon by the voice, Vince met me with another lovely plaything. He introduced me to Tish. She met my specified requests to tee. Five and a half feet tall, red hair, green eyes, and ample curves in just the right places. She dressed casually, but sexy, nonetheless. However, when she opened her mouth to say hello, I barely contained my laughter. Her voice sounded almost exactly like Fran Dresher's character on *The Nanny*. While she was certainly something to look at, I didn't know how long I could tolerate that nasally voice.

Vince handed over the keys to the rented Ferrari; I found that I was to drive a year old F430 Spider. This car has been hailed as one of the best Ferraris ever built. Originally sold in the neighborhood of a quarter of a million dollars, this rental would to be my first taste of a true "supercar." Two beefeaters opened the door for me and my companion. I couldn't believe the sound of the engine when I started and revved it a little bit. It had attracted some attention from the other hotel guests, and we had drawn a crowd. Some people actually applauded when they heard it start. All mine for a mere $1500 a day. Not a bad deal in my present condition.

I put the car in drive and hit the accelerator, smacking straight into a parked limousine. I have never been so embarrassed in my whole life. The people who were just previously applauding were now taking pictures of me on their camera phones and video cameras. This wreck would be on YouTube within five minutes. I remembered that Vince said that full coverage insurance was mandatory with the rental, but I chose a $50,000 deductible to save a few bucks on the premium. I guess this one is going to come right out of my pocket. Vince ran right up to me and told me not to worry, that he would take care of everything. The damage didn't look too bad, but what did I know? I had only driven that beauty for a total of 2 seconds, which unfortunately for me, covered an area of nearly 100 feet. It left tire squeal marks from the curb right into the side of the limo. The limo driver was an independent entrepreneur who was also the owner. He didn't cuss or rant. All he did was stand there and smile. I guess it is fun to watch rich guys act stupid.

Tish and I went back into the hotel to figure out what to do next. We had a couple of drinks, and I made the mistake of asking her a question. All I heard for the next twenty minutes was the Nanny telling me about how she came to Las Vegas to be a show girl but realized she didn't know how to dance well enough.

"Trish, how long..."

"Tish," she said, correcting me. "My name is Tish."

"Sorry." I said. "How long have you been a companion?" I asked realizing that I had just invited her to talk some more. When was I going to learn?

Thankfully, Vince walked up just as Nanny was about to speak again. "Mr. Rigsby, I think I have it all worked out. The owner of the limo is willing to settle for twenty-five thousand dollars." No wonder he was smiling. He was seeing dollar signs! I sat there for a moment contemplating everything and decided that I really didn't want to have to go to court in Las Vegas over something like this. I didn't have anything to hide, but I just assumed that rich people paid other people off to keep from being hassled. "Alright" I said. "Can you pay him and charge it to my room?"

"Of course we can." I've got the rental company man here, too. He thinks the repair will be fifty-five thousand dollars."

"Well, of course he does." I said. "Pay him, too, and I'll be done with it, right?"

"Right. Since it took place on private property, there is no need to get the police involved."

"Just make sure everyone signs a release, so that they can't come back and sue me later."

"Already done," Vince said with an eerily similar smirk as the limo driver.

Good gravy. I had been out of bed for a little over four hours and my mistake had already cost me seventy-five thousand dollars! I hoped the rest of the day doesn't go as poorly as it had started out. "Vince" I said, "why don't we go with a hotel limo for this evening? I'd like to look around a little bit. I'd especially like to see where the James Bond movie was filmed."

"Give me a few minutes and I'll arrange everything."

I decided that if I left the hotel, I ought to have a little spending money, so I went to the cashier's booth and swiped my room card to get some cash. While I had gotten the money out to buy Momma's Caddy and gave her the backpack with the rest of the cash, I realized I didn't have any cash on my person. I thought that twenty-thousand dollars would do it and I put the two bundles of $100 bills in each front pocket. I could feel the money pressing against my legs. I liked it.

Vince retrieved Tish and me from the lounge. Parked in the same VIP parking place where the now wrecked Ferrari had been a classy, black, stretched Cadillac limo. I told Vince that I didn't want a white limo and I didn't want anything that looked redneck and he delivered. It reminded me of the limo in New York City that took me to the Plaza Hotel. The beefeaters were at their posts again to open the door for me and my companion.

As the doors closed, the phone in the back of the limo rang. It was the driver. He introduced himself as Julio and asked where I'd like to go first. I told him that I wanted to see the "Whyte House" from *Diamonds Are Forever*. He told me that it was filmed at the Las Vegas Hilton, and it would only take a few minutes to get there. As soon as I replaced the phone, Tish was all over me like a hound dog on a June bug. I was actually a bit put off by her aggressiveness and told her to wait until later. At this point, seeing the James Bond locations meant more to than having sex with a beautiful prostitute.

Julio pulled the limo into the palm tree lined drive of the Hilton. It was just like I remembered, except, of course, it had the Hilton "H" logo instead of the movie name. As we arrived, Julio called again and asked if I wanted to go inside or only look at it from the outside. I figured as long as I was there, go ahead and go inside. The door of the limo was opened by an attendant at the Hilton and Tish, and I went in for a look around. She told me that Elvis had the entire penthouse when he played in Vegas back in the early 1970's which, she told me was "way before I was born." I didn't recognize any of the interior of the hotel, but I couldn't remember very many scenes being shot there, so it was okay. I didn't know that Elvis had the same penthouse as Willard Whyte; I wondered if it was the real penthouse they had shown in the movie, or merely a set on a stage. I noticed Barry Manilow was headlining, but I didn't care to see him that night. We left the hotel and found Julio waiting for us. I told him I wanted to go to Circus Circus. He said it was just a few short blocks. I didn't bother making myself another drink for the ride.

Arriving at Circus Circus, I was amused at what I saw. The main entrance on Industrial Boulevard was right across the street from a forklift company. Real life meets fantasy separated by four lanes of traffic. Industrial Boulevard was appropriately named. It wasn't the glamorously posh side of Vegas, that's for sure. The Nanny and I walked into the hotel and found our way to the midway, where the scenes of the Bond film were filmed. It thrilled me to realize that I was actually standing where they made the movie. I didn't like the atmosphere, though. It was even louder than the Peninsula. I walked around a little bit and tried to find the water balloon game that Tiffany Case played to win the stuffed animal full of diamonds. I never did find it, but it was exciting to be there.

I spied a watch on a man's wrist and noticed it was nearly six o'clock. No wonder I felt hungry. I asked Tish where she'd like to go eat. She told me her favorite restaurant in Vegas was the Top of the World at the

Stratosphere. I told Julio where to go once we reached the limo and he said he'd call to arrange a table for us. It turns out that sunset is a very popular time to eat at this restaurant as it is in the tall tower that you see in skyline images of Las Vegas. We had a twenty-minute wait once we arrived, but I slipped the maître d' a hundred-dollar bill and we were seated within three minutes.

The view was simply spectacular. The Top of the World is a revolving restaurant at the top of an 800-foot tower. The food met my expectations. The service exceeded my expectations. The ambiance was incredible. The company, however, left a little to be desired. Tish was nice enough, and very pretty, but I wanted to say, "Can't you speak without talking through your nose?" After considering my options, I excused myself to go to the bathroom. I called Vince and told him what I thought about Tish. He apologized but actually sounded a bit frustrated, although only a hint of it came through on the phone. He said that he would arrange for another companion, and I could meet up with her when I returned to the hotel after dinner. I told him it was a little awkward with Tish to tell her about it and he said to give him five minutes and she wouldn't be at the table when I returned. Sure enough, she was gone when I got back. I finished my dessert and ordered an Irish coffee to pass the time while I looked at the myriad of lights as the city came alive at night.

Arriving back at the hotel, Vince met me curbside. He asked me if I was ready for some high stakes gaming where I could stand to win a lot of money. The thought finally went through my head where I was able to grab hold of it for a moment: "or stand to *lose* a lot of money." Despite this being the first glimmer of reality, it departed as quickly as it came. Vince led me back into what you can only describe as the "High Rollers" section of the casino. We passed through doors manned by security guards in uniforms and guns. We traveled down a long, paneled hallway accented with gaudy, Italianesque statues, fountains and paintings. It almost felt like a scene from some gangster movie. I started to get a bit nervous just before we entered into a room with a few tables and even fewer gamblers. Vince told me I could play any game I wanted, that if it wasn't in the room, they'd bring it in.

He said that in this room, there were no table limits, meaning I could bet as much as I want. All of the main casino games have table limits. Most normal people don't worry about those limits, as they are higher than what most folks are willing to lose. This room, however, was the whale room. A whale is a high roller who has access to large amounts of money and is willing to bet it in large sums. Several months later, after watching a program on the Discovery Channel, I figured out that the hotel considered me a whale and Vince hauled me in. Each table in this room included a card reader where I could simply swipe my room card and keep playing. Mighty convenient for the casino, I'd say.

Greed is a curious thing. There I was, a man with millions of dollars. Yet I was about to embark on a reckless extravagant journey. I swiped my card and entered in the amount of $200,000. I chose the roulette table, despite my losses at a similar table the night before, but roulette was a game anyone could play without much skill. If you bet on a number, say "black seventeen" and the roulette ball falls on that number, you win 32 times the amount you bet. I played "black seventeen" for a dozen or so times and lost one hundred, twenty thousand dollars, betting $10,000 per spin of the wheel. I decided to spread my bets out a bit. If you put your chips between two numbers, you can win 16 times the amount you bet if one of the numbers comes up. If you put your chips on the corners of four numbers, you can win eight times the amount bet.

This new strategy worked for me a while. I hit one number "full on" and won $32000, but I was losing at a higher rate than I was winning. I decided that I should change games. I remember playing blackjack with my friends back in Tulsa, so I took what few chips I had and headed over to the blackjack table. I knew the basic rules, but I didn't know about "double down" and "splits." I felt more involved in this game and therefore enjoyed it more.

The Whale Room was something special. It wasn't as loud as the main floor and the waitresses that served the complimentary drinks each wore a skimpy costume that had a see-through blouse. Each table had fine leather seats or stools, depending on the game for the gamblers to be comfortable. There were specific lounge areas where overstuffed leather chairs invited the tired gambler to rest a moment. I looked around and counted a half dozen other gamblers. Most were older men with what looked like companions accompanying them. One older woman decked out in diamonds stood at the craps table accompanied by a young man that looked like her son, except that he kept touching her on the rear end. It dawned on me that the hotel provided male companions, too.

I took a little break after I had lost close to half a million dollars and settled into one of the lounge chairs. Not all of my losses came from my original Lottery money; some of it I won from the casino. If I counted right, I was very close to being halfway through my million-dollar line of credit. I went over to a special kiosk and inserted my card to access my hotel account. It displayed my current balance as "$522,619.42." Wow. Could I have really spent half a million dollars in the matter of a couple of days?

I remembered Vince telling me that I would meet my companion when I got back from dinner. However, as soon as I arrived, he ushered me into the Whale Room. He didn't make mention of my companion, nor did he offer an explanation. What was this I was feeling? Was I being used? Was I allowing someone to tell me what I was going to do? I almost had a moment of mental clarity, a respite from the mind-altering greed of big stakes gambling, when Sondra approached.

Where do they get these women? They looked like they stepped right out of Playboy Magazine, the next one more beautiful than the one before. Sondra introduced herself and leaned forward to kiss me on the cheek while placing one hand on my waist and the other on my chest. I was immediately smitten. We sat in the lounge area and chatted for a few minutes. She suggested that we go dancing at one of the hotel's clubs. I thought it was a good idea.

I had no idea what time it was. No clocks in the casino, you know. I knew that I returned to the hotel at about seven-thirty or so after dinner and reckoned it to be about eleven. I looked at Sondra's watch and was amazed to find it was one-thirty in the morning. As we arrived at Club Noir, the line to get in surprised me. Vegas truly is a city that never sleeps.

Sondra took me past the front entrance to an unmarked door around the corner and down the hall. She pressed a five-digit code into the security lock and the door opened right up. She turned around and smiled at me as she led me into the rear entrance of Club Noir. I turned around to look at the door we had just entered to find it was an emergency exit down the hall from the club's restrooms. As we approached the main room, she motioned to the bartender who called for a waitress to seat us.

I have never been a good dancer. I felt foolish at my high school dances trying to "disco." John Travolta I am not. I told Sondra that I wasn't very good, and she dismissed it as modesty. I insisted the only dancing I knew was from my school dances. She looked right in my eyes and told me it would be alright. We ordered some drinks; an imported beer for me and a White Zinfandel for Sondra. Club Noir was loud like any night club. It seemed to be the place for the younger patrons of the hotel and city. Most were in their late twenties and thirties. I didn't feel too far out of place at thirty-nine.

As we sat and talked and watched the gyrating crowd of people hopping and moving to an indistinct musical beat, I didn't really know what to think. It was all dreamlike to me. I was a millionaire at a trendy night club in Las Vegas, being treated like a High Roller VIP, yet it still wasn't enough. I loved the attention that I got from the hotel. I liked being able to have a different woman each day. I liked having my own valet. I loved being rich. But somehow, I wanted more. It was a deep feeling, really, down where I didn't understand what was going on myself - a familiar need that was being unmet. I imagined that anyone else in my situation would feel on top of the world. But not me. What was wrong with me? Why did I feel this way?

I realized that I wasn't listening to Sondra anymore and she had quit talking. It wasn't awkward. She actually gave me my space and didn't intrude on my thoughts. I liked that about her. Our eyes locked and we smiled at each other. Warily, I asked her if she wanted to dance. She agreed and reluctantly I escorted her to the dance floor.

I realized and lived out my greatest fears on the floor that night. I'm pretty sure the club is going to name an appetizer after me and call it the "Blooming Idiot" because that is the way I felt. I stepped not just on Sondra's toes but managed to step on my own about five times. My arms flung about as if controlled by a maniac with a remote control in another room. I accidently hit three different people "doin' my moves," which unfortunately, hadn't been done since the Disco Era. Someone forgot to tell me that Disco was dead.

Sondra was a sweetheart and didn't appear embarrassed nor did she complain about my two left feet. When my best John Travolta impression died on the dance floor, I decided that I could try out the Robot, which only brought disaster. After four or five songs, I told Sondra that I needed a rest. She quickly agreed and we left the dance floor to the relief of the other guests.

Arriving at our table at the same time as the waitress, I started to order another beer. Sondra objected and ordered us a bottle of champagne. She told the waitress that we'd take the bottle in the private booth. I had no idea what she was talking about but as long as I didn't have to dance anymore, I was fine with whatever she had in mind. She took me by the hand and led me to a door beside a big mirror. She entered another security code to open the door. Going inside, I found that it wasn't a mirror, but a one-way window. We could see out, but no one could see in. She closed the door, cutting the noise level in half, making it only a little loud instead of ear-shatteringly loud. Inside the room was a couple of nice chairs and a couch with a table. A knock on the door announced the arrival of our champagne by a fancy waiter who uncorked it and served it in crystal stemware. He also delivered a tray of hors d'oeuvres which turned out to be pretty good eating.

It was a relief to be away from the incredible noise level of the club. Was I turning into an old fogey? Surely not. We sat on the couch and drank our Champagne and ate our fancy little petit fours. Sondra told me that she was from Sacramento and had been in Vegas for 3 years after a nasty divorce which lead to a restraining order and a time in safe house. She had decided to come to Las Vegas to live with her sister who was a blackjack dealer over at Caesar's Palace. She had a job as a waitress in the MGM Grand when she was approached by someone to begin accompanying unescorted gentlemen around Las Vegas. She was reluctant at first, but the promise of big money convinced her to give it a try. She said one thing led to another and now here she was.

I wanted to ask her about how it all worked and who employed her. I wanted to ask her about how many different men she had accompanied, but then I decided that I'd rather not know. The thought of her as a prostitute was a turn off, but her seductive good looks kept me from thinking about any of that. As I was drunk with money, I was also drunk with lust.

We stayed in the private room about two and a half hours, enjoying each other's company. I asked her if she wanted to go for a walk and she agreed. We left the club at about four-thirty or so in the morning, with it still going strong. The breath of fresh air was exhilarating. We walked along the path to one of the hotel swimming pools. The stars were obscured by the bright lights of the city. I knew they were there; I just couldn't see them. We held hands as we walked and, since there was no one around, decided to go swimming. To be perfectly honest, there wasn't a whole lot of swimming going on. I had never done anything like that in public before. Not that there was anyone around, but someone could have come by at any moment. When we got out of the pool, I saw three surveillance cameras literally following us as we went to get dressed. No privacy in Las Vegas either. I'm sure we gave quite a performance for the late-night security staff. I wonder where that video will end up.

I was exhausted. Approaching six o'clock in the morning, the sky was no longer completely dark. I told Sondra that I needed to get some sleep. Without hesitation, she took my arm, and we went back to my suite. I had made good use of my companion that evening for my own physical pleasure, but now I just wanted her for the pleasure of holding someone as I slept. She, like the others, was gone when I woke up later that day.

CHAPTER NINE

# The Cigar Club

I hadn't left a breakfast order for Karl and there wasn't anything to eat when I woke up. Right after I came out of the bathroom, he greeted me with a newspaper and a serving tray with coffee. At least he anticipated that correctly. I wasn't hungry and said as much to him. While I sipped my coffee and left the newspaper where it lay, Karl actually went in and laid out my clothes for the day. I wondered if he'd be interested in moving to Tulsa. I doubted it.

For the first time since arriving, I turned on the big screen TV. It was programmed to start on the hotel information channel. It gave information to turn to channel such and such to see how to play some of the casino games. I turned there just in time to hear the rules and strategy for playing craps. It sounds easy enough, but I get all confused when I actually play it. Maybe it would be better if I didn't try that one again. I turned back to the hotel guide and watched for twenty minutes before it repeated itself. I saw it had a spa with massage tables. All of a sudden, getting a massage sounded really good to me.

Honestly, I was hoping for more than a massage. I had Karl call for the earliest available appointment. They could take me in half an hour. I hurriedly dressed myself and set out looking for the spa. The hotel was huge, and it took me nearly twenty minutes to find it. I was greeted by a young woman who was a bit flirty. I accepted this as a good sign. Another woman led me through a door marked "Men" back to my private room. It was handsome. It had a shower, toilet, table with two chairs and a professional massage table; the kind where you put your face down through a hole.

The woman showed me the workings of the room and asked if I'd like to place a drink order. I asked for a Mexican beer and a sandwich. Disappointment arose when I realized I'd be showering alone. My beer, sandwich, and a bowl of fresh strawberries were waiting for me when I got out of the shower. I sat in my towel drinking my beer and nibbling on the sandwich. The knock at the door startled me. My masseuse entered and said her name was Sandy. She was attractive, but not a knock-out. She sat in the other chair waiting for me to finish my meal. Before finishing, I told her that we could begin.

She asked me to get on the table, face-down. I dropped my towel, on purpose, as I climbed onto the table. This was my first massage, and I was hoping to make the most of it. I situated myself with my face in the hole. I wasn't prepared for what happened next. She picked up my towel and placed it over my exposed derriere. Maybe this was just propriety at work. Perhaps she wasn't allowed to do anything until the end. I was just going to have to wait and see.

Since I had never had a massage before, I didn't know if it was a good one or not. However, I liked it, so I guess it was good. She kneaded my calves into jelly. She worked my back into sheer delight. I cannot even describe what she did with my neck and shoulders. When she was finished with my back, she told me to roll over. While rolling, she held the towel in place so that I didn't expose myself. She placed something over the hole in the table so that my head wouldn't be hanging down. I figured it was just a matter of time until she offered a more personal massage.

That time never came. She rubbed my arms and feet. She massaged my chest and my upper thighs. I was sure that her fingers would stray and "accidentally" touch me where I so desperately wanted to be touched, but it wasn't to be. She ended the hour with a splendid face and scalp massage. When she announced that she was done, I said that she had missed a few parts. She smiled and politely told me that she didn't give that kind of massage. I asked her why and told her I would be happy to tip her accordingly. She told me she was happily married and wasn't going to jeopardize what she had with her husband. She was polite about it and wasn't putting me down in any way. I respected her for that. I slid my room card, even though the spa treatment was "on the house" and left her a five-hundred-dollar tip. I decided that I would do that again before I went back to Tulsa, but next time would relax and actually enjoy the massage knowing that it would only be a massage.

I hadn't really been out and around very much since arriving in Vegas and I decided that I'd leave the hotel and walk around a little bit. I ended up at "Ripley's Believe It or Not" and paid the admission price to see the fantastic and sometimes funny oddities from around the world. I stopped in a Baskin-Robbins and ordered a Banana Royale. The shop was right on the strip, so I found a window seat and watched the world walk by. That can be just about as entertaining as any other diversion Las Vegas has to offer. I continued my walk and ended up at the incredibly wonderful fountains at the Bellagio. I was thunderstruck. I still cannot believe anything like that exists!

Since it was starting to get dark, I sauntered off toward Fremont Street, the original Las Vegas strip. Part of the street has been converted to a covered pedestrian walkway, employing millions of LED lights to create a spectacular light show. Arriving there before dark, I realized that the chase scene from *Diamonds Are Forever* was filmed right there. I found Binion's Horseshoe Casino and the Golden Nugget. I was standing in the middle of James Bond movie history.

Crowds began to assemble under the light show. I joined them and found a place right in the middle where I thought I could see everything. After the show started, I realized that I could have been anywhere under the canopy to enjoy the technological wonder officially known as the "Fremont Street Experience." It was a party atmosphere in the street. As far as "fun" goes, I think I enjoyed Fremont Street more than anything else I did while in Vegas.

As long as I was in the neighborhood, I decided to go into the Horseshoe Casino. I still had several thousand dollars in my pocket from the night before and thought it might be fun to win some of their money. That, of course, is not how it worked. I lost the rest of the cash I had playing roulette and high dollar slots. Like the Peninsula, they offered free cocktails to the gamblers. I found that to be the case in every casino I visited. As long as the booze flows out, the cash flows in.

I found myself back at my hotel at nearly nine o'clock. Within moments of entering the front door, Vince found me.

"How about another go at the high stakes games this evening, Owen?"

"I've already lost a lot of money today, Vince. I think I'd like to lay off the gambling for this evening and maybe take in a show. Can you get me tickets to see Frank Sinatra?"

"Mr. Sinatra died in 1998, sir."

"Oh. Well then, who's playing?"

After showing me the headliners currently playing in Vegas, I settled on Tim Allen. Vince ordered a limo and introduced me to my companion for the evening, Noel. I don't think she said three words to me all evening. She looked to be about sixteen years old, but she told me she was twenty-two. She was dressed in a gaudy, gold-sequined party dress, about six inches too short in the hem and about six inches too deep in the neckline. This one looked like a call girl.

As I sat with a pretty woman, albeit prostitute, while watching my first, real-live celebrity show, I realized I was no longer paying attention to the performance. Inexplicably, my thoughts turned to my life. I was losing count of the number of women I had been with in just a few short days. I had to check a computer to see how much money I had blown. What did I have to show for it? Watching people back at the Baskin-Robbins was more fun than anything I had paid for. People were treating me like royalty, but it was only because of my money. Is this how it was going to be for the rest of my life? I had everything the man in the street could ever ask for, yet I wanted something different.

What was this inside me that was never satisfied? Why wasn't anything good enough? Why did I continually seek to be filled with more stuff, or the next thrill or the next woman? At 39 years old I was set for life, wasn't I? Was I ever going to get married? Was I ever going to have anyone to share my life with? Was it always going to be high dollar call girls? These thoughts nauseated me, and I excused myself to go to the restroom.

I passed a little kiosk selling fine cigars and tobacco. For some reason, I stopped and decided that I needed to buy a cigar. Having never smoked one before, I asked for the recommendation of the cute brunette behind the counter. She suggested an imported brand that was one hundred twenty dollars for a single cigar. I balked and she assured me that there were none finer and that to truly appreciate it, I needed to smoke it while drinking a cup of brandy.

The image she pitched to me excited me and I forgot about my nausea and heart-searching. I bought my high dollar cigar and went in the Cigar Club and ordered a brandy. The waitress brought it and a cigar cutter and what seemed to be a mini torch to light the cigar. It was quite an unsettling sensation as I drew the hot smoke into my mouth, then inhaled too deeply and thought I was going to choke to death right there in the lounge. The other patrons looked at me with disdain, but I didn't really care. I was richer than anyone one of those yahoos and nothing in my life had been more humiliating than wrecking that Ferrari. Coughing and choking in front of a bunch of strangers was nothing compared to what Vince, and I have come to call "the unfortunate incident."

The waitress brought me a glass of water. I drank the whole glass before she left the table and asked for some more. She smiled as she went to fetch a water pitcher. A distinguished looking older man in a suit sat at the table close to mine and smiled as he asked me "Are you all right?"

"I suppose. This is my very first cigar."

"Welcome, then, my friend, to a life of simple yet sophisticated pleasure."

"The girl outside sold me one of these" I said as I showed him my cigar band.

"That is a good cigar, although quite a bit overpriced. You don't need to go expensive to enjoy a full-flavored smoke."

"At this pace, I'm not so sure I'm actually enjoying the smoke."

He smiled and held out his hand. "My name is Franklin. Lewis Franklin. But you can call me Frank".

"Hi Frank. My name is Owen Rigsby. I'm from Tulsa."

"It's a pleasure to meet you Owen. I'm originally from Cincinnati, but I call Phoenix home now. What brings you to Las Vegas, Owen?"

"I'm on a little vacation," I said. "I've had a," I paused trying not to tell too much, "change in my life and I'm out here having a little fun while I decide what to do next."

"Sounds exciting. What kind of change? Did you find religion?"

I laughed to myself as I contemplated how to answer. Did I find religion? What kind of a silly question was that? "No, I quit my job and I'm just taking some time to figure out what I want to do with the rest of my life."

"What a marvelous opportunity!" Frank said, as he took a sip from his brandy sniffer. "Everyone should be able to do that at some point in life."

"What do you do, Frank?"

"Oh, my boy, I'm retired now. I spent most of my life as a commodities broker in New York. I retired to Phoenix a few years ago, but my wife died last year, and I really don't have anything to do with myself, so I come to Vegas about once a month for a few days."

"I'm sorry to hear about your wife. How long were you married?"

"Only 4 years. She was my fifth wife. I seemed to have a wondering eye and couldn't keep a wife very long. I was married to her longer than any of the others and we were doing pretty good until the cancer."

"Do you have any kids?"

"Not that I know of," he said with a wicked grin. "It gets kind of lonely in Phoenix and you can only play so much golf. I'm fortunate to have a good retirement income so I can come to Vegas, or anywhere else for that matter, any time I please."

We sat and chatted for a quite a little while untul Noel found me. When she came in, Frank stood up and actually kissed her hand, just like you see in the movies. As she sat down, he gave me a sideways wink of affirmation with a smirk that indicated he knew exactly what was going on. I just smiled back at him.

Noel said she wondered what had happened to me and didn't really like Tim Allen anyway, so it was fine if we didn't go back. As Frank and I sat smoking our cigars, Noel coughed and looked as if she was going to be sick from the smoke. I decided that I wanted to stay and smoke, drink and enjoy a little good conversation and if she didn't like it, well, she could just lump it. She excused herself to go to the ladies room. While gone, Frank looked over at me and said, "Wow! Where did you find that little girl?"

I didn't really want to spill the beans about my arrangements while in Vegas, so I played coy. Frank was nice enough, but I didn't really know him. In fact, he seemed rather pitiful. An old man, divorced 4 times, widowed once, living out his last years lonely and desperate for companionship. Suddenly, I was struck with a premonition that I could end up like that. Was I destined to be old and alone?

Noel came back from the restroom and announced she was hungry. Come to think of it, I was hungry, too. We bid farewell to Frank. He watched us all the way out the door of the lounge. We called our limo and decided to head back to the Peninsula for supper. The driver called ahead to make reservations at The Oasis, the Peninsula's super swanky restaurant. As we arrived, the beefeaters were there to open our doors. I escorted Noel into The Oasis where we enjoyed a spectacular assault on our taste buds.

The Oasis was a middle eastern themed restaurant complete with belly dancers. I ordered a two-pound lobster and a one-pound T-bone. I tried to order some wine but ended up taking the advice of the wine steward again. One day soon, I needed to take some sort of a wine class, so I didn't feel so stupid in these circumstances. We both ate in relative silence and enjoyed the belly dancing. That was another thing I had only seen in the movies. At the very least, I was expanding myself culturally; even if it was only in the casinos of Las Vegas.

Noel excused herself again but was back fairly quickly. This time I noticed that there was some white powder on her nose. I mentioned that she had something there and she quickly rubbed her nosed and sniffed hard. The last thing I needed was an under-aged, junkie prostitute in my life. As we finished, I told her that I wouldn't need her any more tonight. I told her that while we had a good time that evening, I decided I was just going to go to my room to get some sleep.

Actually, that sounded like a really good idea. I was greeted by the creepy elevator voice as I made my way back to my suite. I figured I'd leave a breakfast order for Karl and maybe catch a movie on the big screen in the bathroom while taking a whirlpool bath. As I began to draw my bath, I went into the bar and got myself a beer. Stepping down into the bathtub as big as a watering tank, I grabbed the remote control and set the bubbles on "high."

I flipped through the channels and then flipped through them again. I didn't see a movie I wanted to watch so I watched the end of America's Funniest Videos. As it gave way to another program, I found myself watching a TV preacher. This one was different; he wasn't asking for money. He was talking about finding peace. I listened to him for ten minutes until a commercial came on, then I flipped through the stations again, settling on a good John Wayne movie.

I must have fallen asleep because when I stirred around the bubbles had gone off, the water was no longer warm, and a Jerry Lewis movie was on. It was nearly three o'clock in the morning when I got out of the tub and stumbled into bed. I didn't fall asleep right away. I kept thinking about Frank and, even though he had money, he was still lonely. I thought about what that TV preacher said about finding peace. I wanted peace. Why wasn't I satisfied with anything? These thoughts bit deep into me until I drifted off to sleep.

## Chapter Ten

# Another Trip to the Whale Room

I staggered into the bathroom as soon I woke up. I realized that the water from last night's bath stood cold and dirty in the tub, along with three floating beer bottles. Gee! What a redneck! I laughed at myself. I drained the tub but left the empties for the maid. Entertaining a bit of a hangover, I made my way into the kitchen area to find a pot of coffee that Karl had left for me. Karl. What a guy!

I sat there reading the paper – well, the comics and the entertainment section – when Karl appeared pushing a cart full of my breakfast order. It didn't occur to me at that moment, but I hadn't dressed from my previous night's bath. While it dawned on me that I ought to at least get a robe on, Karl gave no indication that he even noticed. Now that's class.

Karl mentioned that Vince would like to have a word with me at my earliest convenience. I told him I would be available in an hour. I ate my breakfast and discovered that I do NOT like kiwi, nor do I like papaya juice. You cannot go wrong with pancakes and sausage. I finished my breakfast, shaved and finished dressing. Vince was waiting for me in the salon.

"Are you enjoying your time here in Las Vegas, Owen?"

"For the most part. I am really enjoying the good food. I never ate this good back in Tulsa."

"Was there a problem with your companion last night?"

"As a matter of fact, there was. Just exactly how old was she?"

Vince looked pensive but answered "Twenty-two".

"She sure looked a lot younger than that."

"You just let us worry about that. All of our companions are of legal age."

"Another thing, did you know she snorts cocaine?"

"Did you see her do that?"

"No, but she came back from the restroom with white powder on her nose and seemed to be embarrassed when I pointed it out".

"Owen, these girls aren't Sunday School teachers. They're companions. They are here to make you look good and to make you feel good. They are a heck of a lot better than what you'd find on the street."

"Probably so, but the one last night looked too young. And, with the drugs, it turned me off."

"I'm terribly sorry if you were upset with the companion we provided last night," Vince said with a bit of harshness in his tone. "Hopefully the next one will be to your pleasing." He changed subjects by asking, "What would you like to do today? Some more high-stakes gaming?"

"I've always wanted to see Hoover Dam."

"Lake Meade it is! I'll make all the arrangements. Would you like a companion to accompany you to the dam?"

"I think that would be nice."

"Would you like a picnic lunch, or would you like for me to arrange a houseboat?"

"The houseboat sounds like the way to go."

Vince looked at his watch. "It is nearly eleven o'clock now. I'll have a limo and your companion ready to go at noon. You can just come down to the lobby and I'll take care of you."

I had an hour to kill while I waited on Vince to make the arrangements. Perhaps I'd mosey down to the whale room and see what kind of trouble I could get myself into.

I found the craps table and thought I might try my hand at that. Who would have thought you could lose a quarter of a million dollars in less than an hour? Hellfire! I just couldn't seem to get my mind around that game. Of course, it didn't help to bet ten thousand dollars on each roll of the die. I guessed that paid for the limo, the houseboat, and the girl.

I kept my eye on my new Rolex watch I had bought the day before. I knew that there weren't any clocks anywhere in the casino and I had always wanted a Rolex, so it seemed like a good thing to do. Of course, I charged it to my room. Another seventy-five hundred dollars plus tax. What did I care? I had money to burn. I strolled out to the lobby to find Vince waiting there with Chloe.

## Chapter Eleven

# Chloe

Chloe grew up in a stable home environment in Austin. The youngest of four children, her parents were tired of raising kids when she came along. They weren't bad folks, but they hadn't planned on having another child so late in life. Her brothers and sister were already grown, married and had kids of their own by the time Chloe arrived.

Her parents disciplined her little and supervised her even less. They gave in to her requests most of the time, just to avoid arguments. She was spoiled rotten, and it showed. Her family wasn't rich, but she had almost everything she wanted. Her siblings tolerated her but seldom let their children play with her. While it appeared she had a dreamlife, she was lonely and craved attention and affection.

She was an average student, at best. She didn't create major problems in class and her teachers liked her, for the most part. She participated in acting and drama from seventh grade and was the star in the junior class play. She was disappointed to only have the role of a supporting character in her senior class play.

From the age of twelve, most people described her has "boy crazy." Her parents imposed few rules for dating, except that her mother took her to the health department and started her on birth control pills when she had her first period. Basically, she had a license from her parents to do as she pleased, as long as she didn't bring a baby home. They even tolerated boys spending the night after she turned fifteen.

Chloe quickly gained a reputation of being easy. She didn't sleep with every boy that asked her; she usually only had sex with her current boyfriend. The problem was she changed boyfriends like a chameleon changes color.

She chose them based on who was giving her the most attention at the time. She picked one up, then dropped him after a few weeks, only to pick him up again in a few months. By the time she was sixteen, she had been treated for chlamydia twice and syphilis once. She was reckless with her sexuality, all the time demanding more from her boyfriends. For them, it was a dream come true. She slept with more than twenty different boys and took the virginity from five.

She was always faithful to take her birth control pills. She viewed that as her ticket to behave any way she pleased. Much of what she enjoyed doing, even at an early age, didn't require birth control pills, though.

She had few friends who were girls. Her one good friend, Melissa, was nearly as promiscuous as Chloe. The summer before their senior year, they happened to be dating boys who also happened to be best friends. The boys suggested a weekend trip to Buchanan Lake. Melissa's boyfriend, Jeff's, grandparents owned a lake house there and gave permission for him to have a "couple of buddies" there for a week. He thought it would be a good opportunity for a little fun with the girls.

The four of them piled in Jeff's car and headed west on Highway 29 towards Buchanan Dam. The drinking started as soon as they left their neighborhood. Jeff only drank two beers in the two hours it took them to get to the lake house. Chloe's boyfriend, Travis, had raided his parents' liquor cabinet, as they were too young to legally buy alcohol. The three emptied a liter of vodka before they arrived.

Chloe and Travis were in the backseat. Travis thought it would be a good idea for Chloe to take her clothes off, which she did with only a little hesitation. She had never been in the presence of other people while having sex. Her promiscuous nature, however, overcame thoughts of propriety. Melissa turned around and watched the whole time. Chloe felt a new sensation of excitement which was hard to come by after several years of self-indulgence. Melissa was aroused as well, and serviced Jeff as he drove. He nearly ran off the road three times. The four of them were out of control.

Jeff's grandparent's lake house was in a development of mostly retired non-residents. They had a dock and a ski boat, which Jeff had used many times before. They described it as their "cabin" which didn't do it justice. It was three bedrooms with a huge upstairs living room. The balcony provided a beautiful view of the lake. The kitchen had every gadget and convenience available.

But Jeff and Travis were more interested in the other amenities. It had an abundantly stocked liquor cabinet and a hot tub. They planned to fully utilize both. The girls went wild over the house. Neither had ever spent any time at a lake and didn't realize that some people had second homes. They unloaded the car and headed to the dock.

Jeff showed off his knowledge of the boat and the other three were impressed. He drove the boat around the lake at top speed, everyone enjoying the sunshine and the beauty of the lake. He showed them different spots where he and his grandpa had fished and what little else he knew about the area.

He slowed the boat and anchored near a couple of islands, one of the few places on the lake that didn't have waterfront homes. They all jumped in for a swim. The water felt good. They played and splashed each other for a little while, then pulled themselves up onto the larger of the two small islands. The girls each pulled their bathing suit tops off and stretched out to suntan for a while. The boys sat back in the shade and enjoyed the view.

After half an hour, Jeff came and took Melissa around the corner for some privacy. Travis took advantage of the situation and he and Chloe enjoyed their moment in the sun. It wasn't the first time that Chloe had engaged in sex outdoors; she was constantly looking for something to spice up her meaningless activities. She and Travis went skinny-dipping afterwards and were joined shortly by the other couple.

The boys were embarrassed to be naked in front of each other. Sure, they had taken showers in the locker room at school, but there was nothing at all sexual about that; just the opposite. The embarrassment they faced came from the circumstances of being naked with each other in front of girls. The girls weren't embarrassed at all. In fact, Chloe and Melissa were almost intrigued with each other's bodies, comparing themselves against what they saw. Like the boys, they had showered after gym class, but their nakedness together wasn't in the context of sexuality.

The boys slipped their trunks back on and the girls put their bikini bottoms back on but rode topless back to the dock. There was a local pizza place that catered to the lake crowd and provided delivery service, so they ordered pizza for supper. They ate on the balcony, had some fun in the hot tub, and then retired as couples to separate bedrooms.

The next two days were almost identical - lots of drinking and lots of sex. The third evening, however, was different. While they were cavorting in the hot tub, Melissa leaned over and spontaneously kissed Chloe. Chloe kissed back. The boys' eyes nearly popped out of their heads as they watched the two girls. It turned hardcore.

Jeff suggested they move the party into the living room. His view obscured by the bubbling water of the hot tub; he wanted a better view of the goings-on. The boys watched for a while, then were again embarrassed to realize they were both aroused and could see each other in that state. Travis timidly suggested they join in on the fun. It was more than they could have ever imagined. The only two that didn't touch, or kiss were Jeff and Travis. It was a bona fide orgy.

The young adults repeated and expounded upon that event for the rest of the week.

Chloe didn't seek out same sex encounters but didn't turn them down when they presented themselves. She always preferred men to women and has never had such an experience, except in the presence of men, who always participated.

Chloe graduated high school and went on to study acting at Austin Community College. Her parents assisted her with tuition while she lived at home. She was immediately attracted to a graduate assistant in her drama department, Les. They dated several times, but he always turned down her sexual advances.

Finally, after what seemed an eternity to Chloe, he gave in, and they had sex. It wasn't the best she had ever had, but he didn't treat her like a sex-object. He treated her with kindness and respect. In her mind, she didn't understand it, but then, in light of every other relationship she'd had, she decided that maybe this is what love was all about. This attracted her to him even more.

They continued to date, but there wasn't a lot of physical intimacy, at least in her estimation. While they would kiss often, they would end up cuddling. She was thrilled to be accepted for being her, instead of being a girl that would put out on the first date. He doted after her every need. He wrote her poems. He presented her with a play he wrote in her honor, which became a campus production the following semester. He asked her questions about herself and actually listened to her answers. He brought her flowers. For the first time in her life, she was happy. And she was in love.

Les proposed to her during the Christmas break of her sophomore year. She eagerly accepted. Her parents were pleased that she was going to settle down and seemed to like him well enough. Les' parents died in a tornado his first year of college. He was an only child and seemed to Chloe to be all alone. He was the quiet, sensitive type. Not too quick to speak; not too loud when he laughed. Very introverted. He wanted to be a playwright after graduate school and live in New York City, writing plays that might make it to Broadway.

Chloe's father decided that she needed to be more independent since she was getting married. While his intentions were good, it pushed Chloe over an edge that no one knew was there. He told her that he was no longer able to pay her tuition and other expenses. He told her that she needed to take a job and start paying rent. He told her that she needed to get a separate cell phone account when the contract period was up for the family account. He told her that she needed to get and pay for her own car insurance. He told her that she needed to take more responsibility for herself, in light of her upcoming marriage.

While he said it all with a loving motive and even with a loving attitude, it upset Chloe. She never had to be responsible before. She knew that she would eventually leave their home, but the wedding date was set for after her graduation, another two years away. She was hoping to go seamlessly from her father's wallet to her husband's wallet. She didn't want to have to work while she was in college. She didn't think it was fair.

The more she thought about it, the more conflicted she became. She misinterpreted her father's intentions as personal rejection. She appealed to her mother, but she stood firm with her husband. Chloe decided that her only recourse was to drop out of college. She didn't want to, but she figured that perhaps she and Les could move the date up and it could work out that way. It was summer break, so she had a couple of months to work on the whole mess.

It was June, between her second and third years of school when it all fell apart. She went to Les' apartment and walked in on him and another man engaging in homosexual activities. There were no other women around. She demanded to know what was happening. Les jumped up from the bed and covered himself while he explained.

"Chloe! I thought you went shopping with your mother."

"What's going on here, Les? Who is this guy?"

"This is Jerry. He's my, uh…" he stuttered, his words tapering off.

"I don't understand."

"Chloe, let me explain."

"I'm listening." She folded her arms and waited.

"Well, I guess there is no good way to tell you. Jerry is my boyfriend. We've been together for three and a half years."

"Three and a half years?" she shouted. "How could you do this to me? I thought you loved me."

"I care very deeply for you, Chloe. You are a fun person to be around. But I can't live a lie any longer. I can't marry you; I'm in love with Jerry. I was going to tell you this fall."

"But why? Why did you ask me to marry you? Why did you lie to me?"

"I don't know. I guess I thought that I could lead a double life. Married to you to appear respectable to my grandparents; carrying on a loving relationship with Jerry. I thought you'd be a good wife who would understand."

"You took me for a fool! You were using me. I can't believe this!"

"I'm really sorry, Chloe. You're a nice person. I hoped you'd be more understanding."

"I hate you!" were the last words Les heard from Chloe as she slammed the door behind her.

Chloe was devastated. She took it to be a personal rejection of who she was, rather than Les having his own issues to work through. She drove to a liquor store and bought some tequila. She drank straight from the bottle as she drove mindlessly through the city. She ended up at McKinney Falls State Park where she spent the next couple of hours crying. A park ranger approached to check on her. She started to tell him about what happened, but all she could do was muster a couple of unintelligible whimpers. He left her alone.

She quit crying and began to think. She got out of the car and walked around to gain her composure. She couldn't continue on like this. She momentarily considered killing herself but didn't pursue those thoughts. Instead, she decided she needed a change. What kind of change, she didn't know.

She thought about what her father told her about becoming independent and responsible. She thought about college but decided that she preferred dancing to acting. Several people had complimented her dancing in the drama department productions. Perhaps she could change her major to dance. No, she didn't want to go back to school. She needed to make some money. As she sat pondering her life and her options, she decided that she might be able to make some money as a showgirl in Las Vegas. Maybe she could get a job dancing while figuring out what she really wanted to do with the rest of her life. She went home to pack and tell her parents.

She left the next day. Her father gave her five hundred dollars for gas and food. Despite their affirmations of love, she mistook their goodbyes as relief that she was leaving. She expected them to try to talk her out of moving away. In her mind, it was another mark of rejection.

She made it to Albuquerque and decided to call it a day. She had never driven so far by herself; she was scared and excited at the same time. The first several hotels she stopped at wanted nearly ninety dollars per night for a room. She found a cheap motel west of town that was more in line with her budget.

She went to a Dairy Queen and bought herself a large, chocolate dip cone. She needed something familiar to comfort her. Getting back to her dingy motel room, she cried herself to sleep.

She was impressed with the excitement of Las Vegas. She didn't have much money but checked into another cheap motel off the strip. She thought she might be able to gamble and increase her stash, but she was carded by a security guard on the casino floor, and they escorted her away before she even made one bet.

She asked the guard where she could submit an application to be a showgirl at the hotel. He directed her to Human Resources. She was looking for the room number when she ran into a man entering the hallway from an adjacent office.

"Excuse me, where's Human Resources?"

"It's three more doors down the hall on your right. What job are you applying for?"

"I want to become a showgirl."

"Do you have any experience?"

"I danced in some of my college productions. They said I was pretty good."

"How long have you been in Las Vegas?"

"I got here about two hours ago."

"Well, in that case, welcome to Las Vegas! Can I buy you dinner to celebrate?"

She thought about it for a moment and said, "Oh, I don't know about that."

"Come on," the man said. "You're making a new start in your life. What do you have to lose?"

"Well, okay. I guess it would be alright."

"Sure it will. We'll have some fun and I can show you around a little bit. I work here, too."

Chloe considered this and smiled to herself. *This may be the break I'm looking for.*

"What's your name?"

"Chloe."

"Chloe. That's a pretty name. I'm Vince."

CHAPTER TWELVE

# Disillusionment

Chloe was about five feet four inches tall and was perfectly proportioned. She was blond and blue-eyed. She had an incredible youthful appearance and a pleasant joy of living. She smiled constantly, but not in a disturbing kind of way. It was the kind of smile that made you smile back. She was from somewhere in Texas, she said, and was 24 years old. I really enjoyed talking with her most of the way to Hoover Dam. It isn't a long trip; but you can't talk the whole way when you are in a limo with all that room.

We arrived at the dam just before one and I enjoyed the tour. I couldn't believe how tall it was; the pictures just don't do it justice. There really wasn't too much to see after we took the tour, so we got back in the limo to go find the houseboat.

It took us about 45 minutes to find our houseboat at Hemmingway Harbor and get completely situated. It came with a houseboat captain and a steward. As we cast off from the dock onto the beautiful waters of Lake Meade, the steward announced that lunch was served. The outside temperature was perfect, so we chose to have a late lunch on the deck. We explored around the lake at a leisurely pace, eating cold pheasant and drinking fine wine. This was really living. I had seen a houseboat or two back on the lakes in Oklahoma, but they were more like RVs on water than the incredible luxury this vessel provided.

The captain situated the boat in a secluded cove where we could swim before sunset. Of course, neither of us had a bathing suit so, skinny dipping it was. We were in fairly deep water and despite my best efforts, I wasn't able to do with Chloe in the water what I wanted to do without one of us drowning so we took our little party back into the houseboat. We completely missed the sunset, but that was alright by me. The captain turned on all kinds of running lights and we headed back to the dock.

Chloe and I just talked the whole way back to the hotel. She told me about her family and how she grew up in Austin, Texas. She went to college two years but dropped out because her family didn't have the money. She had been engaged to get married but found out her fiancé was gay. Then she came to Las Vegas five years ago to find herself and maybe get a job as a showgirl. I wanted to ask her why she became a companion, but I didn't really want to know.

We pulled into Las Vegas well after nine P.M. The city lights gleamed, and I thoroughly enjoyed my good time with Chloe. She was a fun girl to be around. We liked the same kind of music and movies; we even liked the same kind of pizza. As the beefeaters attended to our doors, something very strange happened. Chloe and I were walking arm and arm into the hotel lobby when an old guy came up to Chloe and started talking to her. She responded politely but seemed extremely embarrassed.

I realized that she had been a companion for this old man. He must have been in his seventies and dressed like Rodney Dangerfield. He sported white shoes and a white belt. He was slobbering drunk and tried to get Chloe to go back with him to his room. I told him to get lost, but that only agitated him.

"Don't tell me what to do, sonny! This here's MY girl. I had her last night and I want to have her again tonight. Now, go away so we can get down to business."

I reared back to slug the old goober right in the chops when Vince came running out with hotel security. He grabbed the old man by the arm and called him by name.

"Mr. Jackson. We need to get you back into the hotel."

"Wait a minute, Vince-baby. You said I could have any girl I want, and I want this one again. She made me feel all young again. I want this one."

It was an extremely awkward moment for all of us, except for Mr. Jackson. He was so plastered that he didn't know what was going on. Chloe kept apologizing to me and Vince acted as if I wasn't a part of the situation. I imagine that this is part of the job for Vince; not exactly a job I would want to have. I didn't really know what to do at this point. Chloe was really something special, but it appeared that she was really something special to a lot of men. That definitely turned me off. I didn't want to be rude to Chloe, but I sure didn't want to take her back to bed after that scene.

Vince had Mr. Jackson back in the hotel and left us standing by the front door. Chloe and I were no longer arm in arm and I didn't think we would ever be that way again. Beautiful and a delight to be with, but quite frankly, I was too grossed out to spend any more time with her. I didn't want to be rude, but I told her that perhaps she could go on home and didn't need to spend the night with me that night. She said she understood and leaned forward to kiss me. I turned so that she only kissed my cheek. I could see the pain in her eyes, but if that is the kind of life you are going to lead, you have to expect regret.

*Jackpot!*

I walked by myself back into the hotel lobby extremely disappointed. My Las Vegas experience wasn't turning out to be all that I'd hoped. Lady Luck, that I had heard so much about, sure wasn't following me around. I wasn't winning any money and without exception, all of my companions scored way less than a perfect ten. I stood near the entrance of the casino deciding what to do. Would I ask Vince for another companion or try to meet someone in the bar?

A spirit of bitterness welled up inside me. I hadn't been anyone important for very long, but felt, as a multi-millionaire, I deserved to be treated better than this. I turned away from the casino and tried to determine in which of the hotel's twelve bars I would look for a pretty girl.

I consulted the posted hotel guide to find a suitable establishment. I knew the Big Rollers Club suited me as soon as I saw the name. Trying to find anything in this behemoth of a building was like looking for a dropped fishing rod in a lake; if you kept at it long enough you just might turn up with something.

After several minutes I stumbled upon a different bar. It was called The Bar. It was quiet but full of people. A pianist along a wall played some songs from the seventies. I didn't see a singer. Small cocktail tables with two leather chairs at each scattered the room. Barstools lined the piano, using it as a table. After finding a chair I ordered a drink. Before the waitress could bring it to my table, a gorgeous woman approached me. She asked me if the other seat was taken. I invited her to sit with me and told her my name. She called herself Marjorie.

I couldn't tell right off if Marjorie was a prostitute or not. To tell you the truth, it's kind of hard to tell what anything is in Vegas; not much is as it appears. Marjorie asked for a B-52. I ordered her one, whatever it was, and we got acquainted. Before long Marjorie started playing footsy with me under the table and suggested we go to my room. How could I say no to that?

She commented when we got on the elevator that she knew these were the "special elevators" and gave me a smirk like the limo driver I crashed into. Her hands were all over me on the short ride to my room. As the doors opened, Vince stood there to greet us.

"Good evening, Owen."

"Hello, Vince."

"Good evening, Rita" Vince said.

"This is Marjorie," I said. "I met her in The Bar."

"Yes, I know you did. That's why I'm here to help you out."

"What do you mean?"

"Rita is a con-artist who won't put out but will get away with your wallet and anything else in the room".

Marjorie didn't say anything. She just stood there, staring at Vince with a look that could have killed a pit bull. She let go of my arm. It fell to my side.

"Trust me, Owen. You don't want anything to do with this girl. I have a nice companion waiting for you in your room. Rita's nothing."

At that moment, two security guards arrived and escorted Marjorie, or Rita, or whoever she was out of the hotel. I guess I couldn't do better on my own after all. The feeling of disappointment rolled over me again. I just stood there and looked at Vince. He wasn't smiling. I didn't care. His job was to please me, not the other way around.

"Let me introduce you to your new companion," he said, turning to go to my suite. "Her name is…"

I cut him off. "I don't want a companion right now, Vince."

"Why not? Sherri's a very nice girl and she will make you feel good."

"I'm sure she will, but just not right now."

"What do you want to do?"

"I just want to be alone for a while. I'll tell you when I'm ready for another companion. I'm gonna head back down to the high stakes tables for a while and try to win some of my money back."

"Very good, Owen. Good luck."

I made my way back to the Whale Room and bellied up to a craps table. I lost money there for about an hour then moved on to roulette. I don't know why I like the roulette wheel so much. It certainly doesn't like me. I played the wheel for another hour or two. The drinks they serve in the in Whale Room are made with high dollar liquor. I thought I might try a martini, shaken not stirred, like James Bond. I don't know why he liked that at all. I left it sitting at a table after only two sips. It was horrible.

I drank four or five beers, quite a few Jack Daniels and Coke and the few sips of that martini. I ordered a hamburger and ate a couple orders of onion rings, but the alcohol started to make me drowsy. After the third beer, I quit keeping track of how much I was betting. No one seemed to be in the mood to tell me to go to my room or to stop gambling. They just kept bringing drinks and kept taking bets. I looked at my Rolex and it said two thirty in the morning. Time for bed.

I staggered down the hall with the creepy statues and headed for my private elevator. I dropped my room card two or three times before I could open the elevator door. The whole lobby was spinning, and I leaned against the wall and passed out in a drunken stupor.

I woke up the next morning with one humdinger of a hangover. I don't remember how I got in my suite. I don't remember going to bed. I don't remember getting undressed. I don't remember much after I slid down the wall next to the elevator. I was extremely distressed to find that I had no clothes on at all. Who undressed me? Who in the world put me in bed naked? I sure hope it wasn't Karl.

I stumbled into the bathroom and then into the shower. The hot water felt good on my face and head. I sat down on the built-in chair in the shower and let the stream run over my body. I'm willing to bet that was the longest shower I have ever taken. The hot water never ran out; I just woke up enough to go ahead and get dressed.

I took the last of the new clothes out of my closet. All of the other clothes had already been dry cleaned and were hanging next to the new ones. I smelled coffee. That made me smile. After dressing, I walked into the salon to find a breakfast tray. It had coffee, the wonderful blend of orange and pineapple juice, sweet rolls, fresh fruit and cheese, and chocolate covered strawberries. I noticed the digital clock in the room had just turned to two o'clock in the afternoon. My head was in a fog. The hangover headache was like a freight train roaring through the room and me with no place to hide. I was about to call for some aspirin when I found a variety of bottles of over-the-counter headache medicines next to the phone.

I took three Tylenols and closed my eyes, waiting for relief to come. I hadn't been that drunk in a long time. If there had been anybody there I cared about, I'd have been a little embarrassed. I was here on my own, as it was, and nobody here cared about me. They only cared about my money. Maybe it was time to go home.

I didn't even have a suitcase to pack. I called Vince and told him that I was ready to head back to Tulsa. He said he would make the flight arrangements and come to my room with the bill. I told him to wait just a little bit, that I wanted to go buy a couple of souvenirs for my mom and a couple of other folks back home. He told me to call him again when I was ready to check out.

I found the nice shops in the hotel and bought Momma a diamond necklace and matching earrings. I bought Granny a pearl necklace with earrings. I decided to buy Marty a Rolex like mine. I found a diamond tennis bracelet for Marty's wife and some t-shirts for his kids. I had no idea what size they wore, but thought they'd be happy with anything. They were good boys. I headed back to my suite for the last time, my arms carrying sacks of goodies for those I cared about. Just before I got to the elevator, I realized that I still didn't have a suitcase, so I went back and found a leather duffel-type bag and then returned to my room.

Karl was there and even opened the door for me. He took my treasures and immediately started packing, without saying a word. After bringing my bag into the salon, he asked me if I needed anything else. I thanked him, but never did ask if he was the one who put me in bed last night. That was just too weird to think about. He told me he had collected my toiletries, and everything was in my bag. He thanked me for the privilege of serving me and hoped to see me again at the Peninsula Hotel Resort and Casino. Instead of walking out the front door, he retreated to the rear of the suite, but I never did see that back door he used to come and go.

I called Vince and he was there in a matter of moments to check me out of my room and to settle my bill. I was floored when he presented me with the final bill of one million one hundred twenty-three thousand eight hundred and sixty-six dollars and thirty-four cents. I was even more exasperated when he said, "I'm sure you might like to include gratuities for some of the staff who served you particularly well."

"I'm at a loss for how much would be appropriate."

"Whatever you'd like to give would be fine, I'm sure. However, for your convenience, I have taken the privilege of making a list and putting in a suggested gratuity."

The list included Karl, of course, maître d's, limo drivers, maids, dealers, waitresses, and of course, Vince. Interestingly enough the companions were not listed. The total suggested tips came to a little under seventeen thousand dollars making the grand total bill right at one million one hundred and fifty thousand dollars.

Vince had a portable electronic device which somehow connected me with my bank in Tulsa. I typed in the amount I wanted to transfer and used one of those electronic pens like Wal-Mart uses and signed my name. All of a sudden, I was a million dollars poorer. Easy come; easy go, I guess. I tried to make out like it wasn't any big deal. Vince seemed pleased. Why not? I had just tipped him over ten thousand dollars.

He told me that I was always welcomed back at the Peninsula Hotel Resort and Casino and to give him a call if I'd like to do this again. He grabbed my bag; I handed him my room card. He told me he had a limo waiting to take me to the airport. Then a private jet would take me back to Tulsa. I smiled as I remembered Cindi and hoped she would make my flight a pleasant one.

Vince left me at the limo; a stretched, black Lincoln. The beefeaters opened my door and tried to put my bag in the trunk. It was only one bag so I told them I would keep it with me. I closed my eyes for the trip to the airport, still hung-over. I must have dozed, for the next thing I knew the door opened and I heard the whine of a jet engine. The pilot greeted me and offered to take my bag. I boarded first, then he closed the door as he entered the plane. He told me to make myself comfortable. I looked around but didn't see Cindi or another stewardess and said as much to the pilot. He told me one wasn't assigned for the flight to Tulsa.

Well, wasn't that a fine how-do-you-do? After I got over my mad, I reasoned that it made sense. They had already gotten my money and there was no need to send me home happy. *Leave 'em wanting more.* Sounded like a good marketing strategy.

CHAPTER THIRTEEN

# The Prado

It felt good to be back in Tulsa. I watched us circle around the city and land at Tulsa International. I'm not really sure why they call it International, as there aren't any international flights that I know of and no passport control. Perhaps they had those in the past and the name stuck.

My private jet taxied to my hanger and the captain opened the door and handed me my bag. I barely removed myself from the steps when the engines whined back up and the plane moved away. I didn't bother watching it take off.

As I walked toward the hanger, the same plump woman who asked for my truck key the week before met me. This time she was accompanied by a goofy looking kid, not more than twenty-two.

"Welcome home, Mr. Rigsby!" she said with a smile. "This is Scotty. He washed your truck and moved it into the hanger while you were gone."

"Thanks, Scotty," I said.

"Think nothin' of it," said Scotty with an "ah shucks" kind of attitude.

I realized that Scotty and the plump woman, whose name I didn't know, seemed to be expecting a tip. I reached into my wallet and handed them both a fifty-dollar bill and thanked them for watching out for me. Their faces told the story; they were both expecting me to give them much more than fifty bucks. I asked for my key and drove off without giving it, or them, another thought.

Driving back to my apartment on South Memorial Drive, I felt different. I felt used. Dirty. Money was changing me into something, someone else. A wave of disappointment came over me as I pulled into my apartment complex. This was not the nicest one in town, but it was a far cry from where I started out on my own and far short of the luxury I experienced in Vegas.

I pulled my truck into a parking place and checked the mail. Normally, I get only bills and junk mail. My mailbox was crammed full of mail, several pieces of which were registered mail notices that I'd have to go the post office to collect. I fumbled with the mail, my bag, and my keys as I unlocked the door to my apartment. I dumped the mail on my couch and noticed that my answering machine light was blinking. The only calls I usually get were from Momma, any girl I happen to be seeing and Marty wanting to go fishing. The message counter read ninety-nine messages; the machine was full.

After getting comfortable in my recliner, I pushed the play button to listen to the messages. The first one was from Jack Somebody or other who said I didn't know them but was in a "real bad way and needed some help" to the tune of thirty-five hundred dollars. I deleted that one. The next was from a local homeless shelter which heard I had won the lottery and thought I might like to share my newfound wealth with those less fortunate. "Fat chance" I said as I deleted that message, too.

Out of the ninety-nine messages, only one of them was from someone I knew. Uncle Allen had called, for the first time in my life, and asked if I'd help them out of a bind. He said that he and Aunt Marge had some medical problems and needed about twenty-five thousand dollars to get things straight. I'd have to ask Momma about that. Just as I finished listening to the last message, the phone rang. I answered it and found myself talking to some guy named Cliff who worked for the National Police Support Fund. I simply hung up on him and then disconnected the phone.

I grabbed the stack of mail and found it was nothing but solicitation for money as well. Every charity in America, and two from Canada, must have read that I was rolling in the dough and wanted to get rid of it. Nothing could be farther from the truth. I had been poor my whole life and it was all mine. Well, maybe not really poor, but certainly poor compared to what I was now.

I sat for a few minutes in my chair assessing my apartment. Perhaps it was fine for me a week ago, but now, after living like a king in Vegas, it wasn't going to do at all. I refused to spend another night there; I needed a nicer place.

I found my phone book and called a local travel agent. Patty from Tulsa Time Tours answered the phone and was glad to book me into a suite at Tulsa's only Five Star hotel, the El Prado Hotel and Suites. It was a newly opened property across the street from Utica Square, Tulsa's upscale shopping plaza, right in the heart of the old oil mansion district. Sounded like a perfect fit to me.

I grabbed my suitcase and began to pack my clothes. I decided that I didn't really want them anymore, except for some of my t-shirts and a couple pairs of jeans that felt good. I did pack my cowboy boots, Nikes, socks and underwear, and, of course, the new clothes from Vegas. I grabbed my trunk with my mementos and photographs from my childhood. I threw in my alarm clock, and then decided that I didn't ever have to get up early again if

I didn't want to, and instead, chunked it in the trash, like an NFL player that just made a touchdown.

Looking around, I realized I didn't have much. I had a ten-dollar clock on the wall in the living room. My TV was several years old. I didn't need anything else in the whole place. What should I do, just abandon it all? No, that wouldn't be right. I'd call Salvation Army or somebody to come and clean the place out.

I pulled up to the front of the El Prado and was surprised to find there was no one to open my door. There was a man in some sort of uniform standing by the door, so I called to him to come and get my luggage. He retreated inside and returned with a fancy luggage cart. He seemed surprised to see my old footlocker and my new very expensive leather case I got in Vegas. I dropped the tailgate so that he could retrieve my bags and handed my truck key to him. He just stared at me with a blank look. I asked him to go park my truck. "Oh!" he exclaimed, and then jumped in my truck to move it. "Definitely not Vegas" I said aloud.

The El Prado Hotel was elegant, but not lavish. Its large lobby bloomed with many varieties of fresh flowers. Several sitting areas were situated in the center of the room with the check-in counter to the left. The entire area appeared abandoned because there was no one in the beautiful room but the clerk behind the counter and a woman behind a travel desk. I had a peaceful feeling in this fine place; one that eluded me the entire time in Las Vegas.

As I moved toward the clerk I spied the concierge desk that had been hidden by a large flower arrangement. A young man stood at attention waiting for something to happen like a guard at Buckingham Palace. His eyes watched me as I approached the registration point.

"Owen Rigsby. I assume you have my reservation," I said with an air of snobbery that came out before I could control it.

"Of course, Mr. Rigsby. We have the Presidential Suite reserved for you. How long will you be staying?"

"I don't know yet. I'm going to be buying a house in the area and need a place to roost until then. It could be a couple of weeks."

The clerk seemed shocked that I'd be staying in their best suite that long. The tag she wore gave her name as Judy. She hadn't introduced herself yet.

"Is there a problem, Judy?" I asked.

"No sir. You do know that the Presidential Suite is twenty-two hundred dollars a night, don't you?"

"I don't really care how much it is. I want the best room in the hotel. Is that the best room?"

"Yes sir. How will you be paying? Cash, check or credit card?"

"Cash, I guess. Or check."

"Just a minute sir. I need to get the manager."

Doug, the day manager, came quickly to greet me. Mr. Rigsby, I understand you'd like the Presidential Suite for two weeks?"

"At least two weeks. Maybe longer."

"I don't want to be indelicate, but you do realize the suite is two thousand two hundred dollars per night? We don't have a weekly rate."

"That's the price Judy told me. Is there a problem?"

"Well sir, two weeks would be thirty thousand eight hundred dollars plus tax."

"Okay."

"Since you are a new customer, the hotel requires an advance payment."

"Oh! Is that all?" I said with a fake, arrogant sneer. I reached into my pocket and pulled out a wad of hundred-dollar bills and counted out three hundred and eight of them and placed them on the counter.

Doug and Judy both looked at me with strange expressions on their faces. "Sir, I must inform you that we do not tolerate any illegal activity in our hotel, paying guest or otherwise."

It took me a moment to realize that they thought I was some sort of drug dealer. I had to laugh. I told them that I was the Owen Rigsby that had recently won the lottery and that they didn't have anything to worry about. Doug's face turned beet red and stumbled all over himself to make an apology. They both seemed genuinely embarrassed to think they may have offended such a rich guest as me. I told them not to worry about it and we'd soon be friends.

We finished the check-in procedure and Doug called for the person I thought was the doorman to take my bags and show me to my suite. He pushed the elevator button and held it open for me before bringing the cart in with us. He pushed the button to the twelfth floor and said his name was Mark. He was about twenty-five years old or so and seemed to be anxious to please. He told me that there were only two suites on the twelfth floor, mine and the Governor's Suite, but mine was the bigger and the nicer of the two. He said I was the first guest to occupy it.

He opened the door to my suite and allowed me to enter before him. I was impressed. It didn't seem phony like my suite in Vegas. This room was spectacular, just like you'd expect in a fine hotel. In fact, it looked a lot like the single room I had in the Plaza in New York, but it was even more grand and, of course, a suite. It had a TV as big as the one in the Peninsula and the furnishings were better quality. It was a tad bit bigger, coming in at thirty-four hundred square feet. Leaning in, Mark whispered "beware of the mini-bar; the prices are ridiculous." He handed me my room key, which was an actual key, and waited for a tip. I handed him a one-hundred-dollar bill and told him to be sure and take good care of me. He left with a grin a mile wide.

This place felt good. It was right in the neighborhood where I would live for the rest of my life. How many old oil mansions just waited for me to move into them? I imagined I'd pop in down at the Prado for a drink, or to entertain some people, or whatever. I'd call it "the Prado" as my own nickname for it. I wondered what in the world a Prado was anyway. I'd have to ask them about that. Utica Square would be where I shopped for gourmet groceries and fine, tailored suits. Would I really be needing suits? Sure I would. I'd need them for all the fancy parties that rich people get invited to. Maybe I'd even get myself a tuxedo. Why not?

I looked at my new Rolex and realized that I hadn't called Momma yet to tell her I was back home and where I'd be staying. She wanted to know all about my trip. I told her I had a good time and had a gift for her. She told me that I needed to quit buying her presents. I asked her if she picked out the new carpet yet and if she had quit her job. She said no to both questions. I told her that she had to quit and that we'd talk about it tomorrow over lunch at the Prado. She hesitated but finally gave in to my request. She said she'd meet me at the Prado at noon tomorrow.

I called Marty and told him I was back in town. I didn't tell him about the girls, either, but did tell him that it had cost me over a million dollars. He was very concerned that I needed some sort of a money manager and that I might lose all my money before I realized it. I reassured him that I was in complete control and that I needed to blow that kind of money to celebrate my newfound riches. I told him I brought back a little something for him and his family and promised we'd get together soon for some fishing.

It hadn't really bothered me before, but now, with all my money, I felt that I wasn't beneath Marty. He never treated me as anything but a friend, but he had a much better life than I did, until now. I wasn't going to hold my money over him; he never did that with me. In fact, he had helped me out numerous times when I got into cash-flow problems. I always paid him

*Jackpot!*

back. Now, I might be able to do something really good to show him and Tracy how much I truly appreciated them.

After I got off the phone, I realized I was hungry. I grabbed my room key and headed toward the elevator. As soon as I pushed the button, I realized I did not miss that creepy elevator voice. It was nice to simply ride an elevator without the hotel knowing where I was going and what I was doing.

I made my way over to the concierge desk. The guy that had been there before was replaced by a perky, young brunette whose nametag said "Brenda."

"Hi Brenda. I'm Owen. What kind of restaurants do you have here at the Prado?"

"Good evening, sir. We have two restaurants. The Tulsan which is our breakfast and lunch restaurant, serving American and Tex-Mex fare and the Santa Barbara, which is our premier steakhouse."

"Do I need a reservation for the Santa Barbara?"

"No, sir. You are a VIP guest. All you need to do is show up and give your name and the number in your party. We'll prepare a table immediately."

"Is it any good? The steaks, I mean. Are they good?"

"It's just been selected as the best steakhouse in Oklahoma. It's a pretty good restaurant."

Being that it was a Tuesday night, there wasn't a great crowd at the Santa Barbara. I presented myself to the seating hostess and she sat me without hesitation. The designer of the Santa Barbara knew what he was doing. It was light and airy and gave the sense of being on the coast of an ocean somewhere. I knew that Santa Barbara was a city in California; maybe this was what they were trying to recreate. It appealed to my recently spoiled tastes. Hopefully, the steak would live up to the atmosphere.

The meal did not disappoint. The steak was perfectly grilled over a real wood fire, just like the cavemen ate it, I guess. They told me it was aged Angus. I don't know much about the aging process of beef, but I do know that aged Angus is just about the best you can get. I'm not sure it was any better than the steak I had in New York City, but it was a close second, if not equal. Far and away the best steak I'd ever eaten in Oklahoma.

I ordered a bottle of red wine, but took the waiter's suggestion, again, because I don't know a Chardonnay from a Cabernet. I'd drunk more wine in the past week than I had in all my previous years. Beer was my alcoholic beverage of choice. Up until now, it was all I could regularly afford. I had a couple of glasses with my supper and ordered coffee with my dessert. Glancing at my watch, I realized it was only nine o'clock. I was totally exhausted.

I called for my bill and signed it to my room. I left a nice tip in cash for the waitress. Finding my way to my suite, I drew myself a bath in the big marble tub. As it filled, I looked at the information book you find in hotel rooms describing the hotel and its amenities. I went in to look at the tub again to see what twenty-four karat gold faucets look like. Pretty fancy, I'd say. I lowered myself into the hot tub and found the remote control for the flat screen TV in the bathroom. I turned it on watched the last part of CSI rerun. I left it there because it was in Las Vegas. I recognized the casinos and the Stratosphere tower and laughed when I thought about the Nanny. My goodness! What a week that was.

My thoughts wandered all over the place as I mentally replayed my vacation in Vegas. I was still unhappy about Chloe and Mr. Jackson. I simply couldn't reconcile that in my brain. I thought of the incident with the Ferrari. What humiliation! My thoughts went back to Chloe and the fun we had on the houseboat. Not just the sex we enjoyed, but the whole evening that led up to Mr. Jackson. I felt my brow furrowing as I became angry first at Jackson, then at Chloe.

As in my Peninsula suite, I fell asleep in this tub as well. I woke up sometime after midnight and made my way all alone into the king-sized bed. I could hear a helicopter bringing someone to St. John's Hospital nearby. That was the only sound I heard. I drifted off into a restless slumber.

Having forgotten to close the drapes the night before, the sun woke me up a little before seven. Where was Karl when you need him? I fumbled for the phone and ordered a room service breakfast of coffee and a western omelet. A knock on the door twenty minutes later announced its arrival. I signed for the meal and enjoyed Tulsa coming to life from twelve stories up. I didn't have Karl and there was no one like Vince, but the Prado was turning out to be a nice place to call home, at least temporarily.

## Chapter Fourteen

# Showin' Off for Momma

At about eleven thirty, I headed downstairs to the lobby to wait for Momma. I made an agreement with Mark for him to open Momma's door and park her new Cadillac. I told him I'd take very good care of him if he took good care of me and my friends. Momma pulled up at ten 'til twelve and was surprised when Mark stopped her car, greeted her by name, and told her I was waiting just inside. Despite him being in a bellman's uniform, it was clear she wasn't going to let him have her new car. I could see she was getting distressed, so I bolted outside and told her it was all okay. I introduced Mark to her and told her that the next time she came to visit me at the hotel, just stop right in front and Mark would park her car for her. She was impressed.

I escorted her into the Prado. All she would say was "oh my." Most of us ordinary Okies don't get to see this kind of luxury on a regular basis. It was Momma's first time in a super-nice hotel like this; I wanted to make it count. We strolled up to the hostess of the Tulsan whom I had already prompted. She greeted us individually, "Hello Mr. Rigsby. Good Morning, Mrs. Rigsby. I have your table ready."

"How did she know who I was, Owen?"

"You're the mother of one of the richest men in Tulsa. They are going to know who you are."

"Oh my."

The Tulsan was another very nice restaurant, in a class by itself. It was thoughtfully decorated to demonstrate the progress of the economic success of Tulsa. Many of the beautiful art deco elements of Tulsa's finest buildings were recreated in the furnishings and decorations. Photographs of parks, museums, famous people and interesting buildings adorned the walls. A mural on one wall was a bigger-than-life photograph of the skyline at daybreak. It was truly breathtaking.

Momma looked at the menu, then at me. I could tell what she was thinking. "Don't worry about the prices; we can afford anything on the menu," I told her with an attitude of confidence. "Money is no object." I remembered that I wanted to say that in Las Vegas, but completely forgot, even when the timing would have been perfect. I realized that when I said it to Momma, it sounded arrogant. She just looked at me with worried eyes.

I ordered a carafe of house wine with our lunch. Momma had a chicken breast with herbs and lemon; I had a pretty good sirloin steak. It wasn't cooked over an open wood fire like at the Santa Barbara, but it was still pretty good. Momma said that in all her born days, she had never had wine for lunch. I told her to come back on Sunday morning and we'd have champagne for breakfast. "Oh my" is all she could say.

We finished our lunch and ordered coffee. "Do you want any dessert?" I asked Momma.

"No, Owen. I'm full. It was delicious!"

"I hear they have a really good fudge cake a la mode. I can order some for us both."

"Maybe I'll just have a bite of yours."

"Momma, there is no reason to share. I'll order us both one."

I told the waitress to bring us two of the double chocolate fudge brownie cake with a scoop of ice cream. It came with chocolate covered fruit on the side and the ice cream was sprinkled with sweet cocoa and chocolate shavings. Momma ate only a bite or two and when I asked her if she liked it told me that she was too full to eat another bite. I was full, too, but I was enjoying being rich. And if that meant eating rich foods, I was all over that.

I relished in the fact that I could give Momma nice things. I sat back and looked at her from across the table and realized how old she was getting. How old she was looking. She never kept herself up after Daddy died. The only time I ever saw her put on makeup since then was at my older sister's wedding. She hadn't let herself go, in the classical sense, that is, she was still petite and didn't smoke or drink. But part of her died with Daddy and she didn't ever seem to get over it. I guess I didn't either. Momma hasn't dated any other man. I don't know if she thought it would upset us kids or if she thought she would be betraying Daddy's love.

"Momma, why didn't you get married again?" I blurted out.

"Well," she hesitated, looking for the right words and failing to find them or deciding not to say them, she said, "I don't know."

I changed the subject. "Momma, I really don't like you working at the dry cleaner. You deserve better than that."

"Honey, I enjoy working. I know practically everyone in town."

"But Momma, you don't need to work now. I really want to take care of you."

"Son, I don't want to quit."

"But Momma…"

"Don't 'but Momma' me, Owen. I have to work; I don't know what I'd do with myself otherwise."

Momma can be just as hard-headed as Granny. You'd think they were mother and daughter. I'd have to think of some way to get Momma to quit. But when she calls me "Son," I might as well stop talking about it and move on to something else.

"Momma, I brought you something from Las Vegas," I said, as I pulled out the light blue box. I didn't know much about jewelry, but I knew that Tiffany was a big deal. I handed it to her. She looked at the name on the box and I thought she was going to cry. She opened it and took out the jewelry case inside. Pulling out the diamond necklace and earrings, tears came to her eyes.

"Owen! You shouldn't have!"

"Momma, you deserve to have the very best. You've always cared for me and the girls and never did anything for yourself. I'm here to tell you that it's time to start pampering yourself. And if you're not going to do it, then I am."

"It's just beautiful! But when am I ever going to wear them?"

"Right now. Put them on and see how they look."

She gingerly removed them from their cases and put them on. I stood up, took her by the hand and led her to the front of the restaurant where I had spied out a mirror when we first came in. "Never in all my life did I ever dream that I would be wearing something from Tiffany's!"

I glanced behind me and to find all the wait staff of the restaurant gathered around watching. I felt like a big shot. I liked that feeling. As Momma turned around, all the waitresses and one waiter made a fuss over her. I liked that, too. We went back to the table. I signed for the bill but left a one-hundred-dollar tip. The whole lunch was only seventy dollars, but I now had a reputation to uphold. I just gave my mother a sixteen-thousand-dollar necklace set from Tiffany's. I couldn't just leave fifteen percent. "OK, now let's go look for some new carpeting for your house."

We took her new Cadillac to one of the ritzy home décor outlets in Tulsa. Since she let me drive, she protested as we pulled into the parking lot that she didn't need expensive carpeting in her house. I ignored her objections. We were greeted by a young, professionally attired woman who asked us to sit in a comfortable office area and offered us coffee or tea. We both declined.

I explained the situation and surprised Momma by telling the young woman that I wanted to re-carpet the entire house, remodel the kitchen and bathrooms and replace the heating and air conditioning. While we were at it, I wanted a new roof, new energy efficient windows and new appliances. As long as they were there, they might as well paint the outside trim and arrange for new sod in the yard. I told the saleswoman that "money was no object." Finally! I was able to use it. Momma just gave me a look with those worried eyes again. I ignored her again.

Momma and I walked around the showroom looking at carpet and ceramic tile samples. She hadn't bought anything new for more than ten years when the washing machine finally ran its last spin cycle. I sensed she was awfully uncomfortable because she only looked at the cheaper products, although not much in that showroom was actually cheap. But I didn't care.

It took us about two hours to decide on everything. Momma was overwhelmed, so I made many of the decisions for her, especially when it came to the appliances. I ordered the top of the line everything, including a new garbage disposal. Momma said her old garbage disposal worked just fine. I told her the new one would work even better. I made arrangements for the work to begin the following Monday. I'd take Momma to a furniture store later in the week to re-outfit everything else.

On the way back to the hotel, I turned into Utica Square and pulled up in front of Saks Fifth Avenue. Momma asked me what we were doing there, and I told her she needed some new clothes to go with her new necklace. She protested all the way into the store and back out again with our arms filled with boxes and totes of new dresses, shoes, coats, purses, and even makeup. We completely filled up the trunk and the back seat of her Caddy. "It just isn't right, Owen. I've never paid more than sixty dollars for a dress in my life! One of those dresses you insisted on buying me cost over three thousand dollars!"

"Don't worry about it, Momma. I've got it covered."

"I know you have a lot of money, but there is no need to spend it all on me."

"Don't worry about it, Momma."

"But I do, Owen. I've heard about how some new lottery winners blow all their money the first year and end up in debt."

I had heard about that, too, but hadn't thought of it until Momma said it aloud. "That won't be me, Momma. I guarantee it," I said with some internal conflict.

*Jackpot!*

I drove across the street to the Prado and stopped by the front door. Mark hurried out to open the door for Momma. "Are you hungry yet?" I asked her.

"Oh my goodness, no."

"I'd really like to show you my hotel suite. In fact, you can move in with me." I said that before thinking that I might want to have a little female companionship in the near future, so I offered the alternative suggestion, "Or I could get you your own suite."

"I'd love to see where you are staying honey, but I don't know about staying at a hotel. It's too far to go to work. The gasoline would eat me alive"

"I completely forgot, Momma! I'm glad you said something about that. I've got something else for you in my suite."

Momma was completely impressed by my suite. She had never stepped into anything better than a Holiday Inn. Now she stood in a bona fide five-star hotel. The very best part of the room, in both of our estimations, was the outdoor veranda. The view of downtown Tulsa was spectacular. While it may not be the skyline of New York City, it is more than just a cow town. The tallest building was designed by Minoru Yamasaki & Associates, the same guys that built the World Trade Center in New York. In fact, until I saw the pictures of the pieces of the WTC towers after they fell, I didn't realize how much they look alike. The resemblance is uncanny.

I asked her again if she would like for me to reserve her a room and she declined again. I showed her around and then had her sit down at the dining table. "Momma, I have something for you," I said as I pulled out an envelope. "It is a credit card. I want you to use it for groceries, gas, bills and anything else you need or want. It has a $50,000 limit, but I'll pay it off each month, so buy whatever you want."

"Owen, I couldn't."

"Yes, you can. You can also get cash advances to pay for things that don't take credit cards."

"Owen, I…"

"Momma, this is something I want to do. You gave me the very best you could all your life and now it's time for me to return the favor."

I showed her the PIN and made her memorize it. It was Daddy's birthday. I made her promise me that she would use it for groceries and gasoline at the very least. She said she would, but it was rather half-hearted. "I'm serious about this, Momma. Spending my money on you is not blowing it. I want you to have everything you couldn't afford for the past thirty or so years. It's okay."

We hugged and she cried, and I felt like a good son. She told me she had to get going before it got too late. I told her that surely after all these years, she could take a little vacation time from work, especially now that we had so many workers coming to fix the place up a little. I finally talked her into spending one night at the Prado. I was really happy about that.

I introduced her to the Santa Barbara, and we enjoyed a late supper together. The food was impeccable, and the service was everything you'd expect from a fine restaurant.

Momma and I chatted a little about Las Vegas. She wanted to know everything I did. I left out a whole bunch of stuff including the women and the money. She wanted to know if I got to see Frank Sinatra. I told her what Vince told me. She said, "Well, of course, he died. I forgot." We both laughed and agreed that we didn't know much about Las Vegas or the world of entertainment.

I told her about seeing the Hoover Dam and a little about the houseboat ride. I told her about the Stratosphere Tower and the light show right out in the middle of the street. I told her we'd have to go out sometime; that anytime I wanted, I could call Vince and he'd arrange everything.

I talked Momma into ordering one of the Santa Barbara's delectable steaks. She selected a six-ounce filet which she could cut with a fork. I ordered another T-bone. There was no steak knife on the table; I used my butter knife to cut the steak. I noticed a cherry pie dessert and ordered one with vanilla ice cream. It also came with chocolate covered fruit. I ate it all, even though I was full halfway through my steak. Momma said she couldn't possibly eat dessert.

On our way back to my suite, I stopped by the concierge and made an appointment for Momma at the day spa. I selected the deluxe option that included massages, mud baths, hair treatment and a makeover. Momma didn't object too much; I think she might have been looking forward to pampering like this.

I also ordered room service for breakfast the next morning. Momma had trouble deciding what she wanted because she was so full of supper. I asked for coffee, pancakes, milk (because you can't properly have pancakes without milk), two eggs over-medium to put on top of the pancakes, orange and pineapple juice mixed (like at the Peninsula), four strips of bacon, two patties of sausage, hash browns, with a side of biscuits and gravy. Momma just stood there and looked at me in disbelief that I would order so much.

"I'll be hungry in the morning, Momma," I said. I also specified Griffin's Waffle Syrup, the pancake syrup of choice for discriminating Okies.

Momma wasn't prepared to spend the night, so I had the concierge get her a new night gown and the necessary toiletries. They were delivered to my suite in a reasonable amount of time. Momma and I sat out on the veranda looking at the lights of downtown Tulsa, not really saying much, just enjoying each other's company and the pleasant evening. Curiously, there are no mosquitoes on the twelfth floor.

I finally got around to asking her, "What do you think Daddy would think of all this?"

"I imagine he'd feel about like I do."

"How do you feel, Momma?"

"I'm happy, confused and worried all at the same time. I'm happy that you have all this and don't have to worry about money. I'm confused with all the newness of it, and I'm worried about you and what this money will do to you."

"Don't worry about me, Momma. I can handle it."

"I certainly hope so. Have you spoken with your grandmother yet?"

"No, not yet."

I hadn't thought to call Granny. I was a little leery of what she'd have to say about all of this. I know she and her church disapprove of the lottery. But surely when she sees how much money I've got, she'll be happy for me. "I was going to call her later this week or next week maybe. I brought her a pearl necklace from Las Vegas. I didn't think she'd wear diamonds."

We stayed out on the veranda until nearly eleven o'clock. Momma was just about asleep when I suggested we better go in. Her bedroom wasn't nearly as big as mine. She had a queen-sized bed, but her bathroom was still very nice. I showed her how her Jacuzzi worked, and I could tell she was a bit excited about it. I kissed her on the cheek and told her good night as I closed her door.

I decided that I didn't want to take a bath, so I stepped into the shower the size of a small bedroom. It had about ten different nozzles, from head to toe and on more than one side of the shower. It was like being in a car wash with the top down. I finally figured out how to turn some of the shower heads off and enjoyed a more subtle showering experience. I remembered to close the curtains and finally went to bed about midnight. I fell asleep immediately.

I don't normally remember my dreams, but I had some really crazy ones that night. I dreamed that Daddy was alive, and he and Momma were flying somewhere on a plane. I missed the flight and decided to catch up to them by flapping my arms to fly. In my dream, I didn't think it was out of the ordinary. I couldn't get them to open the door on the plane. As I looked into the window, Momma was replaced by Cindi and she and Daddy were getting all cuddly on the bench in the back of the plane. I couldn't figure out where Momma was, but then I saw her falling to the ground without a parachute. Just like Superman, I swept down to try and save her, but she hit the ground before I could reach her. She looked up at me before she died and said, "Why, Owen, why?" I asked her "Why what?" but she died before answering.

This dream really upset me. I often dream about Daddy, but never something like this. What did it mean? Did it mean anything at all? Was Momma in trouble? Was she going to die, too? I just couldn't bear the thought of that.

CHAPTER FIFTEEN

# Oriental Sweetheart Massage

Momma enjoyed her nearly day-long spa treatment. Most of the things she encountered for the first time. It must have been interesting to be one of the women serving her. While she was having all this done, I went out to look for a new car. The short time I had behind the wheel of a super-car only whetted my appetite. I had to have a Ferrari. It had to be mine.

I was extremely disappointed to find that Oklahoma had no Ferrari dealer. The local luxury import car dealer said they could make arrangements to find me one, but at a premium, I'm sure. The nearest dealership was in Dallas. I'd have to make arrangements to get down there to get one, but I was too busy to go today. I had to persuade Momma to quit her job.

I wasn't very good at convincing Momma of doing anything she really didn't want to do. I had a wild thought to go and burn down the dry cleaners, but that would be wrong on many different levels. Then I had a good idea. I'd bribe the owner to let Momma go. It would be hard, but it would be for her own good. Ten thousand dollars ought to do it. I'd go see the owner soon.

I made it back to the hotel in time to find Momma coming out of the spa with a new hairdo and wearing a new face. She was showing off some of the new clothes I bought her last night and honestly looked like a million bucks. She was beautiful. She thought so, too. I could tell it made her feel good. I offered to buy her supper, but she said she needed to get home to see about her cat.

I called Mark to bring her Cadillac around and I kissed her on the cheek as she was getting in. She stopped and moved forward to hug me. "Thank you, honey," she said. "I've had a great time with you here. When are you coming over to see about the house?"

"I'll be over tomorrow or the next day," I said. "I have a few things I need to do first."

"Thank you for my new clothes and all the nice things you've bought me, Owen. I hardly know what to say."

"You don't need to say anything, Momma. I'm really happy to be able to do something nice for you."

"Your Daddy would be so proud," she said, starting to dribble tears down her cheeks.

At the mention of Daddy, I couldn't say anything else. Tears began to well up in my eyes and I turned away before she could see me cry. I heard the car door shut and turned around to see her pull out of the hotel drive and onto 21st Street. She would be home in about half an hour.

All of a sudden, I found myself without anything to do. Let's be honest; there isn't much to do at all after you've lived like a king in Las Vegas for several days. There are clubs and Indian casinos, movie theaters and things like that, but I didn't feel like doing any of those things. It was just after six and there was still plenty of daylight left. Perhaps I'd go look for one of those oil mansions I had my mind on.

I told Mark to fetch my truck. While he was getting it, I walked over to the concierge desk to find another person, an older man with a nametag that read "Jasper". "Hello, Jasper. I'm Owen."

"Good evening, Mr. Rigsby. How might I help you tonight?"

"Please, call me Owen. I'm in the mood to look at some real estate. You might have heard that I recently won the lottery and I'd like to buy myself one of the fine old oil estates in this part of town. Do you know this area very well?"

"I've lived in Tulsa my whole life and not too terribly far from here."

"Do you know the best place to look for an oil estate?"

"You might want to consult a real estate agent, Mr. Rigs, I mean, Owen."

"I will eventually. I just wanted a head start to see what might be out there. Do you know any of them for sale?"

"No, sir, I don't. I know that most of the estates will be generally between Peoria and Harvard Avenues, and 21st and 41st Streets. Back when most of the homes in this area were built, 36th Street was the city limits. Now, this is all known as 'mid-town.' I know there are some nice places over by Philbrook."

I thanked Jasper and thought about what he said. Philbrook is the former estate of Waite and Genevieve Phillips. He was the younger brother of Frank Phillips, for whom Phillips 66 was named. It is a 72-room mansion built in 1926 on twenty-three acres of land smack-dab in the middle of Tulsa. In 1938, he surprised everybody by giving it to the city of Tulsa to be used as an art museum and now houses one of the finest permanent collections of Renaissance and Baroque art in the world. I remembered visiting there on a school field trip and was overwhelmed with the ornate gardens, fine tapestries and the incredible pipe organ. I remember it even had a lighted dance floor that everyone seemed to think was a big deal because it was built back in the 1920's. Maybe I'd just take a drive over to South Rockford and take another look at the place.

By the time I arrived, the Philbrook Museum of Art was already closed for the evening. I drove completely around the property which indeed looked like an Italian Renaissance Villa, complete with sculptured terraces and manicured gardens. From the back of the property, you could see the fountains, statues and, of course, the grand terrace. Or as we Okies might call it, the back porch. Some back porch this was. It was magnificent. I wondered if they would sell it to me and how much it might cost.

I drove around until it got dark looking for mansions for sale. I had no idea what any of them would cost, but I figured I had enough to buy what I wanted. I felt out of place, even though most of the folks that live even in these neighborhoods are good, decent people, I guess. They didn't seem too snobby. Actually, I really didn't see anyone to know if they were snobby or not. I saw a few Porches and quite a few Cadillacs and Lincolns and a few Mercedes. I didn't see any supercars. Maybe I'd be setting the trend.

It was getting about eight o'clock, but I wasn't ready to go back to the hotel, just yet. I thought about driving over to see Marty and giving them their presents from Las Vegas, but the idea didn't appeal to me. I thought about going to see Granny, but it was probably too late. She usually goes to bed right after Wheel of Fortune.

I pulled into a Sonic Drive-In and ordered a 'brown bag special,' upsizing my fries and drink to a large. I sat there listening to the radio, almost feeling guilty for having a hamburger and fries instead of a steak. The carhop came by and offered me some more ketchup or other condiments. She smiled at me not knowing I was rich. That felt good. Everyone was treating me differently than they did just ten short days ago. My entire life had changed. I liked some parts of the change and didn't like other parts. But my head wasn't clear. I remained drunk with wealth.

I slurped the last of my Dr. Pepper and tossed the trash into the can as I left. I realized I had been two whole days without the company of a woman. I decided I'd go try out a massage, Tulsa style.

I had never been able to afford a massage before, so I didn't know where to go in Tulsa to get what I wanted. I knew they had the Spa back at the Prado, but it was probably completely legitimate. I wasn't looking for a legitimate massage. I finally drove by a place on Sheridan called "Oriental Sweetheart Massage." It sounded like a place where I might have a little fun.

Rick Boyne

I parked and locked my truck and then walked to the door. It was locked, but the blinking neon sign said they were open. I saw a doorbell, so I rang it. The door buzzed and popped slightly open from an electronic security lock being triggered from the inside. I pulled the door open and stepped inside the dark room.

It was a small entryway of some sort with one chair and a darkened window with a money slot and a whole cut for talking. I approached the window, and an Asian female voice asked me what I wanted.

"I'd like a massage."

"You a policeman?"

"What?"

"I say, you a policeman?"

"No, I'm not a cop."

"Show me ID."

"What?" I was getting increasingly nervous about this whole set up.

"Show me you ID or you no get massage."

I pulled out my driver's license and pressed it up against the darkened window.

"Put it in slot."

I dropped it into the recess below the window and saw it disappear and then quickly reappear. "How much is a massage here?" I asked.

"Fifty-dollar cash money. No check. No credit card. You pay first."

"What do I get for fifty dollars?" I asked.

"You get massage. Anything else you arrange with girl."

"Do I get to pick the girl?"

"No. You get first available."

I figured I could at least try it out, maybe it would be something I could do regularly and therefore wouldn't feel so gross. I pulled fifty dollars out of my pocket and pushed it through the slot under the window. "Okay" I said. "Give me the first available girl. But make sure she's pretty."

"All girl pretty," the voice said. "You wait and see."

I felt uncomfortable sitting alone in the small dark room waiting for the first available masseuse. No telling what in the world I was getting myself

*Jackpot!*

into. It was a far cry from the swanky massage I had at the Peninsula. I had just about talked myself out of staying when the door opened, and a youngish woman said to "come on back."

I followed her through the door and down a hallway lit by painted light bulbs. You could hear people enjoying one another's company from behind the closed doors. You could, however, barely see anything. I noticed that the shape of the woman I was following was not as nice as the companions I had in Vegas, but this wasn't Vegas. She stopped at a door near the end of the hall and told me to go in and take my clothes off. I obeyed.

The room was nearly as dark as the hallway and front foyer. It was very uncomfortable, but I stayed anyway. The woman told me to take a shower, so I got in and started bathing. She just stood there looking at me with hardly any expression on her face. She handed me a towel. I dried and positioned myself on the massage table. This one didn't have a hole for your face. It had a towel that was shaped like a horseshoe. I guess it would have to work.

The woman began massaging my calves and thighs. She hadn't bothered to cover my naked rear end. I knew what I'd be getting myself into here. She ran her palm over my buttocks and up to my back and continued the massage for a total of five minutes. She quit the massage and asked me if I was a cop. I told her I wasn't. She then gave me a price list for different sex acts. I hadn't ever paid for sex before, so I had no idea about the going price. These prices sounded a little high, especially for the expected quality. I tried to bargain with her and got the total price down about sixty bucks less than she told me.

She told me I had to pay 'up front.' I did. She took off her clothes then asked if I had a prophylactic. I said no. She swore under her breath and began her part of the bargain. We finished and I realized that there had been no prophylactic used at all. Holy cow! Did I just have unprotected sex with a prostitute? What in the world was I thinking? I jumped up from the table and ran to the shower. She scolded that I could only have one shower, that it was going to cost extra to take a second shower. I told her what she could do with it and that she better have not given me any disease. I dressed as quickly as I could and literally ran down the dark hall.

Finding myself in the foyer, I jerked on the front door, but it wouldn't open. I banged on it and the voice behind the window said something uninterpretable and buzzed me out. I fumbled with my keys the way you do in a nightmare where the bad guys are after you and you can find the key or dial 9-1-1. My heart was beating fast, and I was sweating profusely. I couldn't believe what had just happened. All my life I carefully protected myself when I enjoyed the close company of someone casually. How in the world did I let this happen with a prostitute? Was I so out of control that I'd literally play Russian Roulette with HIV? I didn't know what to do.

Roaring my truck back to the Prado, I wheeled into a Walgreens Pharmacy that was open late. I ran back to the pharmacy part, but it was already closed for the night. Beside myself with fear, I knew I needed to do something. I got a carrying basket and headed over to the aisle with alcohol and iodine. I looked and looked but couldn't find any product for "unprotected sex with a prostitute." I bought a bottle of rubbing alcohol, hydrogen peroxide, tincture of iodine, witch hazel and Betadine solution. I bought a couple packages of gauze and tape. I went to the family planning area and, much too late, bought a large box of condoms. I wasn't going to be unprepared next time.

I kind of settled down a little bit and walked around the store as I tried to think of what I should do. Should I go to a doctor? Should I go to the ER? I simply didn't know. I mindlessly put things in my little blue basket as I walked up and down the aisles. When I got to the checkout, I found I bought chocolate covered peanuts and smoked almonds, a word search book, a travel mug and two sticks of antiperspirant.

I drove back to the Prado, but Mark wasn't there to park my truck. I found a spot for it and headed back to my suite. On the way, I decided to stop by the hotel bar, The Derrick. It was nearly deserted. I didn't want to sit at a table, so I just stood at the bar while the bar tender fixed me a bourbon and Coke. "Hey buddy" I said, "I need to ask you a question."

"What do you need?" asked the bartender.

I had no idea how I was going to phrase this question without looking like a complete idiot, so I just said, "never mind." I guzzled my drink and asked for another one. I signed for both of them, left a ten-dollar tip and asked if I could take it with me to my room. The bartender hesitated, and then gave me a nod of permission. I gathered up my medicine kit from Walgreens and headed to my suite.

Admittedly, I didn't know the first thing about STD's or HIV. Never one time in my life had I ever been so reckless. While I had been sexually active in my life, even more so lately, I never once had unprotected sex. I situated myself over the bathtub and began to pour the liquids directly onto my genitals. The hydrogen peroxide was okay, but the alcohol stung like fire. This couldn't be good. I took the soap from the dish and washed myself well, then tried the alcohol again. It still burned. I got sick at my stomach from worrying and actually threw up. I washed again and tried the iodine. It didn't burn as bad, so I got a cotton ball from the hotel amenity tray, soaked it in iodine and then used the gauze and tape to hold the iodine

*Jackpot!*

cotton ball in place where it burned. Maybe this would take care of it. Maybe not.

I cleaned up around the bathroom as best I could. I brushed my teeth and gargled with some hotel mouthwash. Wearing only my shirt, I went into the living room and sat down to watch some TV to take my mind off the events of the evening. Hell fire! Why me? Why this? Why now?

I had already finished off my drink from the bar, so I opened up the hotel mini bar. I didn't care if it was expensive; I could afford whatever I wanted. Just saying that in my mind made me feel better. I found a quality beer in the mini-fridge and pulled out the smoked almonds. My confidence level was back so I took my field dressing off and put my pants back on. Everything was going to be alright. *Next time, just bring your own protection, dummy.*

CHAPTER SIXTEEN

# Looking for a Tulsa Oil Mansion

The next morning held the exciting promise of a new day. The sun was shining; the birds were singing. Actually, it was nearly noon. I had emptied the mini fridge of all the quality beer the evening before and was rudely awakened by the phone. It was Marty. He wanted to know if I'd like to go fishing that weekend. I thought it was a great idea and told him that I'd meet him at his house bright and early Saturday morning. I could give him and Tracy my gifts.

I remembered the self-treatment I administered in the bathtub the previous night. I thought, to be on the safe side, I better do it again. It didn't burn at all when I poured the alcohol on myself, so I figured everything really was okay. I breathed a huge sigh of relief.

Getting dressed, I thumbed through the phone book for a realtor. I didn't know any realtors personally, but I did notice that there were many large homes with one yard sign in particular, so I dialed the number to Chitwood and Oldham Real Estate Brokers. A perky, but professional, young woman answered the phone. I told her who I was and what I wanted. She told me she would meet me at the Prado in one hour. I told her I'd meet her in the lobby.

I rushed downstairs to have breakfast or lunch or whatever meal it was supposed to be before the realtor arrived. The Tulsan had a nice buffet, so I decided to take advantage of it. It would be quick, and I could get enough to last me until supper. I'm not normally a buffet person, but this one wasn't bad. A man stood at a huge hunk of meat, slicing off what you wanted. He tried to get by with just one scrawny little piece, but he cut two more just like them and made it a decent hunk of beef. The potatoes were good, but I passed on the veggies.

I was elated to find a large dessert bar. I found some of the best chocolate mousse I had ever tasted. They offered a berry and ice cream dish that had some hard liquor in it. I didn't care for it too much. I took a healthy hunk of cheesecake with cherry topping; it was pretty good. I was sipping my coffee when Mark arrived with a man and woman both attired in business suits. "I'm Roger Chitwood of Chitwood and Oldham Real Estate" the man said as he held out his hand for me to shake. "This is my partner, Priscilla Oldham."

"Howdy" I said, trying to see how they'd take me. I was wearing my jeans and one of the shirts I bought in Vegas. I certainly wasn't gussied up like they were.

"I understand you are in the market for an older home in this area."

"Yep, I am" I said with a decidedly hick accent. I wasn't aware that I needed to talk like this, but it was already out there, and I guess I would have to go with it. "I won the lottery and I want to buy myself a great big oil mansion. You got any for sale?"

For the next half hour, Roger tried to talk me out of buying an older mansion. He tried to tell me that for the same money, I could have a brand-new house with all the fineries, and some of them were right here in the same area. I told him that I had heard about some of the new houses he was talking about. There had been stories on the news about people selling an old estate and a builder dividing the property and installing three or four giant houses where only one had previously stood. Many of the neighborhoods sought injunctions to have this practice stopped. I was inclined to agree with the established neighborhoods and didn't want any part of a new house in the area.

Roger then tried to convince me to buy a home in the southern part of Tulsa where there were some large homes on large lots. I was impressed with a lot of what they had to say. Pricilla told me that there were very few places in America where a dollar went farther in real estate. She said that some of the very same estates that sell for less than two million dollars in Tulsa would sell for anywhere between fifteen and twenty million in the Los Angeles area. Of course, the people in L.A. wouldn't want to live in Tulsa, even if they gave the houses away, and no one in Tulsa would ever even care to step foot in Los Angeles.

I told them that I had my heart set on an older estate in this part of town and didn't care to look at anything else. They could tell I meant business, so they offered to show me some of the properties they had listed. I asked them about Philbrook, and they completely ignored my question. I asked them if any of the available properties were famous or had been owned or built by famous people. They named a few architects, but I had never heard of them.

The first property was an eight thousand square foot, five-bedroom home on just over an acre. The asking price was two and a half million dollars. They told me it had been on the market for several months and that the owner had died, and the children would probably be willing to come down on the price. As we pulled into the drive, I was drunk with wealth again. The entrance had a small waterfall just outside the gate. The drive to the house was lined with oak trees covered in English ivy. They said it was built in 1931 during the Great Depression at a cost of over thirty thousand dollars. It was three stories tall. The woodwork throughout the house was exquisite. It had been fully remodeled during the last oil boom in the 1980's and was still quite livable. It had a swimming pool and pool house.

The second property was just east of Philbrook, and you could look out over the Philbrook gardens from the living room. It was a six thousand two hundred square foot beauty built in 1926. It also had five bedrooms, but only about half an acre. They were asking one million seven hundred thousand dollars for this home. The third, fourth and fifth properties were similar in nature. All around seven thousand square feet; all built between 1930 and 1935. Asking prices were in the one and three quarter million range.

I was getting overwhelmed, but I told Roger and Pricilla I was getting tired. I did enjoy riding in their Rolls Royce, however. It was nearly supper time, and I simply didn't feel like looking at houses anymore. Also, I knew that Philbrook was open until 8 pm and I wanted to look around. Who knows? Maybe they would sell it to me.

The dark blue Rolls pulled into the Prado a little after six P.M. Mark snatched the door open for me and greeted me by name. I told them that I'd like to look some more, but probably not until next week. They told me they would send me a list of all available properties that met my criteria, and they would be happy to show any of them I wished to see. We thanked each other and that was that. To be honest, Roger was a little bit too prissy for me and Pricilla was a little too cold. I bet they had fun times around their office at Christmastime.

I stopped by the Santa Barbara and told them I wanted a table, but that I'd be back in about half an hour. I went to my room and showered. Housekeeping had been there and made everything fresh again. The mini fridge was restocked and ready for another binge. I put some of my Las Vegas pants on and made my way back to the restaurant. My table was waiting.

I ordered a bottle of house wine and enjoyed a leisurely supper of steak and lobster. I perused the brochures of the homes I had visited. Any of them would be just fine. One of those fleeting moments of lucidity told me that I didn't need a house that big for just one person. The description of the gardens, greenhouses and guesthouses took care of those thoughts. None of the homes that I had visited were furnished. I'd have to go buy furniture. I have never liked shopping, but it was because I couldn't afford what I wanted. Now, I could afford the whole store. Things were looking up for Owen Rigsby.

## Chapter Seventeen

# Giving Gifts

Saturday's arrival made me glad. I spent Friday doing not much of anything. I watched some TV, ordered room service and got a haircut. I woke up early to get to Marty's house by six thirty.

We already agreed to take Marty's boat out this time. I kept my boat in storage not too far from my old apartment. I'd have to take care of that, too. When I pulled up, Marty already had his boat hooked up to his truck and was carrying out an ice chest.

"Morning, Marty."

"Morning, Owen. How are you doing?"

"Man, I'm great!" I've got the world by the horns and I'm not letting go."

"Well, let's just see if all that money makes you a better fisherman."

"It probably doesn't. But it makes being a bad fisherman stink less."
"I'll bet it does, Owen. I'll bet it does."

I loaded my rods and tackle into Marty's boat and helped him secure everything for the drive to the lake. He brought a thermos of coffee and a couple of cups, so I poured while he maneuvered the boat out onto the street. "You hungry?" I asked.

"I had a banana."

"La-ti-da. A banana. Why don't we drive by the donut shop on the way, and I'll get us some breakfast?"

"Sounds like a plan."

By the time we finally arrived at the lake it was nearly eight in the morning. I backed the boat down the ramp and Marty fired it up and drove it off the trailer. I pulled his truck up to the parking area and joined him on the dock after he did his traditional driving off without me gag. I love Marty like the brother I never had. "What are we fishing for today?" I asked.

"Anything that will bite," was his usual answer, but that day he said, "I heard the sand bass are running. Let's troll and see what we come up with today."

We both rigged up our poles and let our white spinner bait drop eighty to one hundred feet behind the boat. I poured some more coffee and helped myself to another donut. We sat in silence as Marty steered the boat along an underwater ridge where the sand bass usually feed. We made two passes before Marty's pole bent under the strain of a small white bass.

He said, "That's one."

I said, "That's barely worth counting."

He said, "I got it in the boat, didn't I? That counts as one."

We caught many more fish on the subsequent passes.

After an hour or so, Marty asked, "Have you given any more thought to what we talked about before?" To save my life, I had no idea what to what he was referring. I sat silently for a moment, trying to figure it out when he prompted me, "You know, about getting saved." I didn't say anything for a while, then finally said, "Marty, no. I haven't thought about it at all. I've been kind of busy. I'm trying to buy a house and get my life situated into my new millionaire lifestyle. I don't have time for God and church and all that."

"I don't want to press you or anything. I was just wondering if you had given it any thought. I only mention it because I care."

"I know you do, Marty." Just then, I remembered I was trying to look up all those Bible verses when I got the call about the lottery numbers. "But what difference would it make anyway."

That must have been the opening Marty was waiting on because for the next half hour he told me about all the things he had been learning about God. How it wasn't religion he had found, but a real relationship with God. He told me about how much God loves us even though we do bad things. He told me that God loved me so much that he sent Jesus to take my punishment for me. In my place. He told me that all of his life he had been looking for a deeper understanding of God and his purpose in life and the real meaning of life. He said he found that when he gave his life to Jesus. "Owen, do you want to do this, too?"

"No. Not now, Marty," I said, trying to be polite. I don't need to anymore. I've got money; I don't need God to meet my needs."

I thought Marty was going to cry. He was visibly overcome with some sort of emotion. I just ignored it and got myself another donut. I reassured myself that I really didn't need God; I was self-sufficient. Everything was going my way. "Hey, Marty. Pull the boat over to the bank. I need to take a leak." Marty steered the boat over to the shore. I hopped out, knowing that it is quite precarious to try to stand on the side of the boat while you do your business. I went behind a tree for privacy.

*Jackpot!*

I screamed like a little schoolgirl. I have never had such a burning pain when I urinated as I did then and for the next couple of days. It felt as if I was passing razor blades. I noticed I was oozing some yellowish puss. This couldn't be good. I gained my composure and returned to the boat. Marty was looking at me with a weird look. "Everything okay?" he asked. "No. Not at all. It burned like fire just now when I urinated."

"Maybe you have a kidney infection."

"Yea, that must be it," I said, hoping for it to be so.

"Do we need to head back?"

"No, I think I'll be okay. It doesn't hurt now; only when I was going."

"Your call, man. If we need to go, just say the word."

We spent the rest of the day catching fish and having fun the way friends can do when they've spent their whole lives together. I had cleaned out the donuts and, since it was getting along in the afternoon, we decided to go in. We spent an hour cleaning over fifty sand bass, three black bass, two crappie and a channel cat. Not a bad haul for a day where it burned to go to the bathroom.

Tracy has a way of grilling the fish with onions, mushrooms and lemon that eliminates the heavy fish taste and just makes it delectable. She cooked while Marty and I got cleaned up. Marty and Tracy live in a comfortable four-bedroom home in South Tulsa. I've never asked him, but I'm willing to bet they paid half a million for it. It has a huge living room, but in the late spring, summer and early fall, they practically live on their back patio. Marty had an outdoor kitchen installed. It has a grill, several cook spots, a fryer and even an oven. There is a big refrigerator with a separate ice maker. They have an outdoor air conditioner for the heat of the summer and two outdoor fireplaces for when it's chilly. Most of it is covered which protects the furniture and his big screen TV closes up and locks to keep it safe. The swimming pool is just past the patio and has a big slide for the boys to play on. Tucked away in a private corner is a hot tub.

I always bring a change of clothes when Marty and I go fishing so that I don't stink when we have our fish dinner afterwards. We gathered around the outdoor dinner table to eat when, for the first time since I've know them, they all held hands and Marty prayed, thanking God for the food, for the fun time that he and I had that day and for several other things. They all bowed their heads and closed their eyes. I know because I kept my eyes wide open.

We passed around the fish and ate all we wanted. Tracy had prepared a pineapple upside down cake; her specialty. I had three pieces. About the time we all finished, but before Tracy started clearing the table, I announced that I had something for each of them. I pulled out the t-shirts for the boys. As expected, they were thrilled to get them and ran off to try them on. Tracy immediately recognized that the fancy light blue box was from Tiffany's and said as much as I handed it to her. She was genuinely surprised and happy to receive the diamond tennis bracelet.

I thought I was going to cry when I handed Marty his gift. I choked up a little and told him and Tracy how much they meant to me and that these gifts were just little tokens of my love for them. I said that I knew that they were just things, but I wanted them to have them and to think of me whenever they put them on. As Marty unwrapped the box and saw the name Rolex embossed on the lid, he sat it down on the table, stood up and hugged me. Before he even opened the box, he thanked me for it and for our friendship. It was truly a memorable moment.

It was getting late, and I thought I better be getting back to the Prado. I invited them over for Sunday brunch. They declined but invited me to go to church with them instead. We both took rain checks. We all hugged each other and said goodnight. I don't know what I'd do without a friend like Marty. In fact, I think he's the only true friend I have.

## Chapter Eighteen

# Marty

Marty was born in Enid, Oklahoma. His family moved to the Tulsa area where his father opened a furniture store. He was the only son, born third of four children. By all appearances, his family was a normal, happy family. But appearances are deceiving.

His father made a successful business selling discount furniture. He was well-respected in the community and was once asked to run for the school board. That respect ended when he walked through his front door.

Marty's mother nearly died while giving birth to his little sister. The trauma of forty hours of labor followed by an emergency C-section affected her emotionally. Mr. Westbrook stepped up and took care of his family while she recuperated. She never fully recovered. Marty was three years old.

She became emotionally detached from her husband and shut him out of her life. He was understanding at first, but in addition to being frigid, she became a bitter nag. This was too much for him and he eventually drifted away from her as well. Unfortunately for their marriage, he drifted into the open arms of another woman.

He enjoyed the other woman's company for several months before committing the physical act of adultery. It only happened once and almost destroyed him. He knew he'd broken his wedding vows. With guilt overwhelming him, Marty's father confessed everything to his wife. She was less than understanding.

She called him everything she could think of and kicked him out of the house. He went to a motel for a couple of days to let her cool off. When he returned, she wouldn't talk to him. He fell on his knees and begged forgiveness again. She told him he could stay because the kids missed him, but he'd never be touching her again. She laid down the law.

Eventually they became cordial and occasionally enjoyed civil conversation. Once in a while, she even allowed him to kiss her cheek. In public, they were the ideal family. At home, they were dysfunctional, at best.

When Marty was seven, his father took up bowling. He bought a custom-made ball, a nice bag and a team shirt with his name on it. Every Friday night, with his wife's blessing, he got dressed up in his bowling shirt and headed to the alley. At least that's what he told his family. In reality, he was meeting a different woman each weekend. His wife's bitterness drove a wedge of indifference between them. She constantly refused his romantic advances. What his wife refused him in the bedroom, he found in a host of willing, lonely women.

By the time Marty was a teenager, he figured out what was going on. He saw how the constant deceitfulness devastated their family. He watched his mother slip further into denial and his father further away from his family. Almost as soon as their youngest child left the house, they divorced. She moved to Oklahoma City to be close to their oldest daughter. He married a woman who had already been divorced three times.

Marty was good in school and excelled academically. As a senior in high school, he was awarded thousands of dollars in scholarships. He decided to attend the University of Oklahoma in Norman to study finance and economics. He pledged the Beta Tau Rho fraternity.

College life suited Marty fine. He liked the independence. He especially liked being away from his family's problems. His parents kept liquor in the house to get through their own troubles, but he wasn't allowed to drink at home. He got drunk his first weekend at college. Part of him liked the way it made him feel, but he didn't like the loss of control.

His father's infidelities adversely affected him and any potential relationships with women. He was so terrified of becoming like his dad that he seldom dated. He was one of the few members of his fraternity who was still a virgin after his freshman year. The behavior of his frat brothers at the wild parties bothered him. He seldom stayed in the fraternity house when they had their orgies. Several times he regretted joining his fraternity, but the hazing he endured to join made him reluctant to leave the house.

He studied hard and did well in all his courses. He was affable and made friends quite easily. In the spring semester of his freshman year, he noticed the prettiest girl he had ever seen in two of his core classes. She flirted with him, but he pretended to ignore her. By spring break, he had asked her out.

Her name was Tracy, and she too was studying economics. She was from Shawnee, Oklahoma, just a short distance from Norman. She was a member of Gamma Mu Kappa sorority and seemed to be popular among her sorority sisters. She came from a well-to-do family; her father owned a string of Chevy dealerships in central Oklahoma. She was an only child and was used to getting her way at home. Despite having the appearance of being spoiled rotten, she was actually an exceptionally sweet girl.

After several dates, Tracy began to get frisky. She was not a virgin. She wasn't used to a guy not wanting to sleep with her. Marty's hesitations confused and excited her. They weren't dating exclusively during their freshman year, but she had her eye on him.

That summer, he went home for the last time to a two-parent family. Tracy traveled with a couple of her sorority sisters to Greece. She sent him a few postcards and even called him once from a kiosk in Athens. He thought about her all summer but was afraid to commit to a relationship with her because he didn't want to fail her like his father failed his mother.

When classes started back up in August, he asked her out on a date. On the way back from the restaurant, she threw herself at him. He rebuffed her advances, and it caused a riff. She interpreted it as rejection; all he could think about was his father's bowling night.

He didn't call her for several weeks. He had a class with her, but she wouldn't even look at him. He felt bad. He really liked Tracy but wasn't mature enough to overcome this glitch in his raising. He saw her studying in the South Oval and decided to talk with her about it. She listened and realized it wasn't about her. Once they were able to talk about it, she understood it was a special kind of respect for her, not rejection. This made her want him all the more.

She quit pressuring him for sex for the rest of the semester and they enjoyed their time together. She loved sunsets and he was constantly pleasing her with a new vantage point each weekend. He went to Shawnee to meet her parents; they liked him.

Christmas was extremely awkward because his parents had divorced. He spent Christmas Eve with his mother and sister's family in Oklahoma City and Christmas Day with his dad and new wife, Julie. Actually, he only had lunch with them and stayed long enough to open presents. He left quickly to go to Owen's mother's house. Owen was there for the day.

They hadn't seen too much of each other since Marty went off to college. They had a good time catching up and realized how much they missed each other. They both promised to make an effort to get together more often, but something always got in the way.

Marty went back to Norman to a nearly empty fraternity house. He was lonely and miserable. Tracy and her family went skiing in Colorado for Christmas and he wouldn't see her again until classes started. There wasn't much to do on campus during the break. He slept a lot and watched old movies to pass the time. He was heartbroken over his parents' divorce and a ruined Christmas.

He was relieved when classes resumed. He threw himself into his studies and was making a name for himself among his professors as a good student. He was pleased with his success.

He and Tracy continued to see each other. He searched out new sunset venues and proudly offered them to her. Late in the spring, they were at Thunderbird Lake, enjoying a sunset picnic. Tracy brought along a bottle of wine and a blanket. They stretched it out on the red, sandy shore. She had waited long enough. That night she was determined to seduce him.

They cuddled and kissed as they often did at sunset. This time, however, she took off her blouse and bra. Marty was shocked but didn't immediately look away. She kissed him while placing his hands on her bare breasts. Marty, defenses loosened with wine, relented.

His first sexual encounter didn't disgust him. He enjoyed it, which troubled him. After taking her back to the Gamma House, he spent the rest of the night in determined soul-searching. He knew that this changed their relationship. He knew that he could easily fall into the same pattern as his father, and it concerned him. Did he love her? Was he going to continue in this physical relationship with no meaning? Was he being ridiculous?

The next morning, he started making arrangements. When everything was ready, he called Tracy and asked her out to dinner. They drove to Christopher's, the most expensive, most romantic restaurant in Oklahoma City. They enjoyed a delicious supper - both ordering lobster. Technically, they were too young to legally order wine, but they got away with it anyway.

When dessert was finished, he stood from the table, moved around to face Tracy and got down on one knee. He declared his love for her, presented her with a small engagement ring as token of that love and asked her to marry him. Her smile would have been enough, but she leaned down, looked him in the eyes and said "yes." The whole restaurant applauded as they embraced and kissed for the first time as a betrothed couple. They didn't notice.

Her parents were delighted but insisted they wait until after graduation to get married. Her father promised to pay for a huge wedding if they would consent to his wishes. Even though this meant a two-year engagement, they decided it would be best to wait. Tracy wanted a big wedding and neither thought they could afford to be married and both continue in college.

Marty justified their two-year intimate relationship with the knowledge they were engaged. They didn't move in together while in college but grew together emotionally. Occasionally, Marty had panic attacks related to the fear of future infidelity on his part. They had no real crisis during the engagement, but they enjoyed the time together as they completed their studies.

As the big day finally approached, the plans become more extravagant and complicated. Marty didn't care what color the flowers were. He didn't care how many bridesmaids there were or what kind of dresses they wore. He wasn't concerned with the wedding ceremony at all. It was the marriage that was on his mind. He decided that each and every day of their married lives, he would wake and up and tell her he loved her. Every night before they went to sleep, he'd tell her the same thing. He was determined to be faithful to his bride.

The wedding turned into the social event of the summer. Tracy's father was a friend of the governor, so he and the first lady were in attendance. The guest list was a virtual Who's Who of Oklahoma movers and shakers. It proved to benefit Marty immensely.

During the wedding reception, Joseph McFarland, president of the First National Bank of Tulsa, decided to hire Marty. Joseph was a college buddy of Tracy's paternal grandfather, who used his connections to seal the deal. Recently graduated and just married, Marty and Tracy would begin their lives together in a new home that her parents gave them as a wedding present. Tracy told them she wanted to live in Tulsa, for a change as much as anything else. They picked out an elegant home in mid-town.

They spent their honeymoon in Barbados. It was Marty's first trip out of the country; Tracy had been there twice before. Marty was impressed with Tracy's ease of travel to a foreign country. He was out of his element but felt he could get used to it. Her maternal grandparents paid for their honeymoon as a wedding gift. It was first class all the way. Marty's family wasn't poor, but because of his parents' marital problems, they had never been on a family vacation anywhere before. Marty didn't know how to travel in style.

They enjoyed the sunsets on the white beaches of the Colony Club Hotel, a property restored from a former private club into a premier luxury resort. They took water taxis between other luxury hotels, experimenting with different cuisines. Tracy enjoyed riding horseback along the beach; Marty just enjoyed being married to Tracy. It was a fairytale honeymoon.

For Marty and Tracy, the honeymoon isn't over. Their love continues to grow. Marty had just received his first promotion at the bank when their first son arrived,. When he was one year old, they moved out of mid-town into one of the big, new homes in South Tulsa. A year after their second son arrived, Marty made junior vice president. His success had nothing to do with his wife's grandfather; they were merit promotions. Marty was good at what he did, and everyone knew it.

They travel as much as possible. He and Tracy have taken the boys all over the United States and through much of Europe. They're planning on a trip to see the Great Wall of China in the next few years. Marty has become an expert tourist. He doesn't speak any foreign languages but is able to communicate using his hands.

Their life together in Tulsa is as it appears. They love each other and are completely devoted to their marriage. Turns out Marty is nothing like his father. He has found it easy to be faithful to Tracy. Their lives revolve around their children and their marriage. They work to make both a priority - and it shows.

A couple of years ago, Tracy got acquainted with Sharon Welch, a woman at her gym. They were about the same age and had children about the same age and were both stay-at-home moms with executive husbands. Sharon was the nicest person Tracy had met in a long time. They became instant friends.

Sharon was genuine. She had an inner peace, almost a glow about her. It wasn't long until she was talking to Tracy about deep things; things that Tracy had never thought of before. She spoke about love, forgiveness, acceptance and confession. Tracy ate it up. Sharon asked Tracy if she'd like to join a group of women who met for lunch and Bible study once a week. Tracy didn't know anything at all about the Bible. She could count on one hand the number of times she'd even been in a church. They were all either weddings or funerals. Even her wedding was outdoors at her father's country club. Her parents weren't church-going people, and she didn't know what to expect.

The study rotated among the ladies' each week, with the host fixing lunch for the rest of them. The first time she attended was at Sharon's home. It was less than five blocks from her own home, but in a different addition. The other ladies were friendly, and everyone wanted to know all about Tracy. She felt accepted immediately.

They ate lunch, shared some prayer, read and then studied a passage out of the Bible. Tracy was embarrassed that she didn't have a Bible. Well, that wasn't completely true. She had taken the Gideon's Bible out of the hotel room as a souvenir of her honeymoon, but she didn't want to bring it to the luncheon. Sharon had an extra one she lent Tracy.

The leader of the group, Mitzy, asked everyone to open to First Corinthians. Tracy just sat there with a blank stare on her face. Sharon showed her where the table of contents was and helped her find the right page. They discussed the topic of love. Tracy enjoyed herself and she felt good about *really* reading the Bible for the first time in her life. She continued to participate in the little group, even offering to host it at her house sometime.

Sharon continued to share deep things with Tracy. Tracy began reading the Bible on her own and discovered that if she died, she didn't know if she'd go to Heaven or not. Sure she believed in God and in Heaven; everyone did, didn't they? But how do you know if you are going to Heaven or not? She asked Sharon these questions and listened as Sharon shared the Good News with her. She gave her life to Jesus that day and was excited to tell Marty about it.

Marty had grown up in church. He got baptized when he was just a kid, but he didn't really know what he believed or why. He was happy when Tracy told him but didn't know what to do with the information. Sharon invited them both to go to church with her. Tracy eagerly accepted the invitation, but Marty was less than enthused with the prospect and decided to stay home. She came home from church with news.

"Marty! Guess what! I'm going to get baptized! Would you come and watch me?"

"Baptized? You mean you have never been baptized?"

"No. I've never been in a church to do it before. I spoke with Sharon's preacher, Pastor Dan, and he said that the next step is to get baptized. And I'd really like it if you and the boys would come to church and watch me."

"Well, of course we will," Marty said. Trying to think of some way to make her feel good, he said, "I'm happy for you, Tracy. Really."

The whole family went to church the next Sunday. It was their sons first time in church, but they were well behaved. Marty hadn't been to church in years. He stopped going when his parents quit making him go as a young teenager. It felt good to be back in church. He remembered singing some of the songs as a kid, which brought back some bittersweet memories. He watched his wife walk down into the waters of the baptistery. The preacher asked her some questions, said a few other words then dunked her down into the water. He remembered when Reverend Chapman baptized him as a kid. The whole congregation applauded when she came up out of the water. He found himself with a tear in his eye. He thought that was peculiar.

He met Pastor Dan after the service was over. Pastor Dan had a few questions for him. He wasn't quite ready to bear his soul to someone he didn't know, so he avoided most of the queries. That didn't stop Pastor Dan. Tracy and the boys attended church over the next several months. Marty either played golf or went fishing. Pastor Dan continued to make contact with him. They had lunch a few times together and even went out for a round of golf. Even though the preacher was persistent, he didn't crowd Marty or make him feel pressure to open up. He seemed to genuinely care about him.

Almost a year to the day after Tracy was baptized, her prayers were answered. She had become faithful to her new church, faithful to the ladies' Bible study and faithful to pray for her husband's salvation. Pastor Dan came over one evening and Marty was ready to talk to him. He finally opened up to Pastor Dan and told him that even though he had been baptized, he didn't know if he was going to Heaven. It scared him. Pastor Dan asked him lots of questions about his childhood baptism and about what he believed. Marty began to realize that he had been baptized out of peer pressure and not out of obedience to God. Pastor Dan showed him verses in the Bible that proved that the act of being baptized didn't save someone from Hell. He showed Marty how to give his life to Jesus and believe in Him for his salvation. Marty fell down on his knees in tears and repentance and confessed his faith in Jesus. He was baptized the next Sunday.

Pastor Dan told Marty that one of the most important things a follower of Jesus needs to do, in addition to prayer and Bible study, is to tell other people the Good News. He asked if he could think of five people to whom he could tell about his new relationship with God. He thought of six, with his best friend, Owen Rigsby, at the top of the list.

CHAPTER NINETEEN

# Oh! The Humiliation!

I drove back to the Prado, feeling pretty good about myself. Then I had to go to the bathroom again. The pain was unbearable. I looked down to make sure I wasn't urinating fire. No, it wasn't fire. But it sure didn't look right either.

I decided I better go see somebody, so I walked across the way to St. John's emergency room. I didn't have to wait too long to see a doctor. I explained my symptoms and they took a urine test. The doctor came in said there was yellowish puss in my sample. I told him that I had been oozing all day and it had even stained my underpants. He said he'd like to run a test.

I cannot even bring myself to describe the awkwardness of the test that some old nurse conducted on me, save to say the doctor wanted a swab of fluid from my urethra. I cannot think of many things worse. It was painful and embarrassing. The doctor came back in a little while and told me that I had gonorrhea. Well, it didn't surprise me. That's what I get for being out of control.

The doctor said it was a good thing that I came in early. He told me horror stories about people not getting treated for it. He gave me a prescription for a ten-day supply of antibiotics. He was adamant about finishing it, even if the symptoms go away. He told me to not have sex until I finish the treatment and to come back after 2 weeks for a follow up visit.

*Gonorrhea. Oh! The humiliation.*

## Chapter Twenty

# Bad News

I didn't wake up a happy camper Sunday morning. I completely forgot about inviting Momma for Sunday brunch at the Tulsan. The suite's doorbell woke me up. I answered the door and was stunned to see Momma looking so good. She was wearing another one of her new dresses and had on her diamond necklace. She wore makeup, complete with rouge and lipstick.

"Oh Momma! You look wonderful!"

"Thank you, Owen. I feel wonderful."

"Come on in while I get dressed. I overslept."

"That's okay, honey. You take your time."

I went back to the bathroom and expelled the cockleburs from my bladder. I must have made some unpleasant noise because Momma asked if I was all right. I told her that I had a kidney infection. She told me that I better go see a doctor. I told her I went last night. That placated her for now. This is another thing that Momma didn't need to know about.

I dressed in my new clothes from Vegas but noticed that housekeeping must have shrunk them a little in the laundry. The slacks weren't so slack, and the shirt was a bit tight around the middle. I'd have to get on them about that.

I escorted Momma down to the buffet like we were royalty or something. There were quite a few people there; it became THE spot for the idle rich to gather on Sunday mornings. The buffet wasn't as elaborate as some of the buffets I saw in Las Vegas, but I guarantee it was more than something for Momma.

I watched Momma's eyes as we went to the front of the queue and were shown a table immediately. While it was a buffet, a waitress took our drink order. We both asked for coffee. I remembered offering Momma champagne for breakfast and ordered some. The waitress asked if we'd rather have Mimosas. Neither of us knew what that was. The waitress picked up on that rather quickly and explained it was a blend of champagne and orange juice. We said we'd be delighted to try some.

I stood up first and pulled Momma's chair out, trying to act like a gentleman or a big shot in front of the crowd. Surely everyone had their eyes on us. The Big Shot Millionaire Lottery Winner and his mother. Having brunch. At the Prado. Certainly everyone was talking about the diamonds that I had brought my mother from Tiffany's. People must be imagining what it must be like to be me.

I called a waitress and told her that Momma needed some help. Momma protested but I didn't listen. I made the woman carry Momma's plate through the buffet line and take it back to the table. That turned some heads, I can tell you.

I felt like I was in hog heaven, being a big shot in front of a bunch of fancy rich folks and a buffet line that wouldn't quit. I perused the line before actually taking anything. I went to the omelet station and ordered a three egg everything omelet with extra cheese. While the chef prepared it, I attacked the pastry table. Everything you could imagine was there. Pan Dulce. Croissants, plain and chocolate. Apple fritters. Cream puffs. Chocolate and caramel éclairs. I took at least one of each.

I dropped my plate of sugar at the table and went to collect my omelet. I couldn't tell if I was supposed to eat it or put it in a museum. I chose to eat it. I didn't realize how hungry I was until I had eaten the first round of brunch food. Brunch is a combination word that means breakfast and lunch. I finished off the breakfast portion of the meal and now it was time to see what they had for lunch.

Momma said she was too full to eat anything else. I told her that I was going to get my money's worth, and they'd have to think twice about letting Owen Rigsby through their buffet line again. We both laughed at my little joke, and I headed over to the beef Wellington. I don't know why you go to so much trouble to cook beef. Can't you just throw it on a grill? After tasting it, I still have to ask that question. Why does anyone need to put pâté de foie gras around a perfectly good tenderloin?

I loaded up my plate with twice baked potatoes, shrimp, a pork chop and some garlic fried green beans. Tracy served those to me once before and I really liked them. I took a second plate just to hold all the specialty breads they offered. I think that Sunday Brunch at the Prado was going to be a regular activity for me.

Momma couldn't believe that I brought so much back to the table after having already eaten so much. "I'm not done yet, Momma. The dessert table is calling 9-1-1 and I'm the ambulance!"

Momma decided she'd go spy out the desserts when I finally made my way to the dessert table. We had been there a little over an hour. We took our time and Momma went to the bathroom twice while I was still eating. They had three chocolate fountains; white, milk and dark. They offered a variety of fruit, breads, and small marshmallows to smother in the delicious flowing rivers of happiness. Momma chose a couple of strawberries and took a dish of chocolate mousse. The dessert table didn't fare so well with me. I loaded up on several different dishes including apple pie a la mode, blackberry cobbler a la mode and a few other things. I wasn't able to finish it all. I was finally full. And a little sick at my stomach.

I asked Momma if she wanted to spend the afternoon in my suite, but she said she thought she'd go home to take a nap and organize the house before the workers started this week. Before we got up from the table, she said she wanted to tell me something.

"Owen, I've been thinking about what you said."

"What's that, Momma?"

"I think I'm going to give my notice to Mr. Reynolds. I think I'm going to retire."

"Oh! Momma! I'm so glad to hear that."

"I've got something else to tell you, honey. John Painter is up for parole review."

"Oh he is, is he? Well, I'll make sure he…"

Momma cut me off. "Owen. I don't want you to do anything."

"Then why did you tell me about this?" I was filled with rage, not at Momma, of course, but at John Leroy Painter.

Momma and I said our goodbyes. I went to my suite and threw up. The news about John Leroy Painter being released made me physically ill. It couldn't have been the six thousand calories I just consumed. I sat on the cushioned lounge chair provided on the suite's veranda. I thought about how this man had destroyed our lives. And killed Daddy. I determined that there was no way I was going to let him get away with being out of prison. No way. I would have to do something, no matter what Momma said. I'd have to do it for Daddy.

I laid on that lounge chair and went in and out of a fitful sleep for several hours. I saw John Leroy Painter in a dream taunting me and laughing at me. I saw Momma at Daddy's funeral, crying hysterically. I saw Daddy in his casket, but he sat up and said, "Get him, son." I woke up with a start and wallowed in grief and anger for a while. Oh yes. I'd get him all right.

I got up and went to my truck. I'd go buy a gun and blow that idiot's head off. I drove to three different gun shops, but they were all closed on account that it was Sunday. Same with the pawn shops. I ended up down at

River Parks, along the Arkansas River that runs right through the heart of Tulsa. The city has spent millions over the past twenty years developing the east side of the river between 21st Street and 71st Street. There are bike and running trails. There are fountains and sculptures. There is a low water dam that creates a lake effect because the river often doesn't have enough water to flow.

I pulled into the lot next to the Pedestrian Bridge, an old railroad bridge that had been converted for walking. I walked down to the riverbank and sat on one of the benches. Clouds had come in and it looked like we might get some rain. I spent an hour in solitude thinking about Daddy, Momma, Shelly and John Leroy Painter. He had spent more than thirty years behind bars already. But Daddy was dead forever. Why did he get to get out and Daddy have to stay in the ground? It wasn't fair.

I think about Daddy every day since he died. I used to be consumed with hatred toward John Leroy Painter. It waned for years, but now it was back with a vengeance. As much as I was drunk with wealth and lust, I was now drunk with revenge. Who knows? Maybe they wouldn't let him out. He'd been up for parole two previous times and didn't make it. Why would this be any different. He still had about twenty years to life left on his sentence. Maybe justice would prevail after all. Maybe it wouldn't and I'd have to take matters into my own hands.

## Chapter Twenty-one

# Making an Offer

Monday morning came a little too soon; it still burned when I went to the bathroom. I was still sick at my stomach from the day before. And now, with all the rich food I ate yesterday, I was a little constipated. I only mention that because Momma has always been a stickler for good digestive health. I'm sure it rubbed off on me.

I drove over to Momma's house to check on things. A work crew arrived an hour earlier and moved the furniture out to start painting and to install the new carpeting. I told Momma that I'd stay here while she went shopping for new furniture. To my surprise, she said that sounded like a good idea, got in her Cadillac and sped away. I didn't really expect her to do that, so now there I was, stuck at Momma's house.

The number of workers impressed me. They could have this job done in a matter of hours. I took the opportunity to poke around out in the garage. Some of Daddy's things were still out there, after all these years. Daddy wasn't much of a mechanic, but he did have a toolbox with his name on it. I opened it up and held the tools Daddy once held in his hands. I felt a strange connection with him and had to move on before tears welled up in my eyes.

I walked around the house and remembered so many wonderful times with Momma and Daddy and my two sisters. I remembered the time when Lizzy brought home a kitten from school. Daddy threw a fit about it, but Momma said it was okay if Lizzy would take care of it. It wasn't really a kitten, but more of a young cat, about seven months old. Lizzy said that it was an indoor cat and was already de-clawed and spayed. It spent the night in Lizzy's closet.

The next day, a Saturday, if I remember right, sometime along in the afternoon, we noticed that we hadn't seen the cat since that morning. Daddy said that he hoped we hadn't accidentally let it outside. What he meant, of course, was that since we lived in a rural area, there could be any kind of animal that might attack it and since it had no front claws, it couldn't defend itself. We searched the house high and low, but never saw "Midnight." We joined Daddy as we looked out in the yard and all around the house. No Midnight.

Daddy said that maybe the cat was still in the house, and we just hadn't found her yet. Lizzy, Shelly and I looked even harder. No Midnight. Lizzy and Shelly started to cry. Daddy told them that it would be alright and that we would find the cat soon. An hour or two went by and my sisters were still upset. Darkness approached as Daddy went out to look for the cat again. Just across the road, he spied her. He jumped across the ditch and the cat took off running. For the first time in her life, she had been outside all day.

Being that we owned the cat for less than twenty-four hours, Midnight didn't know Daddy yet. He called "here kitty, kitty" as if the cat would come. He chased it up our road, then back again. He finally caught it in a fence corner of the place across the way. It hissed and tried to scratch at him as he picked it up and held it tight. Her eyes wide and her tail puffed; she was inconsolable. Daddy tried to comfort her and pet her. He sat her in front of the water and food dish, but she just ran away. Daddy took her in the utility room and did his best to calm her. After twenty minutes or so, she finally began to relax. We kids wanted to go in and pet her, but Daddy said to leave her alone for a little while and she'd come out on her own.

Sure enough, within a few minutes, Midnight came walking into the living room and hopped right up into Lizzy's lap. Daddy smiled. We noticed that Midnight had a little white patch on her breast. Daddy looked at it kind of funny, then walked back to the utility room. We heard him exclaim, "For Pete's sake." We ran to see what he meant when we met him carrying another black cat about the same exact size. Daddy had gone out and accidentally brought back a stray cat because he thought his kids' cat was missing. Midnight had been asleep somewhere in the house all along.

We laughed about that for many years, even after Daddy was gone. That stray cat stayed around our house for several years, meowing to be let in our house, where it could be loved and spoiled. I chuckled aloud again at the thought of Daddy running up and down the road, calling out "here kitty, kitty." What a father won't do for his kids.

As I thought that thought, I realized that I was already older than Daddy was when he died. I didn't have any kids, or any that I knew of. I wasn't even married. A melancholy feeling overshadowed me.

Interestingly, my thoughts turned to Karen from high school. Did she marry? Surely, she'd look at me now since I was rich. I resolutely determined in my heart that she didn't go for me because I was poor. Things were different now.

I sat on Momma's couch, which was now out in the front yard. I turned it around so that I could see the house and the work going on. Momma fixed up the coffee pot out in the garage, so I sat with a cup and just watched. The workers were doing a great job. The driveway was full of pickup trucks, vans and delivery trucks. I didn't have any idea how long Momma was gone. I needed to get us both mobile phones. They had been too expensive before and I really didn't see a need for them. Quite frankly, I was technologically challenged. I didn't own a computer. The little 12:00 still flashed on my DVD player.

A man approached me. "Mr. Rigsby?" He didn't look like he worked there, but I took him for someone who did. "Yes?" I answered.

"I was wondering if I could have a moment of your time."

"What is it? Is there a problem?" I figured he needed to know about something in the house.

"Yes, sir, there is. My name is Hanna, Chance Hanna."

"What do you need Chance?"

"My wife took ill about three months ago, and the doctor bills have been piling up. I was wondering if you'd be able to.."

I cut him off. "Which one of these companies do you work for?"

"What companies?"

"The ones working on this house."

"I don't work for any of them."

"What are you doing here?"

"Like I said, my wife has been sick, and we need some help with the doctor bills."

"Let me get this straight. You came here looking for me to give you some money? We've never met, but you come here to my Momma's house looking for a handout? Get out of here before I call the sheriff!"

"But Mr. Rigsby…"

"But nothing. Now beat it!" I yelled. "Go on and don't come back."

Chance Hanna left looking like a scolded puppy. He got in his twenty-year-old pickup truck and drove on down the road. I watched him. He never looked over at me as he passed by. *The audacity of some people.*

It was getting along about two in the afternoon when Momma returned home. She told me she bought new furniture with the leftover money from the backpack when I bought her new car. She said it would all be delivered on Wednesday. I asked her why not today or tomorrow and she said that it wouldn't be good to bring it while the workers were painting, repairing, etc. I hadn't thought of that. Momma's a smart cookie. I asked her about spending the night at the house and if she wouldn't prefer to pack a few things and come with me back to the Prado until the work is done. I told her I had that second bedroom, and I wouldn't even notice her. She hesitated, then decided that it might be a good idea.

The workers finished laying the new carpet and the house started to look like something was going on. The new refrigerator and stove were already in the kitchen and the men worked to install the dishwasher and sink. I ordered Momma one of those instant boiling water devices along with a new deep stainless-steel sink. The new countertop was already in place. I don't know how the men found room enough to work; there didn't look like there was enough room for them to all turn around at once.

I drove into town and bought Momma and me a hamburger. Neither one of us had eaten lunch and I was getting hungry. I bought us both a cherry turnover; I knew how much Momma likes cherry turnovers. I was surprised when she turned it down. "Owen, I ate too much rich food yesterday. I don't think I ought to eat the turnover. But thank you for thinking of me." I wasn't about to let it go to waste, so I ate hers, too.

Momma packed a bag, and we had the men put all the furniture back in the house before leaving. We finally left a little after six. I followed her back to the Prado and let Mark park Momma's car. I pulled in a spot by myself. Momma was waiting for me in the lobby. Mark put her suitcase on a luggage cart and knew what to do with it. We went on up to my suite. We sat out on the veranda and talked for quite a while.

I told Momma about me being older than Daddy when he died and the fact that I didn't have any kids and wasn't even married. She nodded and didn't say much. I told her that I was tired of all the different girlfriends and wouldn't mind settling down. Her eyes really lit up when I said that. "Owen, I think that is a wonderful idea. But you need to consider the fact that with all this money, you're going to have every kind of woman after you to get to it." That thought had not yet entered my mind. "You need to be careful," she continued.

I mentioned that I really liked Karen back in high school and wondered what became of her. I told her that I met some pretty women out in Las Vegas, but they really weren't the marrying kind. I'm afraid she knew what I meant. For the first time in my life, I began to be open and honest with my mother about my feelings and my fears. We both laughed when I said that at least I wouldn't die alone; I could afford a nurse to be with me. But the stark reality was I *was* alone. I wanted a real relationship with a nice woman not based on the bedroom. I wanted more than to be physically gratified; I wanted to share my life with someone. It shouldn't be too hard, I reasoned. I was Tulsa's most eligible bachelor.

"Are you hungry yet, Momma?"

"I could eat a sandwich or a salad."

"Would you like to go down to the Santa Barbara or would you like room service instead?"

"Is it okay with you if we just order room service? I'm exhausted."

"Of course it is. We can eat right out here on the veranda if you like."

Momma ordered a bowl of soup with half a club sandwich. I ordered a sixteen-ounce sirloin with a loaded baked potato, house salad and a piece of chocolate cake for dessert. "You sure have quite an appetite lately, honey," Momma said.

"Yes, I've eaten burgers too long. I'm ready to eat like a millionaire," I replied.

"You better watch it, or you'll blow up like your great aunt Bertie. She started an eating binge and gained fifty pounds in six months; all in her hips."

"Don't worry about me, Momma. I've got it all under control."

Momma went to bed shortly after we ate. I stayed up past midnight watching TV. Momma was already gone when I woke up the next morning. I found a note that said, "Gone to supervise the work on my house. Call me if you need me. Love, Mom." I smiled at seeing her handwriting. It had been a long time. She used to leave us notes all the time; sometimes in our lunch boxes. "Hope you're having a good day at school. I love you, Mom." It is funny how the little things like that make such a big impression.

I decided to call Roger and Pricilla and look at more homes. Roger begged me again to look at some of the newer places south of town. I told him I'd be waiting in the lobby at ten o'clock to look at the old homes. I think he finally understood I wasn't going to budge. I also don't think he understood why I wanted an old place. I didn't just want to come and say it, but I really wanted the prestige that accompanied an oil estate.

Roger arrived promptly at ten in his Rolls Royce. I might have to get me one of those, too. We looked at six more estates, mostly like the ones I had already seen. There was variation with style, acreage, decoration, and the like, but they were all splendidly grand. The seventh estate we looked at was the most spectacular. It was about fourteen thousand square feet and looked a lot like Philbrook. It was nestled on five acres just two blocks from Philbrook. A ten-foot wall enclosed the entire property except for the front where an imposing wrought iron fence kept out the undesirables.

We turned into the drive and Roger punched a code into a box and the electric gate opened, then automatically shut behind us. As we entered, I saw a small sign that said, "Deliveries Use Rear Gate." I saw a security camera at the main gate, too.

We pulled into the drive-in front of the mansion. A huge water fountain stood in the middle of a small fishpond circled by the driveway. Roger said the home was built in 1925. The owners refurbished it in 1952 and again in 1999. I could see a rose garden from the front drive. I was in love before I ever stepped foot inside the house. I knew this would be my new home.

Getting inside, however, I was overwhelmed by the sheer luxury of the home. A black and white cut marble floor welcomed the visitor into the foyer. A winding staircase with exquisitely detailed woodwork on the banisters and railing graced the far wall and assured any woman could make a "grand entrance." A gold statue with an actual natural gas flame adorned the base of the staircase.

Each room was better than the last. Instantly, the study became my favorite room. Built in bookcases with carved wood lined the room. Twelve-foot ceilings exaggerated the size of everything. French doors opened from the study onto the back veranda. A swimming pool waited patiently for someone to make a splash. Through the windows, I could see an old-fashioned glass greenhouse. A separate bungalow provided relief from the pool and sun for weary partiers.

Twelve bedrooms, fourteen bathrooms and a professional kitchen made this house huge. But the incredible attention to minute details made it a mansion. Roger told me the name of the estate was "The Haven." It would soon be either "Rigsby Manor" or just simply "The Rigsby."

"What's the asking price? How long has it been on the market?"

"Four million two hundred fifty thousand dollars. It's been for sale for just over a year."

"What do you think they'll take for it?"

"I'm sure you'll be able to negotiate a little bit."

"That's what I'm asking you, Roger. How much do you think I can get it for?"

"Offer them four million."

Four million. Of course he said four million. He stood to make a huge commission off this sale. "I'll tell you what. Make an offer of three million dollars. I'll write a check for it, and you can hand it to them."

"What? You're going to write a personal check for three million dollars?"

"Why not? I'm good for it." I whipped out my checkbook and wrote a check for three million bucks. It felt good, but scary at the same time. In the memo line I wrote "Oil Mansion."

Roger disappeared, presumably to make a phone call. He returned in ten minutes. "They counter-offered at four million."

"Offer them three and a half, take it or leave it," I said, sounding like a big shot. I hoped they would take it, not because of the money, but because I didn't want to compromise any more. I was more than willing to pay their original asking price, but I know you aren't supposed to do things like that.

Roger went off again and returned with the news, "They will give you an answer tomorrow."

*Tomorrow? I want to know now.*

Roger dropped me off at the Prado. It was just after four o'clock. He promised to call me as soon as he heard whether they would accept my offer. I called Momma to see how the work progressed. She told me the men all but finished the kitchen and all the interior painting. She said she scheduled the furniture to arrive at noon the next day. We scheduled the lawn overhaul to begin the week after. No sense to make all the indoor workers traipse around people working in the yard. She told me the paint fumes still filled the house. I told her to come back to the Prado and spend another night.

We ate at the Santa Barbara where I enjoyed another delicious steak. Momma ordered some grilled shrimp. I ordered a bottle of wine, and we spent a leisurely evening together again. I immensely enjoyed spending so much time with Momma. We reconnected; I liked that. So did Momma.

My urinary problem was getting better. Instead of passing razor blades, I was now only passing little bits of molten lava. I didn't know how much more of this I could take. At least my digestive problems ended.

Momma left before I got out of bed, again. She left me another little note on the counter. I went downstairs for breakfast. I stopped at the front desk and told Judy I was expecting an important phone call and I'd be taking breakfast in the Tulsan. She acknowledged me and said she would certainly get me if there was a call.

I ordered a large breakfast, even by my standards. I liked the Mimosas that Momma and I drank on Sunday, so I ordered several of those. They didn't put out a breakfast buffet throughout the week and many of the things on the buffet weren't available, except at the Sunday Brunch. I'd have to wait until next week to experience all the wonderful breads. I ordered another omelet, but this time I requested a four-egg omelet with extra ham and cheese. Since I couldn't order biscuits and gravy at the Plaza in New York City, it delighted me to be able to have them here. We may not be as sophisticated as other places, but we know how to eat well in Oklahoma.

While I was on my second serving of grits, the hostess brought me a cordless phone. It was Roger calling about my offer. "Congratulations Mr. Rigsby. They accepted your offer of three and a half million dollars. I'd like to suggest a closing date in thirty days."

"Thirty days? Why wait so long?"

"It will take a while to draw up the necessary papers. Thirty days is standard. They would also appreciate payment other than a personal check."

"See if we can't do this in ten days. Two weeks on the outside."

"Mr. Rigsby, that is quite a lot of work to get done in ten days."

"Roger, that is quite a lot of commission are you are receiving for this sale. Make the arrangements to do it in ten days."

"I'll try."

"Don't try. Do," I said, with my best Yoda imitation. I hung up the phone. "I just bought an old Tulsa oil mansion" I said aloud, but to no one in particular.

"Congratulations," a voice said from behind me. "Perhaps we'll be neighbors."

I looked around to find an elderly couple enjoying coffee after having finished their breakfast. I smiled and the man stood up. "My name is Albert Crenshaw. This is my wife, Lillian."

"Pleased to meet you, Mr. Crenshaw. Mrs. Crenshaw," I said also standing. "My name is Owen Rigsby."

"Ah, the lad that recently enjoyed winning the lottery, am I right?"

"Yes, sir. I collected it about two weeks ago."

"Two weeks ago you won the lottery and today you bought yourself a Tulsa oil mansion. Sounds like you aren't wasting time."

"No, sir. I've lived like a poor man long enough."

"I understand. I spent the first thirty years of my life scratching out a living, barely making it from one paycheck to the next. But that was a long time ago."

"I take it you don't have to scratch anymore?"

"No. I made a fortune in the petroleum business. I retired about fifteen years ago and sold the company ten years ago. I don't have to scratch anymore."

"I'm looking forward to a life of leisure."

"Oh, that's fine for a while, Owen, but it gets old quick. You need to find something to keep you busy. Are you involved in any civic clubs or organizations?"

"No, that doesn't interest me at all."

"Do you go to church anywhere?"

"No, I haven't been to church in years."

"Would you mind if I shared a little wisdom from many years of experience?"

"Of course not. Share away."

"In the course of this life, you will find many wonderful things and many horrific things. One of the worst things that can happen to you is to get to the end of your life with nothing to show for it. When I earned my first million, I thought I was secure, that nothing could touch me, and I wouldn't ever have to worry about anything again. But I lost my first million. In fact, I lost a million dollars several times over. Wealth is fleeting, but there is one thing that will never leave you. Do you know what that is, Owen?"

I thought about it, but shook my head no.

"That one thing is God. I know, I know. You're probably saying, "I don't need God." But son, you need Him more than ever. The world knows your name and is calling for your attention 24 hours a day, seven days a week. You're going to be disappointed by people pretending to be your friends. You're going to be swindled by charlatans. You're going to be hurt by people you love. The only One Who won't leave you is God."

"My best friend was saying something along those lines just last weekend."

"Smart man. You should listen to him. Quite frankly, Owen, I have more money than you. I earned it all the old-fashioned way; I worked for it. As wealthy as I am, all the money means nothing to me if I don't have the Lord."

"Thank you, Mr. Crenshaw. I'll remember what you said."

We continued our conversation a little while longer but switched subjects to talk about my new mansion. It turns out we were neighbors. He has an estate on the same street, a couple blocks away. He told me that he and his wife had no living children. He said they had two sons, but one died in Vietnam and the other died in a motorcycle accident, both before either married or gave them any grandchildren. I told them about Daddy being killed by a drunk driver. They seemed genuinely empathetic. Before I knew it, an hour passed by while we talked. I thoroughly enjoyed our conversation. Somehow, I made a cross-generational connection and looked forward to seeing them again.

Chapter Twenty-two

# Albert Crenshaw

Albert Crenshaw grew up on a farm in southern Indiana. He was the seventh child of twelve his share-cropper parents raised. He didn't own a new set of clothes or shoes until the Marines issued him his first uniform when he was 18. His parents were poor, but they always managed feed their family and make sure they knew they were loved.

His father had no formal schooling but was wiser than most educated men. He taught his sons the arts of agriculture and animal husbandry. He imparted a high standard of work ethic and demanded the highest levels of personal integrity from his children. Most importantly, in his estimation, he taught his children about God. Albert loved the land but hated the lack of opportunity it afforded. He received his draft notice with enthusiasm and relief.

He was assigned to the 1st Marine Division and reported to Camp Pendleton in July 1952. Boot camp was as difficult as he expected, but he was strong from having worked hard on a farm his entire life. His good nature and pleasant disposition made him popular with his platoon buddies, some of which he remained friends with for the rest of his life.

He was seasick the entire journey to Korea. He often said in retrospect, that the month journey there and back was almost as bad as any combat he saw. His unit arrived mid-October to join the 8th Army in Operation Mixmaster.

Private First-Class Albert Crenshaw took his duty seriously. He was proud to wear his country's uniform. He spent the first 18 years of his life having never traveled more than thirty-five miles from home; now he was halfway around the world. He was amazed to see the poverty of war-torn Korea. These peasants were even poorer than his family back home in Indiana. He was rich compared to any of them.

For most of the winter, his unit saw only limited action with few casualties. There were some skirmishes, but nothing noteworthy. Albert found it exhilarating to shoot and be shot at, but he didn't like the killing. He and his buddies passed the time playing cards or writing letters home. He didn't have a girlfriend waiting on him like the rest of the guys. He wrote to his mother and to his youngest sister, Madeline.

*Jackpot!*

Madeline was four years younger than Albert, but he felt closer to her than any other sibling. She contracted polio at age three and couldn't walk. To be honest, she was a burden for her family, but she made up for it with genuine love for each person. She couldn't help around the house like the other kids but taught herself to sew. By the time she was twelve, she turned her financial burden into an asset. She took in repairs from her neighbors and started to generate a small income for the Crenshaws.

Madeline wrote Albert every week. She kept him up to date on the family, his friends and anything else she could think of to write. She'd send him handkerchiefs and secondhand comic books. He wrote back and told her about the land, his buddies and the different sights he encountered. He was careful to never talk about the killing. He sent her what few things he could find. She looked forward to each letter or small parcel.

March of 1953 saw the North Korean and Chinese forces advance across the United Nations line in a fierce display of aggressiveness. What had previous amounted to a waiting game turned into a full-fledged battle.

Albert's unit was caught by surprise in a dawn assault. The North Koreans launched heavy mortars into their makeshift camp. Sixteen men died within the first five minutes of the battle. Albert's lieutenant was killed by flying shrapnel - the unit was in total chaos without their leader. Keeping a cool head, Albert grabbed a .50 caliber machine gun and headed straight out to meet the enemy. He found a high point where he could have an advantage, then started firing.

The North Koreans immediately fired back with small arms, but Albert's position allowed him to mow them down. A couple of his buddies arrived with more ammunition and bazookas to support his efforts. They noticed a line of five Chinese tanks advancing on their position. Albert grabbed a bazooka, and despite pleas from his buddies, he ran down the hill toward the tanks. Just as the first tank was turning it's turret to fire on him, Albert let loose with a bazooka shot and disabled it. Fortunately for him, it hindered the advance of the four remaining tanks.

Albert crept closer and managed to take out two more tanks. They were sitting ducks. The fourth tank shot and took out the .50 caliber and his two buddies. Albert couldn't get in position to shoot at the two remaining tanks without exposing himself to enemy fire. He realized that ground troops were filing in behind the two remaining tanks and his situation looked hopeless.

The tanks could fire directly into the camp from their positions. With each shot, he saw his friends killed. There was no way to stop them. He figured he was a dead man with nothing to lose. The only thing he had going for him was the enemy didn't realize he was behind the rocks that hid him. He prayed for wisdom to know what to do. He noticed the North Koreans filing over a small ridge because the three burning tanks blocked the easy passage. He began to shoot them one-by-one with his carbine rifle. He was an exceptionally good shot, having hunted all his life back on the farm.

When the soldiers quit coming, he made his way over the ridge toward the two remaining tanks. He shot his bazooka just before the tank fired in his general direction. The shell went fifty yards away from him. The commander of the remaining tank ordered it to reverse direction. It aimlessly fired three shells, but none were close. By the time Albert fired his final shot, six of his fellow platoon members arrived to watch the tank explode. They immediately attended to their fallen comrades and set up a secure perimeter.

Albert was bleeding. Adrenalin allowed him to continue to fight, even though he had been shot three times. He collapsed just after seeing reinforcements arrive.

He woke up in a field hospital. They told him he was lucky to be alive, that one bullet had nearly nicked his heart, one his liver and the other had passed through soft tissue in his shoulder. Several doctors came by to ask him if it was true what they had heard about him single-handedly destroying six tanks. He told them he couldn't have done it if his buddies hadn't taken over his machine gun position to give him a little cover and if God hadn't given him the ability to do it.

Two months later, General Douglas McArthur awarded Albert Crenshaw the Marine Corps Medal of Honor for "conspicuous gallantry and intrepidity at the risk of his life above and beyond the call of duty." He also received the Purple Heart. It made Newsreel and all his friends back home got to see it.

Of course, by the time it was in theaters, Albert was home to watch it with them. The entire theater gave him a standing ovation. His town honored him with their version of a ticker-tape parade; they threw torn up pieces of paper in the air. He was invited to dinner at the governor's mansion and had his picture on the front page of every Indiana newspaper.

The biggest event of all, however, was being invited to lunch at the White House with President Eisenhower. Albert was allowed one guest. He chose to bring Madeline. It was a thrill of a lifetime for them both. They had their picture taken with the President in the Rose Garden which appeared in Life Magazine. She lived for a year and a half longer before succumbing to complications from pneumonia.

The fame didn't go to Albert's head. He was the same lovable guy he had always been. He consistently downplayed the events of that March morning saying that any of the other guys would have done it had they had the chance. To be honest, he didn't like to talk about it. He continues to have nightmares about it to this day.

Albert did reap a personal gain from being awarded the Medal of Honor. Aside from the legislated benefits, he met Lillian. She was the single most beautiful woman Albert had ever seen. She was about five feet, four inches tall with bluer eyes than he thought possible. Albert was immediately taken by her and hoped that they would one day marry. He courted her for almost two years before proposing. The wedding came the following summer. Their firstborn son came just over nine months later.

Albert and Lillian are a living love story. Single-mindedly devoted to each other, they have been a tribute to fidelity in marriage for fifty years. Whether in wealth or poverty, their undying love for each other has been their stability, no matter the circumstance.

And they encountered difficult circumstances in their lives. Albert didn't have a formal education. Even though he was a Medal of Honor recipient, he wasn't able to land any high paying jobs. While he was charismatic, he wasn't a good public speaker, so companies weren't keen to hire him as a spokesman. He lacked the skills that came from a college education, so many technical positions were unavailable as well. He did catch a break by having someone partner with him to open a television and appliance store. He trusted his partner, to his detriment.

By all counts, their store was the most successful TV and appliance store in South Bend in the late 1950's. Albert's celebrity status aided sales to begin with, but people quickly forgot the war and its heroes. His partner, Jimmy Remington, kept two sets of books. Albert only knew about one.

Albert wasn't stupid; just trusting. He believed Jimmy when he told him that the profit margin wasn't wide enough. He believed Jimmy when he told him that they were nearly finished paying off their store loan. He believed Jimmy when he said he'd be back from a vacation to Florida. Albert quit waiting when the creditors showed up demanding payment.

Albert nearly went to jail. Many people said his Medal of Honor kept him from it. He vowed never to be taken for a ride again.

Albert's being in the news turned out to be a good thing for him. A buddy from his old platoon saw the clip, called and offered him a position in his oil company as a vice-president in charge of some made-up division. Albert and Lillian were thrilled. It turned out, that when he had an opportunity to take care of things himself, he exceeded his, and everyone else's, expectations. Albert began to invest in the company and even ventured to buy stock in the drilling of new wells.

He traveled to the oil fields of Venezuela and the Arabian Peninsula. He was doing quite well for himself. He decided to go solo on the funding of a new well. It was dry. Albert and Lillian lost more than a million dollars. It wasn't long until he earned it back though and tried it again. This, too, was dry. A few more years and another dry well. He decided he'd give it one more try. This time, he hit an old-fashioned gusher.

The money started flowing in and he directed it straight into a diversified investment portfolio. That money made more money and before he knew it, he and Lillian started their own oil company. He moved his company to Tulsa to be closer to the center of the American petroleum industry. He was a member of the exclusive Petroleum Club atop one of Tulsa's skyscrapers, until the oil bust of the early 1980's.

The day-to-day management of Crenshaw Petroleum Enterprises became too much for Albert after a light heart attack in the mid 90's. He retired from the office of President and CEO and decided to travel. He and Lillian explored exotic places and saw the things in person that they had only seen in pictures. Their favorite vacation, so far, was a trip to Italy, walking the beaches of the Adriatic Coast.

While they are financially secure now, they realize how far they've come. They don't forget their humble beginnings and wish they had children and grandchildren with which to share their fortune and wisdom.

Albert was so proud of his firstborn son, Teddy. He passed out cigars to everyone in the hospital waiting room, including nurses. He and Lillian knew that their son wouldn't have to have hand-me-down clothes and secondhand shoes like they both did. Albert was determined to provide his son with everything he needed. He was delighted to see that he was a natural at baseball. CPE sponsored his little league team providing new uniforms and equipment each season. After every game, Albert loaded them up in his station wagon, win or lose, and took them to Dairy Queen. If they lost, they got a cone. If they won, they each could have whatever they wanted. Most of them usually got a banana split.

Teddy was a good kid. When he was six years old, his little brother, Lewis came along. He could hardly wait for Lewis to start walking so they could play ball together. Albert and Lillian taught the boys to be grateful for their blessings and to never take anything for granted. Growing up, they knew they were rich, but they never flaunted it in front of their friends. They went to private schools and had private tutoring and music lessons.

Teddy received his telegram from the President requesting his services in Vietnam. Lillian had a bad feeling in her heart that when she said goodbye, she'd never see her son again. Unfortunately, her feeling became fact. Teddy was among the first American casualties of the Tet Offensive. The Crenshaws received a second telegram from the president expressing his condolences.

Lewis didn't take his brother's death well. In fact, it drove him away from his parents and from God. He ran away from home. He drove away from home on his motorcycle. His journey took him into the hippie drug culture of the early 1970's, in Southern California. He assuaged his pain with LSD and heroine. He chased his first high never to find it again. A bad acid trip and a motorcycle didn't mix well, and Lewis died after running his cycle into the back of a parked truck on the side of the freeway. The police estimated his speed more than one hundred miles per hour.

Lillian and Albert were crushed. They lost both of their sons within the span of a year. Lillian nearly lost her faith, but Albert was there to help her through. She kept asking why God would allow both of her sons to die. Albert didn't know but kept assuring her that God was there to walk through the "shadow of death" with them. They tried to have another child, but Lillian didn't conceive.

She had trouble coping. For a while, she started buying liquor and hiding it from Albert. They had never had any alcohol in their home before that. Albert found half a bottle of gin in the back of the pantry while he was looking for a pot to make some chili. It scared him. He didn't know what to do.

He confronted Lillian, "Why do we have a bottle of gin?" Lillian pretended not to hear him. He repeated his question, "Lillian, I asked you a question. Why do we have half a bottle of gin in the pantry?"

"Oh, the maid must have left it."

"Marie doesn't drink."

"Oh, well, the lawn boy must have put it in there."

"Why would the lawn boy be in the house? Lillian, is this your bottle of gin?"

"What? My bottle? Why would you ask a silly thing like that?"

"Lillian, I've suspected it anyway. You've been acting funny lately. Have you been drinking this gin?"

With that, Lillian broke down and cried. Albert sat the bottle on the kitchen cabinet and held his wife and cried with her. He told her that she wasn't alone in this and promised to get her some help. He didn't put much faith in the Freudian quacks, but that was just about all the professional counseling available at the time. He inquired around and found a Christian who practiced counseling. He was licensed in the State of Oklahoma but didn't subscribe to all the popular mumbo-jumbo that secular counselors practiced.

He spent nearly two years with Lillian. He helped her work through not only her grief, but her anger at God. Albert attended sessions once every two months. It brought them closer together and most likely saved their marriage, if not Lillian's life. The process inspired Albert to fund a network of professional Christian counselors, first across Oklahoma, then the Southwest and finally the whole United States. He established scholarships for worthy university student candidates and established the Crenshaw School of Christian Counseling at the Midwest Divinity School in Oklahoma City.

The Crenshaws are wealthy beyond imagination and generous to a fault. He has never forgotten his humble beginnings; growing up in rural Indiana as the son of a sharecropper. He knows it truly is more blessed to give than to receive.

## Chapter Twenty-Three

# Private Detective, Pete Langford

As I returned to my room, my conversation with Momma came back to my mind. Mr. Crenshaw's comment about "getting to the end of your life and having nothing to show for it" only highlighted my thoughts. *I need to get married.* I went to my trinket trunk and pulled out my high school senior annual. I turned to find Karen's picture. "Karen Wilson: Adv. Chorus, Dev. Club, StuCo." I found several other pictures of her in the School Choir, at a Student Council Meeting and as president of the Devotional Club. I found my picture. "Owen Rigsby: woodshop." I completely forgot that I took woodshop in high school. I didn't do much else, as the yearbook testified. I only found one other picture of me in the yearbook. It showed me and Marty in Mr. Griffin's history class. Marty had his arm around my neck in some sort of a pro-wrestling move and I was acting like I was dying. At least I think I was acting.

I turned back to Karen's picture. I thought long and hard about it and decided to act. I grabbed the Tulsa phone book, which included our small town, but I couldn't remember Karen's dad's name. There were thirty zillion "Wilsons" listed in the phone book. This would be impossible. I turned to the Yellow Pages and looked up private detectives.

I called the number to Tulsa Trackers, specializing in person location. A woman named Julie answered the phone and transferred me to Pete Langford. "How can I help you, Mr. Rigsby?" he asked after I introduced myself. I told him that I was looking for Karen Wilson, and when she graduated from high school. I didn't know her birthday, social security number, if she was married or anything else about her. He told me the rate was one hundred twenty dollars an hour, plus expenses. I thought it would be a bargain at any cost. Pete said the company required a five-hundred-dollar retainer. I told him I'd give him a thousand. He told me he'd be right over.

He sure didn't look like your typical TV detective. He was tall and skinny, about my age but with a full head of red hair. He wasn't wearing a hat or a trench coat. I was a little disappointed. He said he had a degree in business with a minor in law enforcement. He said he had twelve years' experience, with the last seven years primarily dedicated to finding missing persons. I showed him a picture of Karen from my yearbook. He pulled out a pocket-sized scanner and copied the picture right into a small laptop. I was impressed.

I handed him one thousand dollars and told him I'd like to make this a priority. He handed me a receipt that he printed out on a little printer from his briefcase. He promised to push this case to the top of his list. I told him I'd give him a one-hundred-dollar bonus for every day short of ten days. He smiled and said, "not a problem."

He left and I had another wild idea. I called a travel agent and booked the first available flight to Dallas.

## Chapter Twenty-four

# The Ferrari

I never flew before my trip to New York City less than three weeks ago. I flew first class on American Airlines. It was nice. The seats were big. But I didn't like all the security that you have to go through just to board a plane. Is it necessary to take off your shoes? How stupid is that? I saw TSA make a woman carrying a baby take off her plastic beach sandals. She had to hand the baby through the metal detector to someone on the other side, then step through herself. The world's gone crazy.

My second flight was aboard a private luxury jet to Vegas. Today, I was flying cattle class to Dallas on a Continental flight. Weren't the stewardess supposed to be petite? What happened to their slogan, "*We really move our tail for you*?" I guess that went out with the complimentary meal service.

I arrived at the cavernous DFW Airport. We pulled in at gate Z-999; it seemed to be the last gate on earth. I'm not sure, but it may have been quicker to walk to Dallas than to try to navigate that airport. I finally made it to a taxi stand and hired a guy named Ahmed to take me to Ferrari of Arlington. I'm not sure where he learned to drive or even if he had a valid US driver's license, but he could just about win any demolition derby. Someone ought to introduce him to that.

Surprisingly, I arrived at the Ferrari dealership in one piece. I paid Ahmed and hoped I'd never see him again. I was met at the door of the dealership by some slicky-boy car salesman who said his name was Todd. He said this was the largest dealership west of the Mississippi, except for Beverly Hills. Since I had no desire to go to Beverly Hills, I'd choose from their stock. Today would be the day that changed my life forever.

As soon as I walked through the door, I saw the one I was going to buy. It was a 2022 Spider SR 90. It was red. It was beautiful. I needed this car. Oh, I looked at some of the other ones, but this one was a convertible. It was a special limited edition of only 499 to be built. Todd said that the guy who ordered this car reneged on the deal, and it had just become available that very day, only two hours earlier. Their selling price was eight hundred thousand dollars. Firm.

They balked when I asked them if they'd take a personal check. They said they could not. However, within a few minutes, we worked out a wire transfer from my bank and they wrote me a bill of sale. I spent the next half hour just learning about my new Ferrari. It would go zero to sixty miles per hour in 3.7 seconds. It had a top speed of nearly two hundred miles per hour. It used only high-octane fuel; anything less than 93 octane could permanently damage the engine. As we finished, I asked if they would throw in a Ferrari jacket. They reluctantly gave me a Scuderia Team jacket they said sold for two hundred and fifty dollars. It was a 100% nylon jacket. Give me a break. I asked about some leather driving gloves, but they wouldn't give those to me, so I popped out one hundred and seventy-five dollars for two red gloves that had the fingers cut off.

They told me how to get back on Interstate 20 and how to get to Interstate 35 North. Very carefully, I put the car in first gear and gingerly gave it some gas. I successfully exited the dealership without wrecking. So far so good.

It drove like a dream. It was dangerously fast. I accelerated onto the Interstate and was doing one hundred twenty-five miles an hour before I got to the end of the ramp. I slowed down and only went seventy or so. I couldn't believe how many stares I was getting. Men and women both stared. I prefer to think that the men were looking at the car. I hoped the women were looking at me. Everyone was looking at the car. I found I-35 and headed towards Oklahoma.

Cruising along at eighty-five miles an hour, I looked up to see red flashing lights in my rearview mirror. I could have probably easily outrun the Texas Trooper all the way to the Oklahoma border, but I pulled over, like a good boy.

"I see from the paper tag that you just bought this car. Is that right?"

"Yes, sir. I just left the dealership."

"May I see the bill of sale please?"

"Yes, sir." I reached into the tiny dash box and pulled out an envelope with the bill of sale.

"Do you have proof of insurance?"

Oh my word! I hadn't even thought about insurance. Just then, I remembered that I carried around the extra proof of insurance card that my agent sends me in the mail in my wallet. I dug for it and handed it to him. "I haven't had a chance to add this car, as I just bought it, but the liability coverage should transfer from an existing car to a new car purchase, right?"

"Yes, sir. It does. Do you have any idea how fast you were traveling?"

"Uh, not really. I probably exceeded the limit though."

"Yes, sir. You were doing eight-five in a sixty."

"I'm glad you stopped me. In a new car like this, it is easy to go to fast. I promise I'll slow it down."

"Tell you what I'm going to do," he said. "If you show me the engine and let me sit in it, I'll let you off with a warning."

"Sure thing, officer. Let me get out so you can get in."

I'm not sure that I liked this arrangement, but what are you supposed to do? It kind of made me feel special to get out of a ticket like that. If I had been driving my truck, I'd be signing for a violation about right now. I told the Texas State Trooper all I knew about my new car; the rate of acceleration and the top speed. He was smiling the whole time. I asked him if he had a camera and I'd take a picture of him next to it. He pulled out his camera phone and I took a couple. He thanked me for taking the time to show him my car and taking his picture. He asked me if I'd show him how quickly the car would accelerate and to go fast to see if he could keep up. In not so many words, he asked to race me.

We waited for traffic to clear a little and I took off down the road like a bootlegger on white lightning. The trooper did his best, but I lost him, and I just kept going. After a minute, he turned off his lights and turned around. I slowed back down to ninety. I needed to buy a radar detector. I pulled into Bucci's and bought the best one they had. The clerk told me it was illegal to use it in Washington, Florida and Virginia. Whatever.

When I returned to the car, there was a little crowd of truck drivers around it.

"Hey Mister, is that your car?"

"Hey Mister, how fast will it go?"

"Hey Mister, how much did that thing cost?"

"Hey Mister, can I drive it?"

If I heard those four questions once, I heard them a thousand times. Everywhere I stop, people continue to ask me those same four questions.

It is normally a four-to-five-hour drive from Dallas to Tulsa. I made it in four with several pit stops along the way. I pulled into the Prado at a little after nine. Mark was all smiles as he came out to park my new car. "Is there a covered, secure place for my Ferrari, Mark?"

"Yes sir, Mr. Rigsby. We have a place that will be just fine."

"I sure don't want it stolen. I don't have any insurance on it yet."

"Don't worry about it, Mr. Rigsby. I promise to take good care of it."

"See that you do. I'd be very disappointed if something happened to it. Be careful when you take off. Don't give it too much gas or you won't be able to control it. Just baby it."

I stood and watched as Mark drove off in my new treasure. I didn't hear squealing tires, crunching metal or breaking glass, so I went on into the Prado. I stopped and asked the night clerk if there were any messages. There was one from Momma. She said that the furniture had arrived, and she'd be staying at home tonight. I sauntered into the Santa Barbara. I was famished from my day in Texas. I was tired, too. As much fun as it was to drive, it really wasn't all that comfortable. My rear end hurt. So did my back.

I passed by someone eating a shrimp cocktail. It looked good so I ordered one, too. I also ordered their largest steak, a twenty-six-ounce sirloin. It was perfect. I didn't feel like wine, so I ordered a German beer. Then another. And another. It was getting late, and I was about the only one in the restaurant. Most Okies don't like to eat too late. I was just about to get up from the table when a young woman approached me.

"Are you the guy that won the lottery?" she asked.

"No, you must be thinking of somebody else."

"No, I know it's you," she laughed, almost hysterically. "I asked around."

"What do you want?"

"I thought you might like some company tonight. I thought you might like a date."

"Get on out of here, lady. I'm not interested."

"Why are you treating me like trash?"

"Because from where I sit, that's what you are."

"How dare you?" she screamed, then emptied my beer glass in my face. "I don't deserve to be treated like that."

By then, the hostess had alerted hotel security and a big burly guy in a blue blazer and gray turtleneck shirt came running up to the table. "What's going on here? Mr. Rigsby, are you all right?"

"Oh sure! Take his side," she said.

"I don't know what this woman is doing, but I know she doesn't belong here. She just poured my beer in my face."

"Do you want me to call the police and charge her with assault or disorderly conduct? We could get her for trespassing."

"No, just get her out of my face."

At that point, just about every on-duty hotel employee came up and apologized for what happened. I tried to brush it off. I told them that there was no harm done and hopefully, it wouldn't happen again. The hotel night manager, Frank, came running up to me as I was leaving the Santa Barbara, apologizing profusely. I repeated to him what I had just said to the other staff. He thanked me for being so kind and assured me it wouldn't happen again. He also offered to have my clothes dry cleaned, at hotel expense. I decided I'd take him up on that offer.

I went to my room and set out my clothes for housekeeping to collect. I was too tired to sit out on the veranda, so I drew a hot bath and soaked my aching body for a while. I turned on the TV and caught the news. What I heard ruined my whole day.

John Leroy Painter had been granted parole. I'm not quite sure why it made the news, but it did. They ran footage from the wreck so many years ago and showed a picture of Daddy and the others who died in the wreck. I completely forgot there were others who died. Daddy was the only adult; the two others were high school kids. Their families must have been hurting all this time, too. I was really shocked when they showed my picture on the news as the recent lottery winner and the child of the man who was killed. This wasn't good. This wasn't good at all.

Just then, the phone in the bathroom rang. It was Momma. "Owen, did you see the news?"

"Yes, Momma, I'm watching it now."

"Please promise me you won't go do anything."

"Momma, don't ask me to make a promise I might not be able to keep."

"Owen, I lost your Daddy. I don't want to lose you, too."

"Don't worry about me, Momma. I've got everything under control."

I found myself gritting my teeth with my brow furrowed. My heart pounded like a coal miner's hammer. I realized I clinched my fists, even though I was supposed to be relaxing in a tub of hot water. I was hatching a dark plan in my mind. I could use Pete Langford to find this jerk when he got out of prison. Then, I'd go pay him a little visit.

## Chapter Twenty-Five

# The Laundry Shrunk My Pants

I didn't rest at all. I tossed and turned and had nightmares all night long. I awoke with a pounding headache. I awoke with revenge on my mind. I awoke a man on a mission. But since he hadn't been released yet and I couldn't get to him, I might as well go eat breakfast. I didn't know when I'd have my little chat with John Leroy Painter, but it would probably be a week or two. I might as well take care of the other things I had going on. I expected to hear from Pete about Karen. I expected to hear from him yesterday.

I was a little distressed when I couldn't fasten my new slacks from Las Vegas. This darn laundry must be more careful. Now I needed to go clothes shopping again. Since Utica Square was across the street, I'd pop in over there and buy what I needed before lunch. My jeans still fit, but barely. I managed to get them buttoned then put on a t-shirt and headed down to breakfast.

As I approached the Tulsan, Doug, the day manager, came running out to greet me. "Oh Mr. Rigsby. I heard about what happened last night. I'm so sorry."

"No big deal, Doug. No real harm done."

"Well, all the hotel staff now knows to report to security if they see her on the premises again. She'll not be bothering you here at the El Prado, I can assure you."

"I've got more important things to worry about. She doesn't really concern me."

I made my way into the Tulsan, looking for my new neighbors, the Crenshaws, but they weren't there that day. I got my table and ordered a big breakfast. I noticed that I had been eating more than I normally did. Momma mentioned it the other day, but I didn't think anything about it. Surely I wasn't gaining weight? I had maintained this weight for the past twenty years or so. I quit thinking about it when my Belgium waffles arrived. There are few things I like more than pecan waffles. These were no disappointment. I polished them off and ordered a second plate, along with six strips of bacon, some hash browns, and three fried eggs, over medium. I knew I needed to drive when I was done eating, so I only had two Mimosas.

*Jackpot!*

Feeling quite full, I left the Tulsan and went to the health spa/gymnasium. I asked the girl behind the desk if I could use their scales. She showed me where they were. I was shocked to find that I had gained nearly twenty pounds in three weeks.

I decided to take my truck to go shopping and to do the other errand I needed to do. I asked Mark to get my truck. He seemed disappointed that I didn't want the Ferrari. I drove across the street and went into Saks. The clerk was some prissy boy that seemed a little too eager to measure my inseam. I told him I wore a 36X32 pant. He brought out a quality pair of slacks, much cheaper than those I bought at the Peninsula shop. I tried them on in the changing room and again was shocked to see that I couldn't fasten them. I told him that these were mis-sized and were too small. He brought me another pair that fit just fine. I didn't see until later that they were size 40.

I bought several pairs of slacks, several shirts and another sport coat. I still had quite a bit of cash on me, so I paid him in one-hundred-dollar bills. I told him to have everything sent to the Prado, across the street. He asked for a room number, and I told him to just deliver them to the front desk. He seemed like the kind of guy that might show up unexpectedly in the middle of the night for a date. I tipped him fifty dollars for his trouble.

Next, I got back in my truck and drove to a gun shop. I had always wanted to own a handgun and now was as good a time as any to buy one. There is no waiting period in Oklahoma, so I was going home with one today. I didn't know much about guns. I knew a few brands, like Colt and Smith & Wesson and Glock. There was another one, but I doubted they would have it here in T-Town. I was buzzed into the store and a chubby man behind the counter offered to help me.

"I'd like to buy a handgun."

"You've come to the right place. Do you know what you want?"

I hesitated and said, "I want a Walther PPK."

The chubby man smiled and said, "So, you're a James Bond fan, are you?"

"Yes," I said sheepishly. "But that's what I want."

"You're in luck. We happen to have a few different varieties; you can take your pick."

He showed me what they had, and I chose one that looked like Bond's gun. He asked me what the purpose of my purchase was, and I told him "home protection." He said that I might consider a bigger handgun, as the PPK was a .38 caliber. He showed me some .45 caliber guns. He also showed me a handgun that shot .410 shotgun shells. "That would do some damage close range," he said.

I filled out the required paperwork and paid cash. I left with three handguns. A Walther PPK, a Colt Army .45 and my shotgun pistol. The store had a very strict policy prohibiting the sale of ammunition at the same time as the sale of weapons. The clerk told me to go out and put my guns in my vehicle, then return to buy the ammo. Whatever.

The first step of my plan for revenge was complete.

Chapter Twenty-Six

# The Visitors

The weekend arrived without hearing from Pete. It was a beautiful Saturday and since autumn was just around the corner, not too hot. Since Marty didn't call me to go fishing, I decided I'd take my new Ferrari for a drive.

It delighted Mark to retrieve the kind of car that most people dream of owning. I heard it start from the front door of the Prado and Mark carefully brought it to me without spinning the tires, a hard thing to do.

I retracted the hard top and pulled out onto 21st Street. Traffic was light, but I wasn't interested in driving in town. I maneuvered the beauty onto the Broken Arrow Expressway and headed East, toward Fort Gibson Lake. The highway from downtown to Interstate 44 has curves and makes it fun to drive. Unfortunately the speed limit varies from 50 mph to 60 mph. It's hard to go much faster because of everyone else obeying the speed limit, for the most part. I did my best and got it up to seventy before having to slow back down.

I enjoyed everyone looking at me in my hometown. News travels fast and I knew there would be no other car like mine in Tulsa, since only 499 were ever made. It was a stroke of luck I happened into the dealership when I did, or someone else would have snatched her up.

I took old Highway 51 instead of the Muskogee Turnpike. In fact, I avoid the Oklahoma turnpikes whenever I can. Oklahoma went back on their word in the 1950's when they built our first toll road. The deal advertised to the citizens was that "as soon as it is paid for, it will be a free road." The road has been paid for many times over and now supports other turnpikes that the Oklahoma Turnpike Authority built but couldn't afford. Somebody ought to investigate it, but I'm sure all the politicians have their hands in the turnpike's pockets.

I drove through the small towns of Oneta, Coweta, Porter, Wagoner and into Okay, on my way to the lake. I always thought that was a funny name for a town. "We aren't great, but we're Okay." I am constantly amazed at the variety of things you can see when you drive through rural Oklahoma. On this morning, I passed a heard of pigmy goats, a flock of Canadian geese on a pond, two bison in among some cows and a couple of longhorns, a covey of wild turkeys on the side of the road and numerous herds of cows and horses, along with loads of the obligatory roadkill. Dead opossums and armadillos dot the roadside; a testament to the failure of slow-moving creatures. I started calling the armadillos "dead-adillos." It makes me laugh every time I say it.

Northeast Oklahoma is beautiful country. We have gentle rolling hills and lots of lakes. If you get much west of Tulsa, hills and trees become a rare commodity. Far eastern Oklahoma gets you into the foothills of the Ozarks. It is hot in the summertime, sometimes reaching 110 ° F. Winter brings the threat of ice storms, but usually not much snow. We don't have too many days below 20° F, but it can get below zero.

I made it to Fort Gibson Lake and stopped at the Dam Overlook to enjoy the view. They had the electricity generation gates open, but none of the flood gates. Fishermen were lined up on the shore with their surf roads trying to snag paddlefish, locally known as spoonbill. It is an odd-looking fish related to the shark. They have become strictly regulated in recent years, as their eggs were being illegally sold as Beluga caviar. I cannot imagine why anyone would want to eat fish eggs on purpose. Spoonbill meat is pretty good if they are cleaned properly. The best way to cook them is to grill them over an open fire.

It was a bit early in the year, but I looked for bald eagles anyway. Many of the great birds winter near the dam and you can often see great flocks of pelicans that arrive to feed for a few days before moving on. I drove across the dam and stopped at The Dam Café for a sandwich. I parked where I could keep an eye on my car. It drew a crowd. "Mister, is that your car?" "Yes." "How fast will it go?" "200 mph." "Hey Mister, how much does a car like that cost?" "A lot." "Mister, can I drive it?" "Absolutely not."

I got in my car and started it up. I had everyone's attention. I revved the motor a couple of times and saw the expressions on their faces. I slammed it into first gear and stepped on the gas pedal. This time it did what I wanted it to do. I burned rubber for a good five seconds as I left the parking lot. Nobody has a video camera when you really want one.

I continued my drive down River Canyon Road. It was empty of other cars, so I opened her up. I just about lost control when I hit one hundred sixty miles per hour. That would have been disastrous. I still hadn't bought insurance for it yet.

Pulling into Fort Gibson, I passed a sign that said, "Oldest Town in Oklahoma." It is built around an actual stockade type fort established in 1824. The WPA rebuilt many of the old buildings and the stockade in the 1930's. It looks like something right out of a movie set. Ft. Gibson also has a national cemetery. It is a miniature version of the famous ones. I drove around, taking in all the history.

*Jackpot!*

Leaving Ft. Gibson, I came across an Indian casino. Cars filled the parking lot. I pulled in the drive and considered going in. My recent string of bad luck in Las Vegas kept me from it. There didn't seem to be adequate security to protect my Ferrari, anyway. I sat for a moment, watching people come and go. There weren't too many people leaving; most were going in. Some of them might be lucky enough to win a few hundred dollars. Most would lose. I pulled out of the drive before I drew another crowd.

It was well into the afternoon when I returned to the Prado. I was very pleased to find a message from Pete at reception. I went to my suite and returned his call. "Mr. Rigsby, I'm happy to report that I found Karen Wilson. Her name is Karen Edwards. She is married to James Edwards and has three children, Jody, 18, Julie, 16 and Jacob, 14. She is a high school Math teacher in a suburb of Kansas City, Missouri."

I was overjoyed! I wasn't happy about her having three kids, but we could deal with that. I had to find out more about this James she was married to. This might be trickier than I first thought. I would have to somehow convince her to leave her husband. Surely the lure of millions of dollars would do the job.

I arranged for Pete to send over all the information he had, and we settled the bill. I told him that I may have another job for him in the next week or so. All of that may have to wait, anyway; I just might have myself a bride in the next few days!

I called Momma and invited her over for Sunday Brunch again. She said she would be delighted to come. Perhaps we'd make this our Sunday morning thing. If I could convince Karen to join me, we could make it a family affair. Maybe we'd send her kids off to boarding school in Switzerland. I've heard that's what rich people do with kids they don't want. We could start our own family. Then again, she might be getting to old to have kids. We might keep the youngest one around. Perhaps he's young enough to accept me as his new dad.

I could drive up on Monday; it would only take four hours. Maybe less. Pete included maps of where she lives and works. I'd have to catch her away from her husband. Maybe she'd leave to come back to Tulsa with me on Monday. I could tell her that she wouldn't ever have to work again. I'd buy her any kind of car she wanted. I'd tell her about my new oil mansion. Oh, this was going to be great. Everything was working out just like I wanted.

All but one thing. I forgot about what the doctor said. He said I was cut off until I finished my antibiotics. I still had three days left. It wouldn't be good giving the love of my life gonorrhea. I'd have to go to Kansas City on

Wednesday or Thursday. That would be okay. That would give me time to buy the wedding ring. At least it didn't burn to go to the bathroom anymore.

So much going on all at once. The millions of dollars, the oil mansion, the new car, John Leroy Painter, gonorrhea and now Karen. It's almost too much to handle.

I remembered how nice the massage was at the Peninsula, but how bad it was at the Oriental Sweetheart Massage. I figured the one here at the Prado should be a nice place. All I wanted was a nice relaxing massage. The Day Spa at the Prado didn't disappoint me. I didn't like the salt rub too much though. It was supposed to defoliate me, or something like that. I made the girl stop; it felt like she was rubbing me with sandpaper. I did enjoy the essential oils and aroma therapy. I'm not sure what it was supposed to accomplish, but it smelled good.

I ordered a two-hour massage and fell asleep during the last thirty minutes or so. I must have snored and woke myself up. The girl was trying not to smile, but I chuckled, and she let out a big, toothy grin. We only spoke a few words to each other up until then, so I asked her name.

"Mary," she said. "What's yours?"

"Owen."

"Are you the guy that won the lottery?"

"One and the same."

"What's it like?"

"What's what like?"

"Having all that money."

"Oh, it's pretty nice."

"Have you bought anything real expensive yet?"

"Yes. I bought a house and a car."

"What kind of car?"

"A Ferrari."

"Wow. It must be nice."

"It is."

I had many such conversations with people. They wanted to make conversation, but they didn't know what to say. Most people have never been around a millionaire before. The money makes them nervous. It's almost an unspoken expectation that I will give them some money, just because I have a lot and they don't. They simply don't know how to relate to someone who looks like they do, talks like they do, thinks like they do and could buy them a hundred times over.

I left the Day Spa and moseyed over to the Santa Barbara. It takes special talent to mosey properly. It's more determined that meandering, not as quick as strolling, but much faster than lollygagging. It's an art, really.

I was ahead of most of the supper crowd. There were a few young couples being cozy and a family with two children. A towheaded boy of about 10 and a little girl that looked to be 6 years old. She had her hair in pigtails and her cheeks covered in freckles. She smiled at me as I walked by. I smiled back. The man and woman at the table looked like they were upset over something, but the kids didn't seem to notice. It wasn't any of my business, so I went on to my table.

I ordered the large sirloin again. To find such a wonderful steakhouse right here in Tulsa made me happy. I could dine here for years to come. I was already becoming good friends with the wait staff. They all called me by name. Well, they called me "Mr. Rigsby."

My thoughts turned to the family sitting nearby. The husband and wife seemed to be over whatever little tiff they had, and everyone ate and chatted with smiles on their faces. I sat alone; but perhaps not for too much longer.

In my mind's eye I retraced every time I ever spoke with Karen. Every time I ever watched her in the school hallway or cafeteria. I tried to recreate every conversation, every blink of her eye, every flip of her hair. She was the only girl I had ever wanted, and I realized I had been mentally comparing every woman I dated to her memory. My memories of her consumed me.

Yes, of course, I knew there was going to be a problem. She was married and had kids. But I had millions. Surely that would persuade her, right? If it didn't, I'd have to take things into my own hands, but I didn't want to resort to that. I wanted her to leave her husband and her kids and come and make her life with me in Tulsa.

Was this a pipe dream? Could this really happen? Would she really leave her family? These thoughts began to chase each other around in my head. I became worried about the prospect of rejection. She turned me down in high school; this was going to be different. Money talks, doesn't it?

A waitress interrupted my thoughts by handing me the cordless phone. It was Momma. She told me she had a big surprise for me and asked if we were still on for Sunday Brunch. Momma with a surprise for me? What could it be?

The next morning, I ran just a tad later than normal, that is, I arrived too late to watch Momma pull up in her Cadillac and Mark park it for her. For some reason, that gives me a little thrill. I guess it is knowing that after all these years, someone is finally waiting on her, for a change. Nevertheless, I spied her walking through the front doors as soon as my elevator doors slid open.

There were several people with Momma who I did not immediately recognize. I looked at the middle-aged woman and only realized who it was when she spoke.

"Hi, Owen. It's been a long time."

"Lizzy!" I said as I gave her an awkward hug. "It's so good to see you. How long has it been?"

"Too long," she said with a grimace. "Too long."

At least twenty years had passed since I last saw my big sister. She had gained a lot of weight and lost all her dark hair. Dark circles under her eyes only accentuated her gray hair. Up close, she looked as old as Momma. Momma had been out to California to see Lizzy on three occasions. Lizzy's husband was a chronic cheater. She left him after the fifth or sixth affair and chose to stay out on the west coast. She had three kids, Robert, who was now serving in the Army in Germany, Betsy, who was unmarried, but had a two-year-old son, and Curtis, who had dropped out of school at sixteen, left home and whose whereabouts were unknown. I was about to meet Betsy and her son, Kyle, for the first time.

"Betsy, this is your uncle Owen," Lizzy said.

"Did you really win all that money?" Betsy asked.

"Betsy! What a thing to say," Lizzy scolded.

"That's all right, Lizzy," I said. "Yes, I really did win all that money. But let's not stand out here in the lobby talking about it. Anybody hungry? Let's go get something to eat."

We headed toward the Tulsan's Sunday brunch. Two-year-old Kyle tried to show the world that the "terrible twos" really mean terrible. Never in my life had I witnessed such an undisciplined child. He screamed at the top of his lungs and neither his mother nor his grandmother seemed to care much. He threw the salt and pepper shakers on the floor, dumped his plate of eggs on purpose, and began to throw bits of other various food items at anyone within range. Momma, me, and everyone else in the restaurant were embarrassed except the West Coast Three. They were oblivious to everything.

Obviously, Lizzy was the one raising Kyle. Betsy seemed to have little interaction with him and deferred all discipline to my sister. Lizzy had done a poor job of raising her daughter and she was paying for it by raising her grandson. It looked like she didn't learn the first time.

I'm no parenting expert, having none of my own, but I know a problem when I see it. And hear it. In fact, everyone in the restaurant knew there was a problem. Momma offered her support and tried to help out, but Kyle was incorrigible.

We muddled through brunch and finally left the restaurant to the delight of the other patrons and wait staff. I was thoroughly embarrassed. I suggested that we go to my suite. Lizzy seemed delighted at the prospect. Once there, Lizzy handed Kyle to Betsy and told her to keep him busy and quiet while the grown-ups talked. Betsy rolled her eyes as she took her son out onto the terrace. I shut the door as my great-nephew began to wail.

We chit-chatted for a while, then Lizzy got down to business. She gave me some sob story about her kids and how hard it is to raise the kids right without help from their father and one thing after another. I knew, of course, where she was headed with this conversation, and she finally got to her point.

"Owen, I was hoping that you could help us out a little."

"How little?"

"Anything you can spare."

"If things are so tight, how could you afford to come back home?" I asked.

"Momma paid for the plane tickets."

"I see." I noticed that Momma wasn't looking right at me any longer. I decided to toy with her. "So, how about fifty bucks?"

A worried look came across her face. "I was hoping for a little more."

"How much more?" I demanded.

"To be perfectly honest," she started.

I cut her off. "Yes, let's be perfectly honest. You haven't been to see us in more than twenty years. Momma tells you I've won the lottery and, let me imagine, you beg her to help you come back to see the family. What a nice little family reunion this is."

"Owen!" Momma said.

"Don't 'Owen' me, Momma. This is ridiculous. She doesn't care about us. She only cares about herself. She didn't even come to Shelly's funeral."

Lizzy began to cry. I lit into her for another five or ten minutes. She apologized through her sobs. She said she had no excuse except that she had been selfish and had to get away from home. She said that she hadn't really ever gotten over Daddy's death and it was just too hard to stay here to be constantly reminded of him everywhere she looked.

At the mention of Daddy, my heart broke, too. I apologized for being so harsh and I began to cry with her. Momma joined in and we all cried for way too long. We were locked in a three person embrace with all three of our heads touching. Our tears splattered on our shoes. We cried so hard together that we weren't able to speak. Our jaws and our eyes ached from the release of bent up emotion. I finally pulled away and said, "you know he's getting out, don't you?"

"Who?" Lizzy asked.

"John Leroy Painter."

"Why? When? How could this happen?"

"He made parole."

"I thought he was supposed to get a minimum of fifty years."

"Yes, me, too."

"When is he getting out?"

"I don't know yet. I haven't looked into it."

"Owen," Momma said. "Please don't do anything. Let's let bygones be bygones."

"How can you say that Momma? He killed Daddy."

"Sometimes you just have to move on, son."

"But Momma, everything changed because of him."

"Honey, you don't have to tell me that. I know it as well as anyone. Your father was the love of my life. A part of me died with him that horrible day. But if I can't get past this, it's like I'm in prison, too. Maybe this is happening so that we can all get over it."

"But Momma!"

"Maybe we all just need to forgive him."

I sat in unwavering disbelief after hearing what Momma just said. Forgive John Leroy Painter? Never.

## Chapter Twenty-Seven

# Granny's House

Lizzy and I made up after our little cryfest. I went ahead and got her and Betsy and the scream-machine a suite, on a different floor, in the Prado. I didn't want to hear him screaming all night long. Momma's house looked so nice after the remodeling and with all the new furniture that I really didn't want Kyle to mess it up. I begged Momma to go get her things and come back and stay in my suite while Lizzy was in town. We could have our own little first-class family reunion right here.

I asked Lizzy how long she was going to stay. She said she had plans to be there a week. A week, huh? That kind of messed up my plans for Karen. I had waited twenty-five years, I could wait a few more days.

There were five of us, counting the Kyle the Horrible, so we couldn't all fit in my pickup or my Ferrari, not that I would want Kyle in my Ferrari. I honestly feared for Momma's new Caddy, so I arranged for a limo to chauffer us around town. Lizzy admitted it was the first time she had been in a limo since Daddy's funeral. Betsy said she thought Kyle was conceived in a limo in Orange County. I really didn't care to hear the details of that, so I changed the subject.

"Would you like to see my new house?"

I told the limo driver how to get there, but no one answered the buzzer when we arrived. I didn't know the security code yet, so we were out of luck. Momma and Lizzy were impressed with the entryway and with the security the estate boasted. I told them all about the property and promised that we'd come back when I could get in. It was only supposed to be a few more days until I closed on it, then I could start buying furniture and stuff to make my oil mansion complete.

I used the limo driver's mobile phone to call Roger, but he and Pricilla were out with a client and would return my call later. I guess I needed to break down and get a cell phone. I'll bet I was the only multi-millionaire in America without a cell phone who was less than ninety years old.

Since we had the car and nowhere else to go, Lizzy suggested that we go see Granny. I hadn't seen Granny in over four months. I knew Momma told her about my winning the lottery, but I hadn't even taken her my present yet. I didn't want to take it and give it to her in front of my west coast relatives, so we didn't have to go back by the Prado. I told the driver how to find Granny's house.

Granny lived in a nice little home a few blocks east of Riverside Drive. I hadn't even thought about her when I previously stopped by the Pedestrian Bridge to think. Daddy's father died before Lizzy was born, so we never knew our paternal grandfather. This wasn't the house Daddy grew up in, though. It burned to the ground after he and Momma were married, but before his father passed away. He died of a stroke at age fifty-two. He bought this house for himself and Granny back in the early 1960's. It was still a pretty good neighborhood.

Granny was delighted to see us, but really doted over Betsy and Kyle. It was her first time to meet both of them, too. Kyle promptly knocked over and broke a lamp in the living room. I finally told Betsy that she was simply going to HAVE to take care of her son. It created a bit of an awkward moment, but Lizzy and Momma both seemed relieved that I said aloud what they were thinking. Betsy gave me a look as if to say, "who are you to tell me what to do," but probably thought of my money, so didn't say anything.

Granny's ability to get around and do for herself impressed me. She was nearly ninety years old, still lived by herself and still drove. She no longer mowed her own grass, but she continued to teach her Sunday School class as she had that morning. She made a pot of coffee and found some juice for Kyle. He fell asleep underneath the coffee table. Finally! Some peace and quiet.

We stayed and visited for several hours. Granny quizzed Lizzy on the past couple of decades of her life and tried to talk to Betsy, but Betsy didn't possess the elementary social graces like conversation and giving the impression of caring. While I could tell that Granny loved her because she was her great-granddaughter, I saw that Granny was extremely frustrated, and possibly a little hurt, that Betsy wasn't trying back. I suppose Granny figured this would be the only time she would ever see them and wanted to make the best of it.

Listening to Lizzy and Granny talk, I discovered that Lizzy called Granny every year to wish Granny a happy birthday. I had no idea that they were in contact with each other. Before leaving, Granny half-heartedly scolded Lizzy for staying away so long, but said it thrilled her to see her again and to meet one of her children and her great-great-grandson. She asked that we all hold hands together so she could pray for us. Betsy held Kyle and he actually behaved fairly well during the prayer.

Granny prayed for us, thanking God for the time spent together and for getting to meet Betsy and Kyle. She asked His blessing on us and some other stuff. I quit listening after a few sentences.

We all had a big group hug and said our goodbyes. Granny called after us as we were getting in the limo, "Remember, God loves you! And so do I." She called me back to her porch before I got in. "Owen, please come and see me by yourself in the next couple of days. I want to speak with you privately."

"Do you need some money, Granny?"

"Goodness, no!" she exclaimed with an air of exasperation. "I just want to visit with you about some things."

"Okay, Granny. I'll call before I come."

"Don't forget, Owen. This is important."

"Okay. I won't. I love you, Granny."

"I love you, too."

That worried me. Granny seemed very serious about something. And she didn't want to tell me in front of Momma or Lizzy. I wondered if she was sick. She said she didn't need any money. But lately, everyone except Momma has been asking me for money. I could trust Granny, though. If she said she didn't need money, then she didn't need any money.

Even though we enjoyed an enormous late brunch, we were starting to get hungry again. It was a bit early for supper, but that didn't bother me. I told the driver to take us to a little Italian restaurant over on Sheridan. We were surprised to find it closed on Sunday. I didn't realize any restaurant still closed on Sunday. I told the family how good it was and since that made us hungry for Italian, I directed the driver to take us to the Olive Garden.

I ordered a bottle of wine. It made Betsy mad when the waiter wouldn't serve her, noticing that she was under twenty-one. Part of me wanted to give a little wine to Kyle to keep him sedated. They do that in Europe; why couldn't we do it here?

Kyle was an unholy terror all through supper. I didn't know if I could stand a week of this. I had no idea how Lizzy put up with it in her own home. I finally asked them to take him outside and paddle his little rear end. Looks of horror met me from two women. Lizzy told me that they didn't believe in spanking. I told her it was apparent, but for the good of the family, the restaurant and the kid, they might re-consider corporal punishment as a means of discipline. Even Momma said that they needed to discipline the child, or they would never have control of him. Our suggestions fell on deaf ears.

The last straw came when the waiter brought our food, told us the plates were very hot, and Kyle touched them anyway. Lizzy went into a tizzy about putting hot plates in front of small children. I told the waiter to bring us a few ice cubes wrapped in a napkin. I told Betsy to take the child and put him in his highchair. I told Lizzy that if they didn't control her grandson that I would never go out to eat with them again. I told them both to keep the kid quiet, that we were in a public restaurant and were making it miserable, not only for us, but for everyone else in the place. I stood up and apologized to those who were directly around us and instructed the waiter to bring their bills to me.

Lizzy was humiliated. That made two of us. She didn't say another word through dinner. Kyle still cried, but at least Betsy tried to attend to him. She fed him bits of spaghetti. The waiter brought some apple juice which seemed to keep him fairly quiet. Our supper was ruined. Everyone was mad. All for lack of discipline.

I had the driver take us back to the Prado. I kissed Momma and told her I needed to get away for a while. I needed some distance between me and Lizzy and the Terror from Torrance.

It began to rain a little bit, so I hopped in my trusty pickup truck. It felt good to be in something familiar. Perhaps I'd keep my old truck, just like Sam Walton kept his. There may be times I want to go somewhere and not be recognized in my Ferrari.

I didn't know where to go and had nowhere in mind. I found myself in downtown Tulsa. Completely deserted at night, it isn't hard to navigate the one-way streets. I drove past the BOK Center, one of the top new venues in the United States. The very first event there featured Celine Dion in concert. Paul McCartney even played there. I couldn't afford tickets before, but now I could go to any show I wanted.

I drove by a coffee shop near Bartlett Square and decided to stop in. It looked like something right out of the 1940's. There were two old men sitting at opposite ends of the counter drinking coffee and a younger couple in a booth near the back eating burgers. I selected a booth and ordered a cup of coffee and a piece of cherry pie.

I'm not a coffee snob. I don't need to pay four bucks to enjoy a cup of coffee. I don't like instant, but I don't have to go to a specialty shop for a cup of java. I think I'm happier that way because I can enjoy coffee from McDonalds or Starbucks. It really doesn't make that much of a difference to me. There are some coffee snobs who refuse to drink Folgers. How ridiculous! Just give me a cup and make it hot and black.

The waitress in the coffee shop must have been two hundred years old. She was petite and moved kind of slow, but she was attentive and kept my coffee cup full. My total bill amounted to less than four dollars, but I left a twenty on the table as I walked out. From behind the counter, she thanked me for coming and told me to come back. I thought I just might do that.

I drove back to the Prado. While not too late, I started to get tired. Instead of going straight to my room though, I went into the bar and ordered a Jack and Coke. I nursed it at my table for a short while thinking about Lizzy and that awful grandson of hers. Lizzy never did give me an amount for how much money she needed. Or wanted. The whole situation turned my stomach. Of course I wanted to help my sister, but under the circumstances, I didn't want to lavish money on her. A hundred thousand ought to do it. I'd have to tell her that I wouldn't continue to give her money. She would have to make this do for a long time.

The waitress came by and asked if I'd like another drink. I thought about it for a second, then told her no, that I was ready to leave. I paid my bill, left a tip, and was satisfied that I was making the right decision about Lizzy. I didn't owe her anything. She should be pleased with what she got.

## Chapter Twenty-Eight

# The Rigsby

Over the next few days, I either got used to the noisy antics of Kyle or he got better. I'd like to think it was the latter, but I cannot imagine that he improved much in a few short days. I had finished my antibiotics and received a clean bill of health from the doctor. I was happy about that. I received a phone call from Roger to say that he had not been able to arrange the closing within the ten days that I preferred, but it would be just another few days. I was not happy about that. Seriously, how hard it is to buy a house if you've got the cash to do it?

Lizzy and I finally got a little time alone to talk and reminisce. It was so good to be with my big sister again. The roles had changed, however; now I felt like the big brother. I begged her to be firm with Betsy better discipline Kyle. She admitted there was a problem but seemed at a loss to know what to do about it. I took her for a ride in my Ferrari. She declined my offer to drive it herself.

Finally, we got back around to the money. "You never told me how much money you wanted, Lizzy."

"Owen, I feel funny asking for it."

"It's okay. How much do you need?"

"I'll just say it. I need fifty-two thousand dollars."

"Wow. That's a lot of money," I said half-heartedly. "What do you need it for?"

"I know it's a lot. I still owe about thirty on my house and I've got credit card bills of nearly twenty thousand. I don't make a lot of money and I'm only living paycheck to paycheck."

"Welcome to the American Dream," I said, my voice dripping with sarcasm. "Tell you what I'm going to do. You asked for fifty-two thousand. I'm going to give you a hundred thousand. Maybe you can get yourself some other things you need."

"Oh Owen! Thank you so much!"

"Now listen, you need to know this. I can't keep giving you money. You need to pay off your debts and then stay out of debt. Use this money wisely," I said, as if I was going to practice what I preached.

"I will. I promise I will."

"Here's what else I'm going to do. Give me your plane tickets and I'll have them converted to first class. Have you ever flown first class?"

"Oh my goodness, no! This is only the second time in my life I have ever flown anywhere."

"Just try to keep Kyle quiet in first class. First class passengers don't appreciate crying kids." I was speaking as if I had lots of mysterious knowledge and experience in this subject. The truth was that no passenger likes to hear crying babies in any class.

"I will. I will. Owen, I don't know how to thank you."

"You can thank me by disciplining your grandson."

I made arrangements to transfer the money directly into her California bank account. I took her tickets to the concierge desk, and they had them upgraded to first class. I ordered a limo to take them to the airport and handed Lizzy a thousand dollars in cash for traveling expenses. I love my sister. She's the only one I have left. We hugged and kissed goodbye. She asked me again to go to the airport with them. I really didn't want to go. Momma was going to ride in the limo there, so I arranged for the driver to be sure and bring Momma back to the Prado.

Paying for everything made me feel like a big shot again. But this time, it genuinely made me feel good to be able to do something for more than just show. I was really helping my sister. As Mark closed the door to the limo, I knew that the drama was over at least for a while. Lizzy gave no indication of when they would come back. Knowing Momma, she'd buy them tickets back out again for Christmas or something.

Before I returned to my suite, the front desk said I had a phone call. I took it on the courtesy phone. It was Roger. We were finally ready to close. He made an appointment for two P.M. that day to finalize everything. I thanked him and went down to Marty's bank to make the withdrawal.

No one could imagine my disappointment when the bank told me that they didn't have three and a half million dollars in cash on hand. The bank manager came and apologized and said that for such a large cash withdrawal, I needed to give them at least 3 working days' advance notice. Why didn't they tell me that three days ago? Since the sellers didn't want a personal check, I was just going to pay for the house in cash. Now, I'd have to settle for a cashier's check.

We met in the law offices of Dewey, Cheatham and Howe to sign the contract. Why do lawyers think they need to be involved in every area of life? No telling what they were charging the poor saps who were selling the house. For my part, however, I handed them the check for three and a half million dollars. I don't know who salivated more; the heirs or the lawyers.

The Haven was now The Rigsby. From the lawyers' office I called a contractor with whom I had previously arranged to change the sign on the front gate. By the time I arrived, I expected it to be a work in progress.

I had a boatload of keys, codes, instructions and the service history of every built-in item in the house. Momma had returned from the airport, was with me and shared my excitement. I couldn't wait to show her the estate. I wish Lizzy hadn't left before I took possession of it.

The signing of the contract and all the other stuff took about an hour and a half. Momma and I arrived at The Rigsby about four. She hugged me and cried when we got out of her Cadillac, and she saw the opulence of the property. She held onto my arm as I unlocked the front door, disabled the alarm system and entered the foyer. Her reaction was much the same as entering into the Prado for the first time. I took her immediately to the study and showed her the view. We took our time as we looked in almost every closet and marveled at the amenities of a fine, remodeled Tulsa oil mansion.

As Momma walked around looking at the different features, I dreamed about how Karen would like it. I imagined her sitting with me in front of the fireplace as we snuggled together, drinking hot cocoa on a cold night. I dreamed of us entertaining our friends by the pool, like Marty and Tracy did. I pictured us setting up the Christmas tree together, laughing as we placed the ornaments on each limb. I envisioned my carrying her up the grand staircase to the master bedroom.

I was overcome with emotion. Momma saw me wipe a tear away and asked me what was wrong.

"Nothing's wrong, Momma. I just can't wait to show the house to Karen."

"Who's Karen?"

"You remember, Momma. Karen Wilson."

"Karen Wilson?"

"We went to high school together."

"Oh, I think I remember her. She was a sweet girl. Have you two been seeing each other after all this time?"

"No. She lives in Kansas City. I'm going to see her later this week or the first part of next week."

"Oh. How does she know about this place, then."

"She doesn't. I haven't told her yet."

"Then why," Momma started, but didn't finish the question. She just looked at me with the worrying eyes of a mother trying to understand.

"I'm going to ask her to marry me."

"Marry you!" Momma exclaimed. "But you haven't been seeing her."

"It's complicated, but I think she'll agree after we talk." *And I tell her about the money.*

"I don't know what to say."

"You don't need to say anything, Momma. I've got it all under control."

Momma and I drove back to the Prado where she packed her things to go back to her house. I decided to go out furniture shopping. Most of the furniture stores are open until eight or nine in the evening. I still had time. I didn't want to go hog wild buying furniture, though. Karen would probably want a hand in decorating. In the meantime, I could buy a bed, a big screen TV and the most comfortable chair in the world.

I found a beautiful king-sized bedroom suit and a comfortable mattress set. I bought the largest big screen TV they had and a beautiful entertainment center to house it. I went ahead and bought two rows of theater-style, leather recliners to fill out my man-room. I also bought a couple of silly neon signs and a big dart board. That room would be my exclusive domain. I paid extra for next day delivery and setup. I figured I could afford it.

I drove back by The Rigsby. I wanted to see what the grounds looked like at night. Lights mounted high up in the limbs illuminated many of the big oak trees in the front of the estate. The previous tenants must have been fairly security conscious because darkness on the property was at a premium. Soft lights lit the pool and pool house area. Decorative security lights lined the back wall. Surely the lighted acreage made prowlers think twice.

Satisfied with the lighted grounds, I made my way back into the mansion. The dark, cavernous foyer eerily echoed every sound. I quickly turned on all the lights to make myself more comfortable. I wasn't scared, but the mansion could make a great haunted house for Halloween.

A noise from the kitchen startled me. I began carrying my Walther PPK as soon as I bought it. I pulled it out of my pocket; just in case. It was small, but since it was good enough for James Bond, it was good enough for me. I quietly made my way into the kitchen and switched on the light with my left hand. My right hand gripped the PPK like a kid holding the safety bar on a roller coaster. I didn't see anything or anyone. I checked the cupboards and the pantry. Nothing. I even looked in the oven and the refrigerator. I'm not sure exactly what I expected to see in there.

I moved from the kitchen into the breakfast room. Out of the corner of my eye, I saw a man standing in the corner holding a gun. I fired three times before I realized I shot out a full-length mirror. Later, I found that it was an authentic Louis XIV mirror worth over $140,000. I hadn't seen the insurance man yet about the house, so it was my loss.

I put the PPK back in my pocket and sat down on the floor. I didn't know whether to laugh or cry. I couldn't help to think how stupid it was to shoot out a reflection of myself in a mirror. Within three minutes of sitting down, I heard the sirens. I took the gun back out of my pocket and laid it on the kitchen counter, since I didn't have a permit to carry a concealed weapon. I took the magazine out and laid it next to the gun, just so the police wouldn't feel threatened.

I hit the manual switch just as the two police cars arrived at the gate. They roared on up the drive and hit the ground running with their side arms drawn.

"I'm Owen Rigsby. This is my home. Everything is all right."

"There was a report of 'shots fired.'"

"Well, yes. I fired my gun."

"Sir, we need to take a look around."

"Come on in. I'll show you the gun and I'll show you what I shot." *Just please don't tell anyone else.* The officers still had their pistols drawn but weren't on point as they were when they arrived. I led them into the breakfast room and showed them the mirror and explained what had happened. I brought them into the kitchen and showed them my PPK.

"James Bond, huh?" one of the officers remarked. "We don't see many of those around."

We talked a while, and I told them my story about winning the lottery and how I had just taken possession of the estate earlier that day. They said they knew the estate well, as there was an old woman who lived here who dialed 9-1-1 every other day about something. They heard she had passed away some time ago. They mentioned seeing the new sign on the gate changing the name to "The Rigsby."

They also told me that it would be good if the police had the code to the gate in case of emergencies. The security code to the gate is one thing, but nobody gets the code to the house. They didn't ask for it. One thing about Tulsa cops; you can trust them. They aren't corrupt like the big city cops you see on TV shows. I could probably give the entire force my home security code and nothing would ever turn up missing.

The conversation turned to the Ferrari parked out front. They wanted to know all about it. I let them both sit in it. It never hurts to be in good with the police when you have a two hundred mile an hour sports car. One of the officers said he saw a Ferrari about like mine on YouTube the other day. He told me some goober got in it and drove it straight into a limousine out in Las Vegas. The other cop laughed and said his teenage son had shown it to him. We all got a big laugh out of that one. I never said a word. The information about "the unfortunate incident" was on a need-to-know basis and neither of these fine officers of the law needed to know.

I thanked the officers for responding so quickly to the call. I expressed surprise that anyone could hear the shots from outside. They just smiled and told me to thank my neighbors. I promised not to shoot out any more mirrors in the house. We actually had a good visit. They weren't intimidated by the money. They were polite. We joked around a little. No doubt my new incident would be all over the station house in ten minutes. Oh boy.

I couldn't find a broom in any of the many closets, pantries and workrooms. I can't believe the heirs took the brooms but left a mirror. I'd have to leave my mess until later. The furniture I bought would be delivered the next day; I'd bring some cleaning supplies along to keep at the house.

I didn't sleep well again that night. I dreamt about burglars and intruders and not being able to dial 9-1-1. The phone was always dead, or I kept getting the wrong number. I must have shot out that mirror a hundred more times in my dreams that night. I woke up dreadfully tired. In fact, a bad mood dominated my whole day. It changed somewhat when the furniture arrived, but I realized that I didn't have cable TV to watch on my new big screen and there were no aerials at the mansion. The cable company couldn't come for three days. I offered to pay them more, but they wouldn't budge. I decided to not even bother staying in the mansion until the cable TV was installed.

I went out and bought a new John Deere riding mower with all the attachments. I drove it around the yard, but then quickly realized that I could just as easily pay someone to mow the large lot, so I parked the mower in the yard shed and never even started it up again.

I admit that I was in a funk. I was depressed about not having cable TV. I was depressed about having to wait on Karen. I was depressed about John Leroy Painter. I still cannot believe I shot a mirror. I was a little gun-shy in respect to female companionship. I needed to make sure I completely healed up from my gonorrhea before I went to see Karen. I guess I needed to save myself for her; if only in my mind.

I thought that buying the huge oil mansion, the Ferrari and having the millions would make me happy. I was wrong. Maybe Karen's accepting my marriage proposal would get me back on the right track. A ring! I needed to buy Karen a wedding ring. I'll bet Jerry or Jack, or whatever her husband's name is, didn't buy her as big a diamond as I would!

I went to Zale's, and then to Kay's, then to Herzberg's, then finally to a local shop that actually stocked big diamonds. I found an eight-carat marquis cut solitaire in platinum for just a little over six hundred thousand dollars. Stunning comes close to describing this ring. Karen wouldn't be able to turn me down; no woman could.

Buying this huge diamond ring made me feel a little bit better. I put it in my safety deposit box at the Prado and strolled into the bar for a drink. I ordered a Crown and Coke. I could taste a little difference between Crown and Jack, but I think I prefer Jack.

The bartender, Jimmy, stood nearby polishing some wine glasses, or whatever bartenders do with a cloth. "Mr. Rigsby. Do you mind if I ask you a question?"

"You just did, Jimmy," I joked. "What is it?"

"I know this is kind of personal, but what are you going to do with all that money?"

I smiled. "Jimmy," I said. "Spend it. I'm going to live like a king. I'm going to spoil my mother and my best girl and I'm going to enjoy it all, every day."

"Sounds great."

"It is great," I said. But I knew that I wasn't happy. Not yet.

"Mr. Rigsby," Jimmy started.

"Call me Owen."

"I couldn't do that, sir."

"Sure you can. I give you special permission."

"Okay, but I'll have to address you as Mr. Rigsby if any manager is near."

"It's a deal."

"Owen, has the money changed you? Do you think it will?"

"No, not really. I'm the same fun-loving guy that my family and friend know and love. But now, I can afford anything I want, anytime I want. I guess that part has changed. I'm just a regular guy that happens to have millions of dollars."

"That's pretty cool," Jimmy said. He left me to wait on another customer. *Change? How could the money change me?*

I went to my suite exhausted and slept like a hound dog that's been out all-night hunting coons. My last thought before dropping off to sleep left me wondering when I would actually go to Kansas City. I didn't realize that my nerves were shot over all the events of the past week and that I didn't really know what to say to Karen when I saw her for the first time in more than twenty years. I guess I didn't need to say much. The ring would say it all for me. I closed my eyes satisfied with that thought.

CHAPTER TWENTY-NINE

# Kansas City

A good night's rest can do a world of good for a weary body. I awoke refreshed and ready to go to Kansas City. Before rushing headlong into something important, I gave it a good going-over in my mind. I decided that I better get a hotel room just in case Karen wanted to go away with me immediately. The concierge recommended the InterContinental on the Plaza. He said it wasn't too terribly far from the suburb where Karen lives and works. I could headquarter there and do my own private investigating.

I took the ring out of the hotel safety box and put it into the tiny storage box in my Ferrari, along with the Walther PPK. A millionaire cannot be too safe, especially in a big city. The Ferrari doesn't have a large trunk either, but it had room enough for my leather duffle from Vegas. The weather was beginning to cool down, so I went across the street to Utica Square and bought a new leather jacket. I picked up some new Ray Ban sunglasses, too. I looked mighty fine if I said so myself. Of course, a two-thousand-dollar jacket would make a bum look good.

I pulled into McDonald's to get a cup of coffee. Nothing like a Ferrari at the McDonald's drive through. Pulling out onto the highway, I wound my way through Tulsa until I found Interstate 44. I'd need to be calm, cool and collected when I saw Karen. It would be a huge surprise to her, and she might not immediately understand what I'd be proposing. I'd need to find a place to watch her for a little bit to make sure it was actually her. I'd hate to propose to some woman I didn't even know.

My mind raced all the way to Kansas City. My radar detector came in handy several times; I averaged about ninety miles per hour. Not surprising to me, I got lost. You'd think that after driving a donut delivery truck for so many years that I could find my way around in a different city. The problem was that I didn't know where I was going and didn't bring a map. I knew that to get to Kansas City, you headed straight north on US 71. I didn't think ahead about which exit to take or exactly how to get to any of the places I needed to go.

After an impromptu tour of downtown KC, I finally found my way back to the Plaza and the InterContinental. I slipped the ring and the PPK into my pocket before handing the car over to the valet. The efficient clerk registered me into my suite, and I was impressed. The Presidential Suite was much smaller than my suite back at the Prado. I didn't need much for my two or three nights; it would be just fine.

I settled into the Oak Lounge for a drink and to settle my plans. For the first time, I realized that my red Ferrari stood out in a crowd. If I wanted to be incognito while stalking Karen, I'd have to be careful. But then again, perhaps the expensive sports car would be a good incentive to draw her away from her husband. My mind reeled with thoughts of what I should say, how I should say it and her possible reactions. The desired interaction would go something like this:

*"Hello Karen. It's me, Owen."*

*"Owen! It's so good to see you. I've been thinking about you since high school."*

*"Things have changed, Karen. Now I'm rich and can give you everything you want. Leave your husband and come with me. I have a ring and want you to be my wife. We'll have a wonderful life together as millionaires."*

*"I've been waiting for this for twenty years! Yes! Yes! A thousand times yes!"*

If only it would be that easy. I knew it would be more complicated than that; I'm not stupid. I decided against driving the Ferrari and rented a car to be more discrete. The rental came equipped with a GPS and the agent showed me how to use it. I followed the digital voice to within a block of Karen's house. It was a modest older home in a better suburban area of Kansas City. I drove around the block several times trying to get a feel for the neighborhood.

She taught math at Horace Mann High School several miles from her home. I mentally pictured her driving the same route twice a day and followed it myself to see where she worked. I reasoned that her oldest kids went to school there, too, and probably rode with her. I drove back to her house. I assumed they were out; I didn't see any cars or lights on. I needed to find out where her husband worked, too. Pete included that information in the research he provided.

James Edwards worked for the Missouri Department of Transportation as an engineer. He was forty-six years old and had worked for the State for nineteen years. He earned a bachelor's degree in Engineering from the University of Oklahoma and a master's degree from the University of Kansas. He served as the president of the local Rotary Club and he and Karen attended Indian Hills Baptist Church where Karen taught Sunday School and James served as a deacon. Their kids were "A" students and Jody had just been accepted into the University of Missouri. Julie wrote for the school paper and Jacob played junior varsity basketball. Karen earned her bachelor's degree from OU, too. That must have been where they met.

My heart pounded and a feeling of nausea swept over me. Could I really persuade Karen to leave all of that for me? Was I crazy? Was I bordering on being a stalker? Self-doubt and insecurities filled my mind. Yet, for all of my grown-up life I'd thought about Karen. No matter what woman I dated, I wished it had been Karen instead. I wanted her more than anything. I wanted her more than the money. I would trade it all if I could have her in my life.

A gray minivan pulling into the driveway disrupted my thoughts. The two front doors opened and both side doors slid open and out jumped four people. Karen was driving. I parked one house down but had a good view. I could tell that she aged, but she was still beautiful. She no longer had long curls but wore her hair short. Her two daughters looked like her; the oldest looked exactly like Karen from high school. The boy must favor his father.

They unloaded the van with bags of groceries. They carried them all in on the first trip. The boy came back to the van to retrieve a forgotten backpack. Within twenty minutes, a black four door Chrysler 300 pulled into the drive. A middle-aged man removed himself from the car. I assumed it was the husband. He was about my height but looked rather skinny. Actually, he looked as if he might run. If worse came to worse, I could probably take him.

Not too long after his arrival, the whole bunch of them exited to the minivan and took off. They passed right by me. I could plainly see Karen in the passenger seat. She was gorgeous. None of them suspected the changes that would be coming. Ole Jimbo didn't know he was about to lose his gorgeous woman to rich man. The kids didn't have any idea they would soon attend a boarding school in Switzerland. And Karen didn't suspect that she could make me the happiest man in the world by saying "yes."

I fired up the rental and followed them to a school football stadium. It must be Junior's football game. I parked several rows away and followed them to the gate. I didn't really want to get that close, but I couldn't help myself. I paid the price of admission and found a bleacher seat a few rows above and to the left of them. I hadn't been to a junior varsity game in many years, and I had no desire to watch one tonight. But Karen was here.

I stood with the crowd for the national anthem and the very politically correct "positive thought" that came in place of the old-fashioned prayer. The crowd cheered as the home team made its way onto the field. Evidently, Junior played wide-receiver for the Panthers and wore number twelve on his jersey. "J EDWARDS" was printed on the back. His family stood and cheered at the kickoff. Every time the ball came near him, his whole family shouted their support. I watched Karen and was enamored with her love for her kids. She would make me a good wife.

I left at half-time and made my way back to the hotel. The GPS made the difference of my getting back to the hotel or getting lost and driving to St. Louis. The concierge recommended The Club if I wanted a truly superb steak. I wanted one and I got one. The only thing that would have made it any better would have been if Karen had already said "yes" and we enjoyed the dinner together.

I finished my steak and went to their lounge for a drink. I didn't recognize their jazz singer, although she impressed everyone there with her voice. I listened to more jazz in the past month than I had my entire life. It seemed like all the fancy places had a jazz ensemble or some such entertainment. I understand why.

A beautiful woman approached and asked if she could sit with me. Here we go again. I told her that I was waiting for someone. She moved on without another word. That just might be my "no thanks" line in the future. I sat listening to music, enjoying drinks for quite a while. I didn't stay too late because I wanted to get a good night's sleep to be ready for the next day's stakeout. I didn't feel my actions constituted a "get on CNN" kind of stalking, but I needed to make sure I pulled this off in the right way.

I left a wakeup call with the front desk for five the next morning. I told them to call back at five fifteen, just to make sure. I wanted to be out in front of her house before she left in the morning so that I would know her routine. My stomach bothered me, and I didn't sleep well. I didn't dream about Karen, but about her husband. He chased me up and down the bleachers at the football stadium, but it wasn't the one in Kansas City; it was the one back home where I grew up. My foot kept getting stuck on protruding boards or I'd stumble over stadium chairs that were left on the bleachers.

The phone woke me like an unexpected cannon shot from my restless slumber. I was brushing my teeth when they called back. I nearly scolded them for calling again, but I remembered that I asked them to do that the night before. I had a feeling it was going to be a long day.

I dressed, ate a quick bite in the Oak Room and left on my mission. I arrived at Karen's house just in time to see her get in her minivan and drive off alone. That was a good thing. I would be able to catch her and talk to her without her kids there. I followed her to a gym. She looked great in her exercise clothes. She stayed fit all these years; me, not so much. I had gained quite a bit of weight in the last month.

I couldn't really see into the gym through the tinted windows, and unfortunately, it was a "ladies only," so I couldn't get in. I patiently waited the forty-five minutes for her to complete her workout. She popped back in her van and took off like lightning to her house. I could tell that I would need to buy her a sports car, too. Maybe a matching Ferrari. Nothing was too good for my wife.

By seven thirty, she and her kids loaded up the minivan and left for school. The Chrysler 300 remained in the driveway for a good ten minutes before Jimbo left for work. This time, I followed him to his office. He had a twenty-five-minute commute to the state building. I pulled the rental in across the street and watched while he parked and went through the doors. I didn't stick around to wait on him.

I returned to my suite to figure out what to do. Knowing that I could get to her alone in a relatively easy fashion excited me. I convinced myself that if I could speak with her privately, she would be persuaded. I reckoned that I didn't have much of a chance if I confronted her in front of her kids or Jimbo. I decided that I'd be waiting at the gym the next morning with a bouquet of roses and the diamond ring. I'd see her before she went inside, well, because she wouldn't be all sweaty.

Happy with my plan, I headed back down to the Oak Room for lunch. I spent the rest of the day relaxing and daydreaming about how our lives would be forever changed by the events of the next morning. I afforded myself a high-class massage at the InterContinental's Day Spa. It was every bit as good as the one at the Peninsula. Since I wasn't expecting any extras, I relaxed and enjoyed the self-gratifying treat.

I decided that I'd do a little shopping that evening. Kansas City's Country Club Plaza has a wonderful selection of fine clothing and other kinds of stores. I bought a new set of clothes so that I'd look presentable when I asked Karen to marry me. This could well happen the way I so desperately wanted it to happen. This time tomorrow, I could be headed back to T-Town with my future bride.

I know we couldn't get married right away. I think people have to wait six months to remarry after a divorce. We'd have to check on that. We could have a big ceremony or stand before a judge; it didn't matter to me. I would arrange a honeymoon to anywhere in the world; all first class. I'd need to get a passport. I'd have to pay off Jimbo; a million dollars ought to do it. I will tolerate her kids to a certain degree, but they are half his, so maybe we could arrange for him to have sole custody and only see them at Christmas. If she gets custody, they'll be getting passports of their own for an all-expenses-paid, extended educational stay in Europe.

My hands started shaking as I thought these thoughts. My stomach tied itself in knots. I called room service and ordered a big bottle of Jack Daniels; the little one in the mini bar wasn't going to cut it tonight. I called and requested another five o'clock wakeup call. It wasn't even six o'clock yet.

Even though my excitement level was high, I felt hungry. I noticed more and more that I ate when I was excited. I needed pizza. I thought about ordering room service, but I hadn't had a good, delivered pizza since I left for Vegas, so I called Papa John's. My favorite has always been double pepperoni with onions, mushrooms and green peppers on thick crust. This time I added extra cheese to the mix. I found *Goldfinger* on the TV in my suite's media room and settled in for the evening. I emptied the mini bar of the beer and finished the large pizza by myself. The combination of beer and pizza made me feel good. What could possibly go wrong?

CHAPTER THIRTY

# The Proposal

I awoke before the front desk called and was already dressed and ready to leave the hotel at half past five. I was too early to go to the gym, so I stopped in downstairs for their buffet breakfast. I decided to drive the Ferrari to make the best impression possible.

I spied out a florist that had early morning hours and pre-ordered a bouquet of two dozen red roses. They were ready when I stopped by to pick them up and I tipped the woman a fifty for doing such a good job. My nerves were so shot that my hands were shaking. Today would be the day that changed my life forever.

I arrived at the gym with five minutes to spare. I parked the Ferrari in a conspicuous place and waited for the love of my life, my future wife, to arrive. I kept one eye on my Rolex and one eye on the street towards her house. Two minutes past the time she arrived yesterday and no sign of her yet. I waited. My mind began to think that perhaps she didn't work out every day and I would miss her today. Thinking the worst, I nearly abandoned my post when I saw her minivan roaring up the street.

She didn't park next to me, but instead found a place a whole row away. I stood casually, leaning against the Ferrari. She couldn't miss seeing me. However, she appeared to focus only on getting into the gym and nearly walked right past me. I called out her name. "Karen. Karen Wilson??" which startled her. She stopped and turned toward me.

"Do I know you?"

"It's me, Owen. Owen Rigsby from high school."

"Owen? What in the world are you doing here in Kansas City?" "Karen, a lot has changed since we went to high school together. I'm no longer poor. I recently won the lottery and I'm a millionaire."

"Good," she said. "Good for you." Her confused look said it all.

I reached into my pocket and found the ring I bought, got down on one knee and said, "For the longest time I have been in love with you. You are the only girl I've ever wanted. You turned me down in high school because I was poor, but I'm not poor anymore. I'm terribly wealthy and can give you anything your heart desires. Karen Wilson,, will you marry me?"

She just stood there with an expression of disbelief on her face. Finally, after a few agonizing moments she spoke. It wasn't what I had hoped for.

"First of all, Owen, I'm flattered," she said, choosing her words carefully. "But I'm a happily married woman. I'm honored that you would feel this way about me after all these years, but I really love my husband. He is a good man, and we have a good life together. I made a commitment to him twenty years ago and no amount of money is going to make me destroy what we have together. I hope you can understand."

"But Karen, I can give you everything you ever wanted."

"I have everything I ever wanted. I have that in my family. I can't throw that away. I hope you are able to find that for yourself one day."

"But Karen, I bought you a ring. It's eight karats. I paid six hundred thousand dollars for it," I said, holding it out to her.

"It's the most spectacular ring I've ever seen, Owen. But I can't accept it. Please understand."

"But Karen, you turned me down in high school because I was poor. I'm not poor anymore."

"No, I can see you aren't. But the reason I turned you down in high school wasn't because you were poor. The reason I turned you down in high school is basically the same reason I'm turning you down now. I wanted a boy who took God seriously. You obviously haven't changed."

"Of course I've changed. I'm rich."

"Owen, you may be rich, but your soul is bankrupt. I have to go."

"But Karen," I started. I watched her trot back to her minivan and leave the parking lot.

"This isn't over," I said out loud.

I stood there a few minutes trying to figure out what to do next. I guess I knew the possibility existed that she would turn me down the first time we talked. I'd give her a day to mull it over in her mind and let her look around at her precious little family and evaluate what she wants more: them or unlimited wealth.

I drove back to the hotel and swapped back to the rental car. The Ferrari was too flashy to follow her in. Both cars remained in the driveway when I arrived at her house. It was almost seven thirty; time for her to leave. She didn't leave and neither did Jimbo. However, what did happen surprised me. A Kansas City police car arrived and pulled up right in their driveway.

*Jackpot!*

The officer got out and went inside when Jimbo answered the door. Surely they didn't call the police on me!

About fifteen minutes later, the policeman came back outside, started his cruiser and pulled out of their driveway. Only he didn't drive off. He pulled out a little way, then backed in the drive and turned his car off. That unnerved me to the point I left to return back to the hotel.

I made my way back to my suite and cracked open the Jack. I drank straight from the bottle. I didn't expect the police to become involved. Why in the world would they call the police? Why did he just sit in their driveway like a guard dog? What was happening here?

I polished off what little was in the bottle and called room service for another. The bed fairies must have finished with my room while I was out because the mini bar brimmed with beer and the covers magically appeared back on the bed. Housekeeping did a good job at this hotel.

I sat and considered my options. My feelings twirled around like a four-year-old girl in a ballerina costume. Anger, confusion, exasperation and longing tumbled in my head like tennis shoes in a dryer. The bourbon didn't help.

I needed to sort this out logically. I made a list in my head:

    *1. was in love with Karen.*

    *2. he was in love with Jimbo.*

    *3. he wouldn't leave Jimbo for money.*

    *4. Jimbo might leave Karen for money.*

    *5. needed to approach Jimbo.*

That was it! I needed to approach Jimbo. If he would leave her then she would have to come to me. I would console her through her difficult time. I've seen it on TV a thousand times before. They always run to the one they turned down. That was me.

My own ability to reason pleased me. What a brilliant plan! Every man had his price. How much would I be willing to pay Jimbo to divorce Karen? A million dollars? Five million? Ten million? Yes. I'd be willing to pay Jimbo ten million dollars to leave Karen. For that kind of money, I could probably convince him to tell her to find comfort in my arms. This was perfect.

She probably told Jimbo what had happened, and he probably was nervous that she might leave him for me. That would set up the perfect storm. He would be jealous and paranoid. He could accuse her of wanting to leave him. I could pay him to leave her without her knowing. He'd leave and she'd come running to me. I'd let them have the rest of the day to have their arguments and set the stage for my phone call to Jimbo the next morning. I could wait another day. I could wait for Karen.

Content with my cunning plan, I strolled downstairs for lunch. I was a little tipsy from the half bottle of Jack; I needed to eat. I ordered two large shrimp cocktails as an appetizer, a twenty-ounce steak and a pound and a half lobster with a loaded baked potato for the main course, and a hot fudge sundae for dessert. It was a struggle, but I ate it all. I wasn't feeling drunk anymore, so I took a stroll around the Plaza confident in my devious device to get the woman I love.

Lunch had been early, and it was still early in the afternoon. I sat on a bench along a little parkway and watched people walk by. About an hour later, a pretty young girl dressed in jogging clothes stopped at my bench and sat down. She wore her hair pulled back in a ponytail and she had on a purple headband. She removed the earphones from her MP3 player and sat breathing heavily. I couldn't help but notice.

"Pretty day, isn't it?" she asked.

"Yes. It's very pretty. So are you."

She turned toward me. I could see she was in her twenties. "It's not an accident I sat down here with you."

"It's not? Is it karma?"

"No, silly. Aren't you the guy with the red Ferrari?"

"Yes. That's me."

"I knew it. I saw you at the hotel. I've always wanted to sit in a Ferrari."

"You have? We'll let's see if we can't remedy that."

We walked the short distance back to the InterContinental and into the private parking garage. I opened the door for her, and she brushed against me as she got in. She ran her hands along the leather steering wheel in a manner obvious to even the blind what she had in mind. What the heck. One more fling before I marry Karen.

"Would you like to see my suite?" I asked.

"Of course I would, silly."

She hooked my arm as we made our way back to the presidential suite. Many of the men in the hotel just stared as we walked to the elevator, and I'll bet I could have told you what every one of them were thinking: *Man. I wish I was that guy.*

Once in my suite, she told me her name was Tammy. She said she was a student at the University of Missouri at Kansas City. I offered her a drink. She asked for tequila. Then the party started.

I must admit I really needed that with Tammy. My nerves were shot, and I had just been rejected. She comforted me in my time of sorrow. Several times, in fact. As we lay exhausted underneath the grand piano, she finally let the other shoe drop. "I was hoping that you might be able to help me, Owen."

"Help you how?"

"Well, like I said, I'm a student at UMKC and I'm having a little financial crisis."

"How little?"

"About ten thousand dollars."

"Ten thousand dollars? What makes you think that I'd give you ten thousand dollars?"

"I was kinda hoping that I pleased you enough this afternoon to do that."

"Listen, sugar. You can't expect ten thousand dollars for a roll in the sack. It was good, but it wasn't that good."

"How much can you give me, then?"

"What makes you think I'll give you anything at all?"

"Well, the police won't like it when they find out I'm only seventeen."

"Seventeen? You said you were twenty."

"Well, we wouldn't want the police to have to look into this, would we?"

*Hell fire. How in the world do I get myself into these kinds of things?* I considered my options then decided that I'd offer her five thousand dollars. She accepted it quickly. As she opened the door to leave she said, "It was a pleasure doing business with you." Just the parting shot I didn't need.

After tomorrow, I wouldn't be dealing with trash like this anymore. I'd have the woman I'd loved for years and years. She'd be all mine and only mine. I wouldn't have to worry about getting gonorrhea or anything else. I wouldn't have to worry about dining alone or sleeping alone or being alone. I'd finally have all that I really ever wanted.

I spent the rest of the evening stewing about Tammy and anticipating my phone call to Jimbo the next morning. I decided I'd sleep in, probably for the last time alone. I felt stupid that I let Tammy get the best of me, but at least I got something in return. Room service delivered my meal, and I had another restless night.

## Chapter Thirty-One

# Jimbo

I woke with a smile on my face. Today would be the day that changed my life forever. I decided that I didn't want to go downstairs for breakfast. I needed the illusion of power, so I ordered my breakfast to be brought to my room. I used several of the little bottles of vodka from the mini bar to turn my orange juice into screwdrivers. I reasoned that I didn't need courage to do what I was about to do; I just needed a little something to sooth my nerves. I even forced myself to watch the news for a little while. It was Saturday morning; Jimbo wouldn't be at work.

I sat in the luxurious sofa in the living room of the suite with the folder Pete had given me. It contained Karen's home phone number. I grabbed the phone and dialed. A man answered on the third ring.

"May I speak with James Edwards?"

"This is James. Who is this?"

"James, I have a business proposition for you."

"Who is this?"

"Never mind who this is. I'd like to offer you the sum of five million dollars."

"Five million dollars? For what?"

"I'd like to give you five million dollars to divorce your wife."

"Is this Owen Rigsby? You've got a lot of nerve calling me here like this. Just who exactly do you think you are? You have no right to bother my wife like you did yesterday."

"I merely made a proposal to her yesterday. Today, I'm making one to you. If five million dollars isn't enough, I can go ten."

"Are you out of your mind? Let me tell you something, Rigsby. The answer is no. My wife's answer is no. We don't want your money. You can't buy us."

"Just think about it. Ten million dollars is a lot of money. You can do fantastic things with a lot of money. Take it from me; I know."

"I know you are certifiably whack-o. Listen to me. Don't ever call us again. Don't ever approach my wife again. And don't ever contact us again. I mean it. I've already called the police. They know about you. If you make any further contact, I'll get a restraining order against you."

"James, think about what you are passing up. Think about the…"

"I said no!" he shouted into the phone. "Look, you obviously have some issues. Just because you have a lot of money doesn't mean you can go around offering to buy another man's wife."

"But I thought…"

"You thought wrong. Now don't you dare ever contact us again. I mean it!"

He slammed the phone down on his end. The line went dead. I sat there completely stunned. My plan didn't work. What was I going to do now? I thought and thought but couldn't come up with an answer. The only logical course of action didn't seem very easy. I'd have to get rid of Jimbo somehow. I couldn't just kill him outright; that might turn Karen against me. I'd have to hire a hit man or somehow make it look like an accident. Was it really worth all this? The first sane thought I'd had in a week was this: *did I really want a woman who didn't want me?*

All this broke my heart. No. I wouldn't hire a hit man. That was ridiculous. Maybe this was all just a stupid delusion to begin with. She turned me down in high school when I was poor, and she turned me down twenty-five years later when I was rich. Maybe she didn't like me at all. Maybe no amount of money would separate her from her family. Could people really love each other like that? I wanted that, too.

I slipped off the sofa and onto my knees and cried like a baby. Disappointment, heartache and depression flew around my head and torso, taunting me with what could have been. My mind went back to the same old thing. *If Daddy hadn't died…*

I became physically ill as I realized that all was lost. She was gone and there wasn't a thing I could do about it. I rushed to the bathroom and barely made it before I made a mess. I sat, embracing the porcelain god of drunks, and cried some more. What was I becoming? Why did this affect me so? Why couldn't I just shake this off? Why was I crying?

I guess there was nothing left for me to do here, so I packed up and checked out. I returned my rental car and headed south to T-Town. I didn't feel like driving fast. In fact, I dilly-dallied along. It took me nearly 6 and a half hours to get home. I passed by the Phillips 66 station outside of Joplin where I bought the winning lottery ticket. I stopped in to say hi and show off my Ferrari. Everyone was duly impressed. Everyone wanted pictures of me and the car. They wanted to hear about what it was like to win the lottery. I told them about my mansion, my trip to Vegas and my suite at the

Prado. I didn't bother mentioning Kansas City. This kind of attention was just the thing I needed to lift my spirits and get me out of this whole Karen thing.

I still had my suite at the Prado, but probably for not much longer. I completely forgot about the cable TV people coming. I hadn't made arrangements to get them into the grounds to make the installation. It was late Friday night, and it probably wouldn't happen over the weekend. No big deal. I really enjoyed living at the Prado. I pulled in and was promptly met by Mark who was delighted just to be able to park the supercar.

I called Momma and told her I was home. I told her that Karen and I wouldn't be getting married after all. I told her that I decided against it since she seemed to be happy in her current situation. I invited Momma to Sunday brunch and told her I'd probably be moving out of the Prado and into my estate on Monday. She said she was enjoying her "new" house and that everything was marvelous. I told her that her happiness made me happy.

But I wasn't happy. Not happy at all. I was miserable. I had been certain that the lack of money was the source of my discontent my whole life. Now, I had all the money I could ever wish for, but I still wasn't happy. Why?

## Chapter Thirty-Two

# The New Boat

I spent the next several weeks moping, banging around in my empty oil estate. I bought a few more sticks of furniture, but I was disappointed that Karen wouldn't be helping me make the purchases. I only bought a cheap dinette set and put it in the breakfast room next to the empty mirror frame.

Autumn came gently. The nights were cool, and the leaves began to change. Momma and I began to make it a habit to brunch at the Prado. I continued to gain weight and be depressed about Karen. I watched college football on my big screen TV and occasionally went fishing with Marty. Except for trips to the Santa Barbara, I became a recluse.

Early one morning, early being ten A.M., while eating a couple packages of cherry frosted Pop Tarts, I came to my senses. *I cannot live like this; this is ridiculous. I have to get over Karen.*

Seventy-five million dollars in the bank and I sat around all day ordering pizza and eating junk food. An idea had been brewing in my mind for several weeks and I decided to act on it. I jumped in my truck and made the twenty-minute drive to Bass Pro. I walked to the back of the store, past all of the stuffed animal trophies, fishing tackle and sunglasses to the boat department. I don't know why they don't call Bass Pro the "Happiest Place on Earth."

I walked right up to the salesman in the department and said, "I want the best bass boat you've got." He showed me several different models with their different options. I decided on a twenty-two-foot ProBass six-seater but upgraded it to a three hundred horsepower motor. We dickered on the price a little bit because that's what you are supposed to do, and settled on just over sixty thousand dollars for the boat, trailer and upgraded motor. I spent an additional two thousand dollars on fishing tackle, including a fancy reel that has a microcomputer built right in, to help prevent the dreaded "rat's nest" backlash. The reel alone was over six hundred dollars.

She was a real beauty. I called Marty and begged him to take the next day off work. "I've got something real important I need to show you," I told him. We agreed to meet at seven o'clock the next morning to go fishing.

Marty was impressed with my new boat as I pulled up in front of his house. He was genuinely happy for me. Tracy and the boys even came out to look at it before we took it out for the first time. I couldn't wipe the silly grin off my face. I felt like the Cheshire Cat.

After several hours out on the lake, we caught several bass. The powerful trolling motor worked like a dream. The weather was great, albeit a bit cool, but the time had come.

"Marty, gimme a dollar."

"What? Why would I give you a dollar?"

"Just give me a dollar, will you?"

"You've got more money than anyone I know, why on earth would I give you a dollar?"

"Would you just shut up and give me a stupid dollar!?! Trust me."

Marty reluctantly reached into his pocket, retrieved his wallet and pulled out a dollar bill. He handed it to me with a look of frustration in his eyes.

"Thank you very much," I said, as I reached into my jacket and pulled out an envelope and handed it to him.

"What's this?"

"Open it and see."

Marty opened the envelope and unfolded the typed document inside. He read it to himself, then looked up at me with an expression of disbelief. "Are you sure about this, Owen?"

"If I wasn't sure about it, would I have fixed it up before we came fishing?"

"But, Owen, I don't understand."

"Well, what does it say? Oh yeah. 'I, Owen Rigsby, for the sum of one dollar and other considerations, sell this boat, motor, trailer and contents to Martin Westbrook.' I guess it means that I didn't want you to take a tax hit, so I'm selling you this boat instead of outright giving it to you."

"What's the 'other considerations'?"

"Thirty or so years of putting up with me as your friend."

"I don't know what to say. I'm absolutely flabbergasted. Thank you, Owen, thank you so much!"

"Don't mention it. After all, it was a business transaction, right?" I winked.

"Right."

A cold front came through about the time we loaded up to go home. Marty already phoned ahead to Tracy, and she met us at the street. She hugged me first, then Marty. The boys were back home from school and jumped up in the boat and pretended to steer. They stayed in as I backed the rig into their driveway. Marty just stood there with a goofy look on his face.

"Why would you do this, Owen?"

"Marty, don't you know? I love you like a brother." I started to tear up just a little bit, so I cracked a joke about flaunting my millions. We both knew that was only a joke because real friends didn't do that kind of thing to each other. "I've been thinking about this for some time now, and, well, I just wanted to do it."

I stayed for dinner. Marty lit their outdoor fireplace. It wouldn't be too long before the cold weather would put an end to our outdoor dining. Today, however, the fire provided enough warmth to make it comfortable. Our dinner conversation was light. The love I felt was real.

It's interesting to me how doing something nice for someone without expecting anything in return can make a person feel so good. I left Marty's feeling better than I had felt in weeks.

On the way home, I stopped at a store to get some more beer. Coming out, a shabbily dressed man asked me for a favor. He said that his wife was sick, and he needed a few bucks to buy her some medicine. I told him to go take a flying leap. The nerve of some people. Isn't that why they have charities? Hell fire.

That episode put my mood off a bit, but it wasn't anything like what waited for me at The Rigsby.

## Chapter Thirty-Three

# Paparazzi

I noticed several cars and vans parked along my street, which seemed unusual for the time of day. As I approached my gate, I saw that a group of people gathered there and blocked my entrance. They had TV cameras.

Surprisingly, I thought there might be more paparazzi hounding me, but no one had even called to interview me about anything before. I had no idea what this was about, but I reasoned that they didn't know where I lived, and they finally caught up to me. I had a little speech all worked out about being a millionaire and the burdens and responsibilities that wealth demanded.

They didn't ask me about the money. They didn't ask me about the mansion. They didn't want to know who I endorsed for mayor, governor or president. To my horror, they wanted to know how I felt about John Leroy Painter being released from prison.

They caught me off guard. I had nothing to say. I blubbered like a complete fool. My first television interview and I came across as a stuttering imbecile. *Why couldn't I ever catch a break?*

I bullied my way through my own gate and forbade anyone to enter. I knew he had been granted parole, but I nearly forgot about it since my trip to Kansas City. How *did* I feel about John Leroy Painter being released from prison?

I sat alone with my thoughts in the TV room. I didn't dare turn on the TV, even though the news wouldn't be on for a couple of hours. I called Momma and she said someone already called to tell her. I told her about all the TV cameras and how I couldn't even get two words together to make a statement. She reassured me of her love for me, and I her.

I thought about Daddy. He would have been retired by now. Probably gray-headed. Or bald. Shelly would probably still be alive because Daddy would have been there to take care of us. Can it really be thirty years? Has he really been gone that long? I wept bitter tears.

How did I feel about John Leroy Painter? I hated him. I hated him with all my guts. I hated him so much that it kindled a fire of revenge within me. I sat in my chair for the rest of the night planning and scheming. Would I really go through with the ultimate act of vengeance?

The gate buzzer woke me the next morning. A woman with a microphone and a news camera stood in front of the security camera. I asked her what she wanted. "A moment of your time" was her reply. I told her that Mr. Rigsby wasn't available for comment. She didn't go away. I kept an eye on the monitor and noticed another news van pull up and actually block the drive. I called the police and complained. They sent a car and cleared out my driveway.

I didn't want to talk to the press, but I felt like I needed to talk to someone, so I called Marty. He admitted that he saw the story on the news but didn't say how stupid I looked. I didn't ask, either. He wanted to know how I was doing. I told him the truth. Not the whole truth; he didn't need to know everything.

He volunteered to come over, but I said it wasn't necessary and that he didn't need to get involved, *especially where the press was concerned.*

I didn't want to be holed up in the mansion all day. A quick glance at the security monitors showed no TV crew at the delivery gate. I fired up the pickup and out I went. I'm glad I decided to keep it.

I needed to go have breakfast at the Tulsan. The Prado has become an escape for me from my empty house. I couldn't believe my eyes when I saw a news truck at the Prado. I kept driving.

My name is well known in Tulsa, but not my face. That works to my advantage when I need to get out and around. In retrospect, I'm glad the media hasn't pursued me until now. Anonymity was comforting in that time of distress.

I drove to Granny's house. She asked that I visit her several weeks previous, but I never got around to it. Although I left her necklace back at the Rigsby, I needed to see what she wanted.

Granny greeted me with a hug and kiss full on the lips. You simply had to get used to it because Granny wasn't going to change. She invited me in for a cup of coffee.

"Owen, you look terrible."

"Thanks, Granny."

"No, really. You look like you haven't had any sleep."

"I haven't. I couldn't sleep last night, so I sat up in my chair thinking."

"What about?"

"First one thing and then another."

"I spoke with you mother on the phone this morning. She's worried about you. And frankly, so am I."

"What are you worried about? Everything's fine."

"Everything's not fine, Owen. We're worried about how you are taking John Painter getting out of prison. We're both worried you might do something unwise."

"What in the world do you think I'm going to do, Granny? What am I supposed to do, just let him walk free while Daddy lies in a grave? I can't do that."

"Honey, you have to forgive and move on. If you aren't able to forgive, you're the one locked in a prison cell. Don't you see?"

"No, I don't see, Granny. I don't see that at all."

I got up to leave. I wasn't really mad at Granny, just mad at the whole situation.

"Owen, nothing you do is going to bring back your Daddy. He's gone. Don't ruin your life, too."

I looked back over at my grandmother. She had tears in her eyes. Her wrinkled hands clutched the collar of her housedress. Worry filled the lines in her face. "I'm sorry," I said being careful to not let the front door slam. Granny never liked it when you let the front door slam shut.

Well, that didn't go anything like I thought it would. It was too early to go to a bar, but not too early to start drinking. I stopped at a liquor store and bought a bottle of bourbon. It fit nicely in the cup holder of my Ford F-150.

I drove aimlessly for a while, having no idea where to go or what to do. Amazingly, I found myself at the offices of Pete Langford, the private investigator. He, too, had just arrived at work for the day and was about to enter his office. He glanced up and immediately recognized me.

"Mr. Rigsby. Good morning. What brings you out today? Was everything satisfactory in my report?"

"Yes, it was all just as you indicated."

"Did you find the subject?"

"Huh?"

"Did you find the woman you were looking for?"

"Yeah, but I'm here about something else."

"Well, in that case, come on inside where we can talk in private."

I entered his small office suite. The whole thing could fit inside my home theater. He introduced me to Julie, his receptionist. She said she was glad to finally meet me in person. Pete ushered me into his private office, a room smaller than the bedroom I grew up in. Again, it wasn't anything like I imagined. There were no stacks of files on the desk; no wadded-up paper on the floor. In fact, the place was immaculate.

He offered me a chair and we got down to business.

"I don't think it is any secret that I've been in the news lately," I started. "It's been about John Leroy Painter, the man that killed my father while he was driving drunk."

"Yes, I saw that on the news and read it in the Tulsa World."

"I'd like for you to find John Leroy Painter for me. I want to know where he is staying. I want you to get a picture of him so that I know what he looks like now."

"Mr. Rigsby, I have to tell you that I'm not so sure about this. I don't think it is a good idea for…"

I cut him off. "I don't care what you think. I'm hiring you to find this guy."

"I can't be party to any investigation which leads to criminal harm against any individual."

"Criminal harm? I'm just asking you to find him, not kill him."

"What I mean is that you appear to have something in mind when you find him, and I can't be a part of that."

"I just want know where he is."

"Why?"

"Because I need to know."

"I have to have certain assurances that you aren't going to use the information I provide in the commission of a crime. My license and my conscience depend on it."

"I swear to you that I'm not going to harm anyone," I said. I had my fingers crossed, just like a five-year-old would when he lies to his parents. "I'll pay you ten thousand dollars up front to find him. Cash. If you won't do it, then I'll get someone else."

Ten thousand bucks is a lot of money to anyone. It probably amounted to two months' salary or more. He sat there and looked in my eyes. I looked

*Jackpot!*

right back at him trying to hide my motives. He pursed his lips and gave an ever-so-slight headshake. I stood up and started to thank him. He stopped me and we made our deal. I knew that he could be bought. I've heard "every man has his price." Pete's just happened to be ten thousand dollars.

I asked him to have the information to me as soon as possible; to make this his highest priority. He said he'd give me the report the next day. I was impressed, not knowing, of course, that much of the research he'd be doing was actually public information. I'd have to get a computer one of these days and learn how to use it.

I left his office and decided that I better get some food in my increasingly large belly. I'd had a package of pop tarts and a half a box of chocolate covered donuts this morning, but the bourbon needed something else to cut it down. I wanted to go to the Tulsan but didn't want to face the media. I opted to try a Tulsa tradition, Jamil's Steakhouse. I drove by but the building wasn't even there. The Interstate 44 widening project purchased a huge amount of property including Jamil's. Emptied out hotels, businesses and restaurants littered the roadside.

I had no idea where they relocated but happened on the new location a mile east on 51st Street. I became concerned at the sight of an empty parking lot. A sign on the door said they didn't open until four pm. Just my luck.

Becoming increasingly agitated by hunger, booze and the desire for revenge, I needed to eat to help recapture my composure. I figured if I could stay in South Tulsa, the news cameras wouldn't find me there. I headed to Restaurant Row, otherwise known as 71st Street, where all the chain restaurants set up shop. Woodland Hills Mall was the anchor at Memorial Drive, but developers sprinkled the restaurants in among the strip malls, shopping centers and retail outlets.

I settled on Tex-Mex. They were very crowded, and my money had no influence at chain restaurants. I asked to sit at the bar and was seated immediately. Not too many folks are willing to eat at the bar, even though there are always plenty of open seats.

I ordered a Margarita and then another. I ate a bowl of chips and salsa. I switched to Mexican beer. My Almuerzo Grande arrived, and I dove right in. I sat at the bar for over an hour drinking, eating chips and salsa and watching the crowd come and go.

I drove myself back to my estate. One solitary news van stood vigil at my front gate. No one covered the delivery gate. I grabbed what was left of my bourbon and headed for the swimming pool. I didn't take time to go in and get a towel or my bathing suit for that matter. I stripped down, even though it was quite cool and stepped down into my heated pool. I made my way over to the built-in Jacuzzi and lifted myself in. I pushed the button that started the bubbles. It felt good.

I swallowed the last of the whiskey and got out to get another bottle of something. I have a good supply of booze and I selected a bottle of 18-year-old scotch. I didn't bother going back outside. I got a pair of sweatpants and t-shirt and sat in my TV room. It was almost a sin to have a beautiful home like this completely void of furniture, save three rooms. The empty house mocked me. Its barren walls reminding me that Karen wouldn't be there to help fill the void in my own life.

The phone rang shaking me into consciousness. I arranged for a new phone with an unlisted number. Only Momma, Granny, Marty and Pete Langford had the new number. I also ordered caller ID so that I could screen what few calls I did receive. This happened to be Pete.

"Good news, Mr. Rigsby. I've found John Painter."

"Where is he?" I asked.

"He's right here in Tulsa."

"Can you bring over the information?"

"I can be there in half an hour."

"Come to the delivery gate. There are news people at the front gate."

"Will do."

I turned on the TV while I waited for Pete to arrive. Nothing on, as usual. The buzzer indicated that someone was at the delivery gate. Pete arrived alone. I pressed the button to open the back gate and saw him drive in. I cannot believe the news people didn't see the sign about the delivery gate and have someone stationed there.

I invited Pete in through the back door. The beauty of the mansion impressed him. He remarked on there not being any furniture and asked if I finished moving in. I gave him some sort of excuse about something and diverted his attention by asking for his report. We sat at my breakfast table which was a first for me since I usually eat alone in front of the TV.

I remarked that his quick results surprised me. He simply smiled and started the presentation. He didn't have a photograph that he took himself, but he took one off the Oklahoma Department of Corrections website. It showed John Leroy Painter as an old, thin, gray-headed man, and starting to bald. He didn't look anything at all like I remembered. Pete told me that someone set him up in a small apartment over in West Tulsa, in the

Carbondale area. He had a few other pieces of information, but the photo and the address was all I wanted.

Pete hesitated as if he wanted to say something else. I told him to speak up. He mentioned that he was concerned about my intentions. I reassured him I was only interested in the sake of curiosity. He seemed satisfied. I dismissed him and told him how to exit the back gate.

I sat looking at the face of the man who killed my father. He didn't look like a killer; he looked like a pitiful old man. But he was free, and Daddy was dead. By the end of the evening, I planned for him to be dead, too.

Carefully, I studied every feature of that man's face. I planned to confront him that very evening in the fashion of <u>The Princess Bride</u>'s Inigo Montoya, "Hello. You killed my father. Prepare to die." I didn't have anything nearly as clever to say. I've thought of that moment for most of my life, but never really crafted a particularly sinister salutation.

What must have been going through that man's head all those years ago to get drunk then go out and drive? How could he have been so careless to have collided with a church van, forcing it into a telephone pole? How could he escape with literally only a scratch and yet my father and two others were killed?

I drained the second bottle of booze and went looking for a third. I needed some liquid courage to get through the night.

## Chapter Thirty-Four

# John Leroy Painter

At a little after five, I ordered a pizza. I didn't keep anything in the kitchen, except for junk food and alcohol. I noticed the news van finally left. I guess I didn't give them their sound bite for the six o'clock news, so they moved on. The order came to a little over twelve dollars. I handed the kid a twenty and shut the door.

I always preferred beer with pizza, but tonight called for something more. I drank Tennessee's finest without enjoying it or the pizza. I was on autopilot; a justified mission of revenge.

I gathered my small arsenal to decide the weapon of death. I looked at my Walther PPK and decided against it because I liked James Bond too much to have it be a constant reminder of this night. I decided against the Colt because I liked it and didn't want to get rid of it. I looked at the shotgun pistol. It was called "The Judge." Perfect for what I needed. It didn't use bullets, so CSI couldn't trace ballistics back to me. It would make a mess. And that's what I wanted. I planned on emptying all five .410 shotgun shells into his head.

Then I'd be free. Free of hate. Free from angst and mental torment. Free from the bastard that killed my father. I could finally find peace. Surely I'd find peace. I had to have peace.

The alcohol affected my mental processes. No clear thoughts tonight. I looked at the clock; nearly nine. I slipped The Judge into the pocket on my sweatpants. The weight couldn't pull it down over my bloated stomach. I grabbed my two-thousand-dollar leather jacket I bought for my trip to KC. The night was cool.

I stumbled out the door and to my Ferrari. I didn't think about the notoriety of a car like that in Carbondale. It didn't matter. Only killing John Leroy Painter mattered now. I took the pistol out of my pants and stuck it in the pocket of my jacket. It felt better there. I started up the Ferrari but had to go back inside to get the address and map of my prey. I'd make Daddy proud of me tonight. He'd finally be able to rest in his grave knowing that I put his killer in his.

Pictures swirled through my mind. Pictures of Daddy. Pictures of Momma. Pictures from the newspaper after the accident. Pictures of funerals and cemeteries and coffins.

*Jackpot!*

I sat in the Ferrari a full ten minutes before starting her. I heard Momma telling me not to do something stupid. I heard Granny saying the same. Something deep down inside told me I was on the wrong track. But revenge yelled louder.

I fired up the Italian beauty and nearly ran into the gate. I maneuvered gingerly through without scraping anything. My vision was off. My judgment was off. The only thing actually on appeared to be my internal burning for vengeance.

I made my way south to catch Interstate 44 which would take me toward Carbondale. I couldn't keep the Ferrari in my lane. Other drivers honked. I considered it to be them cheering me on to my life's purpose; to avenge my father's death.

A bitter guile stirred in my stomach with the bourbon. Sweat soaked through my shirt, even though it was fifty degrees, and I had the convertible top down. I missed my exit.

I pulled off at the next exit which took me out of my way. Carbondale is a small area completely surrounded by highways and interstates. Not being in a good frame of mind didn't help me find my way back. I had never really been in this part of town before; I never had a reason.

Fortunately for me, traffic was light. However, because of my state of mind, it took me nearly an hour to make the ten-minute drive from my house. I found the address and pulled into the driveway with my lights off.

I sat in the car for another several minutes steeling my nerves. My hands shook like leaves in a stiff breeze. The gun pressed through my jacket and against my body reminding me of the task at hand. Could I really do this thing?

No lights shone through the windows. John Leroy Painter had gone to bed for the last time. Soon, I'd send him to Hell.

I opened the car door and literally fell to the ground, the alcohol numbing my senses. Picking myself up, I accidentally slammed the door alerting a nearby dog to bark. It really didn't matter. There was about to be more noise in the neighborhood.

I staggered to the door of the cheap renthouse where my enemy resided. I almost threw up. I could feel the front porch moving, just another effect of the booze. I rang the doorbell.

I rang it again. And again. I pounded on the door with my fist. I could feel the wood on my knuckles, but no pain.

Finally, after what seemed an eternity, a light appeared in the front window. I aroused the murderer from his peaceful slumber. The show was about to start.

The door opened and an old man stood there in light blue boxer shorts and a white t-shirt.

"Yes? What do you want?"

"John Leroy Painter?"

"Yes. Who are you?"

"May I come in?"

"It's late and I was asleep. What's this about?"

"I just need a word with you. It won't take long."

Reluctantly, the old man opened the door and let his executioner into his small living room. A broken-down couch, a couple of chairs and an old TV made up the furnishing. Quite plush compared to his room for the past thirty years.

"My name is Owen Rigsby. You killed my father," I said, pulling out my gun, "and now it's your turn to die."

He actually put his hands up, just like you'd see in a movie. If I had been sober, it might have been funny. All the blood drained from his wrinkled face. He took a deep breath and said, "May I say something before you kill me?"

"Make it quick," I said. *A condemned man's last words.*

"I'd like to say two things. The first is that I'm so very sorry for killing your father so many years ago. There isn't a day that goes by that I don't think about him and the two others that died because of my recklessness. I know I've destroyed your life and all I can do is say I'm sorry and beg for your forgiveness."

"Well, if you think that saying you're sorry is going to make everything better, you're dead wrong. I don't forgive you. I hate you. Tonight, I am your judge, jury and executioner."

"In that case, the second thing I'd like to say is I forgive you."

"You forgive me? What in the world are you talking about? Forgive me for what?"

"For killing me. You see, after about eighteen years in prison, I finally received forgiveness from God. I repented of my old ways; of getting drunk and only caring about myself. I was born again and became a Christian. I got a whole new lease on life. I knew that one day we were likely to run into each other and I wanted to make sure that you know I was sorry and to beg your forgiveness. Now that I'm about to be see God, I don't want to face Him with hatred in my heart. So, I forgive you for killing me. You need to hear it just as much as I need to say it. I hope you understand."

My head was spinning. Nausea overwhelmed me, but only tears came out. I gritted my teeth so hard that I thought I might break them, or my jaw. My whole body started to shake, but especially my arms. I slowly lowered the gun. I couldn't believe that he wasn't lying on the ground bleeding.

He never broke eye contact with me, but he wasn't staring me down. His eyes were filled with compassion and pain. A small tear trickled down his cheek. He didn't look scared. He didn't look smug.

My breathing was labored, my chest heaved with each breath. I couldn't say anything; I was at a complete loss for words. Confusion accomplished what the alcohol couldn't. He started to say something but decided to keep quiet. His hands were still in the air, even though the gun pointed to the floor.

I turned and left him standing there.

## Chapter Thirty-Five

# The Get-away

Making my way back to my car, I jammed the pistol back into my coat pocket. I fumbled for my car key and dropped it on the dark driveway. Stooping down on my hands and knees, I found it just underneath the carriage.

Backing out onto the street, I laid rubber all the way down the block running three stop signs and a traffic light before entering back on I-44. My vision was extremely blurred. I'm sure the alcohol was a cause of the problem, but my eyes were wet from those bitter tears. I came face-to-face with my father's killer but was unable to take revenge. I was angry at myself and angry at him.

The gun poked my side as if to taunt me, reminding me that I was a coward. I took it out of my pocket and threw it off the Arkansas River Bridge. It was gone forever. When I threw it with my right hand, my car swerved wildly, and I narrowly escaped smacking the concrete. I regained control, at least of the steering wheel, but continued to speed to my exit. I took the Riverside Drive exit way too fast and scraped the curb with the side of the car.

Finishing the circle ramp, I pushed the accelerator to the floor and fishtailed onto Riverside. I let up and slowed down. I only saw her a fraction of a moment before she jumped out of my way. Some young woman was out walking her dumb dog and was jay walking the wide avenue. I nearly hit her. That would have been just great.

It's only three and a half miles, at most, from I-44 to my street up Riverside. I made it almost two miles before I saw the red and blue flashing lights. That's all I need. From my experience with the Texas State Trooper, I knew I could outrun this squad car from TPD. But I also knew that I might end up killing myself if I did.

I pulled my Ferrari into an open driveway and turned off the ignition. A second police car arrived. I'd probably end up on the TV show COPS if I didn't watch myself. I opened my door as the first officer approached. I don't remember too much from this point on. I vaguely remember trying to touch my nose for some reason and singing the ABC's.

CHAPTER THIRTY-SIX

# Rock-bottom

I awoke face down on a concrete floor, laying in my own vomit. At first, I had no idea where I was, but then I saw a metal toilet in one corner and a drain in the center of the floor. Otherwise, the room was empty. A large gray iron door drew my attention. It was locked from the outside.

Reality slammed into my consciousness. Having never been arrested before, it took a while to realize that I was in the drunk tank at the police department.

Had I really sunk so low? I had a huge headache from my hangover. I made my way to the toilet which, above it, had a built-in sink. I ran the cold water and splashed my face. It helped. I washed out my mouth and cleaned up the best I could. At some point during the night, I lost control of my bladder. My shirt was covered in vomit; my pants soaked in my own urine. What a lousy start to a bad day.

My Rolex was gone, along with the contents of my pockets, my belt and my shoelaces. There was no clock. What time was it? Did it really matter?

I sat on the cold cement floor in the corner alone with my thoughts. It all came rushing back to me. I went to kill John Leroy Painter. What was it he told me? Oh yeah, he forgave me. The room spun.

I replayed the whole event over and over the best I could trying to remember every detail. I remembered Momma telling me to not do anything stupid and my telling her not to worry, that I was in control. I clearly was not in control. I yielded control to the bottle of bourbon the night before.

As I thought about a lot of things (a drunk tank is a nice quite place to think). I didn't understand how I had fallen to such a place. I thought I *was* in control. To think, a multi-millionaire with an historic Tulsa oil mansion covered in vomit and urine in a Tulsa drunk tank.

For the first time since I won the lottery, I saw clearly. I saw how my selfish behavior in Las Vegas did not work to my advantage, but to my shame. I understood how my going to Kansas City to try and buy Karen served no purpose other than my own pride-filled fantasy. I realized my actions traumatized her and her husband.

My own actions embarrassed me when I realized I nearly paid to have my mother fired from her job just because I wanted her to retire. I thought again of Mr. Jackson in Las Vegas, and how disgusted I became with Chloe. I remembered the humiliation of my gonorrhea. Oh dear God! My heart is evil!

For the first time in my life, I came to grips with my own wickedness. People had been trying to tell me this for years, but I was too proud to listen. Marty was trying to show me a way out the day that I won the lottery, but I didn't want to hear what he had to say. Granny's preacher even told me about it, but I was too hard-hearted to recognize it. Granny tried to get me alone to tell me, but I turned my back on her as well.

Somewhere, somehow, I lost my way. As long as I was in control, it didn't look like it was going to get much better. As long as I called the shots, I could end up a killer or being so self-absorbed that nothing else mattered. How do I get out of this mess I've created?

I moved from a sitting position to my knees. My heart was truly broken for the first time in my life. I fell on my face and heard myself calling out to God.

> *I've made such a mess out of my life. You've been telling me for years that I couldn't do it alone, but I was too stiff-necked to listen. I've been really bad. I've been with prostitutes. I've been living only for myself. And last night, I intended to kill someone. I wanted to kill him, but You were there, too. You sent me a message. I was too drunk to hear you last night, but I hear you right now. I'm sorry, God. I'm so very sorry. I can't do this on my own anymore. I just can't do it right. That day on the boat, Marty told me how his life was changed because he asked Jesus to save him. I want to do that right now. I ask Jesus to save me and to forgive me. I promise that with Your help, I'll change. I don't want to be like this anymore.*

When I finished talking to God, a wave of peace overwhelmed me. I smiled. I hadn't felt peace in a long time, maybe ever. It was a kind of peace that defies description, like being on a boat on a lake without wind or waves, just sitting there enjoying creation. Only this was much deeper. My slate had been wiped clean. I had a fresh start.

I wanted to tell someone. I needed to tell to tell someone. I wanted to tell Granny first, then Marty. I wanted to tell Momma and Lizzy. I wanted to tell everyone I knew that God saved me.

## Chapter Thirty-Seven

# Trying to Obey God

The passage of time is a strange thing. When you dread something, time flies. When you look forward to something, it crawls like molasses. I felt like I was in a barrel of molasses. I passed my time by talking to God some more. I told Him about all the bad things I ever did, some of which I had completely forgotten about. But, when I spoke with Him, I wanted to tell Him everything. I was still ashamed, but somehow, it felt right confessing them. I've always heard that confession is good for the soul; I can agree with that.

For some strange reason, I felt like singing. I couldn't think of any songs, except *Jesus Loves Me*. I learned that when I was a kid.

> Jesus loves me, this I know,
> For the Bible tells me so.
> Little ones to Him belong.
> They are weak, but He is strong.
>
> Yes, Jesus loves me.
> Yes, Jesus loves me.
> Yes, Jesus loves me.
> The Bible tells me so.

I sang that song a million times waiting for someone to let me out. I didn't know what kind of charges I was facing. Did John Painter call the police on me? Was I looking at attempted murder in addition to drunk driving?

Drunk driving! Just like John Painter. It was drunk driving that killed my Daddy, and I did the same thing going to kill the perpetrator. How could I have done that? I vaguely remembered the woman walking the dog the night before. Did I hit her? Is that why I was in jail?

*Please hurry up so I can know what I did!*

The wait was killing me. Drunk tanks weren't equipped with phones. They'd let me out when they were good and ready. Obviously, they weren't ready.

The hours passed. Hunger started to rear its ugly head. I drank water from the sink.

Finally, I heard the metal clank on the big iron door.

"Mr. Rigsby, I'm Lieutenant Johnson," he said handing me a blue jumpsuit. "Put this on. You'll be more comfortable."

"Thank you."

He waited for me as I changed from my nasty clothes into the dry, clean inmate clothes. While it felt good to be out of my soiled things, I wasn't too excited about wearing the uniform of the incarcerated.

"What am I being charged with?"

"Driving Under the Influence. You're in luck. Court is still in session, and they've added you to the docket. Your car's been impounded, though, so you'll have to pay to get it out, but the impound lot's closed until Monday morning. I'll get a patrolman to give you a ride home after we get everything done here."

"Is that all I'm being charged with?"

"Yes, this time. Mr. Rigsby, you of all people should know what happens when you drink and drive. Wasn't your father killed by a drunk driver?"

"Yes. His name is John Painter. He is genuinely sorry for what he did, too."

It took more than two hours to be processed out. A little bag held my pocket items. I re-laced my shoes before leaving. A young officer drove me home in a patrol car. I rode in the front seat. He remarked on The Rigsby saying that it was a beautiful place. I thanked him but knew that it stood almost empty. I asked him if they wanted my blue jumpsuit back, but he said to keep it. I would keep it; as a reminder.

I went inside and headed straight for the shower. The hot water felt good. I wadded up my dirty clothes and put them in the trash can. I didn't need them as a memento of my time in the tank.

After I dressed, I paused and opened my footlocker to find my Bible. I opened it to look up John 3:16 and read it again for the first time. God really did love me. He had been waiting for me for all these years. I continued to read but started at the beginning of the book of John. I read fourteen chapters before my stomach reminded me that I hadn't eaten since last night and it was practically six P.M. I closed the book and told God how happy I was that He showed patience with me.

I sat and looked at my big, empty mansion. While I still loved it, it didn't mean as much to me as it did the day before. In fact, the Ferrari and even the money didn't mean as much to me either. I wasn't prepared for the change of heart that took place. It surprised me.

Since the Ferrari was in the impound lot and I couldn't get it out until Monday, I drove my truck to a hamburger joint. For the first time since I was a kid, I thanked God for my meal before eating. I didn't make a big deal out of it, but I did close my eyes. Eating made me feel better, but I finished quickly so I could go talk to Granny.

My visit delighted her. She smiled, as always, and invited me in. She asked me to have a seat, but instead, I fell to my knees and hugged her around her legs. I told her how sorry I was that I neglected her. I told her I loved her and would try to show it in the future. I told her about being in jail the night before and how that very morning, God saved me.

She knelt down with me, right on the floor and cried. She told me she prayed for me my entire life and saw the answer to her prayer this very moment. She prayed and thanked God for His mercy on my life.

Gaining back our composure, she asked me more about what happened to land me in jail. I told her the whole story. I saw the shock in her eyes, but watched it disappear as I related the story of how John Painter forgave me and how I couldn't go through with it. She smiled and we both praised God for working things out like that.

Granny asked me to go to church with her the next morning. I said yes. We were both happy about that.

I told Granny I needed to go see Marty and tell him. She hugged and kissed me. It was the best visit ever.

I headed over to Marty's house. I didn't find them home. While disappointed, I knew that I'd see him soon. I went back to The Rigsby and enjoyed the best night's sleep in my life.

I picked up Granny the next morning and I escorted her to church. Shelly's funeral was the last time I'd been there. It didn't bring back good memories. I endured Granny's old lady Sunday School class. They all doted on me as if I were their own grandson. Granny introduced me to everyone we met. She was happy.

I sat with her during the service. I enjoyed the singing. We sang songs that came rushing back to my memory from my childhood. That felt good. It pleased me to sing more than just "Jesus Loves Me." The pastor had an interesting message from James 2:14-20. I listened to every word. He spoke about good works and how they to prove your faith, even though they can't save you.

They offered an invitation at the end of the sermon. It's a time where people who want to can go down front and ask for prayer or join the church and other things. I thought it was a good opportunity to practice what I just heard, so I walked down the aisle.

The preacher met me with a handshake and let me tell him about my decision. I told him that after listening to his sermon, I decided to give his church a million dollars. I took out my checkbook and wrote out a personal check. The preacher looked confused and called another old man from the audience. They spoke for a moment, then the preacher came back over.

"I don't want to insult you, but we can't take your money."

"Why not? It's a million dollars. It can do lots of good things for your little church."

"Yes, but we cannot accept it. It's lottery money."

"So?"

"It's the devil's money. We can't take it because it would bring a curse on our church."

"Are you saying that you are refusing to take a check for a million dollars? That's the dumbest thing I've ever heard of."

"Well, I'm sorry. We just can't take it."

I walked back up the aisle crushed. And confused. Granny met me with a smile until she saw my face.

"What's wrong, Owen?"

"I tried to give the church some money, but they wouldn't take it. He said it was 'the devil's money.' I only wanted to help your church. I didn't know I had money from the devil."

"Now listen here, Owen. Don't get all upset about this. Let's give it some time and think about it and ask God to help us understand."

Normally, I would have been angry and left in a huff. But this made my heart heavy. I didn't want to do anything to upset Granny, so we waited and left during the prayer. I didn't think I'd ever be back at that little church.

I took Granny to The Tulsan for lunch. It overwhelmed her, just like Momma. I enjoyed treating her to such a banquet, but something changed. I wasn't trying to show off or act like a big shot. The wait staff doted on Granny, just like her Sunday School class made a fuss over me. I liked watching her feel special.

I dropped her off at her house and went to see Marty. Tracy opened the door and invited me in. We sat inside their living room since the weather had turned during the night and a light drizzle was falling. The outdoor patio looked closed for the season.

We sat together and made some small talk. Finally, I blurted out, "Marty, Tracy, I got saved yesterday!"

"What? Owen, praise the Lord! We're so happy to hear that. Tell us all about it."

I told them about my encounter with John Painter and being in jail. I told them how I felt I finally made it to the lowest point in my life and the only hope I had was God. They both stood up and hugged me. I thanked Marty for telling me about his story on the boat and how that played a huge part in giving my life to God. Marty teared up. So did Tracy.

I told them about going to church with Granny that morning and what happened with the preacher during the invitation time. Marty's face showed the alarm he felt.

"Owen, I know you are new to all this, but you're going to have to be careful how you deal with people."

"What do you mean?"

"Well, peoples' attitude about the money to begin with. People may not understand the change that's taken place in your heart. They may not understand your intentions."

"I still don't understand, Marty."

"They may have thought you were trying to draw attention to yourself by giving the money down front to the preacher."

"I was just trying to put into practice what I just heard the preacher say."

"Look, I'm fairly new at all this, too. Let me call my pastor and maybe he can help us both understand what the Bible says about this."

Marty called his preacher and to my surprise, said he could come right over. He arrived twenty minutes later.

Dan pastored Woodland Hills Bible Church. He looked to be about fifty. His demeanor allowed me to be at ease; his smile won me over immediately

Marty asked me to tell Pastor Dan my testimony. I told him I didn't know what he meant. He explained that a testimony was my salvation story. I told Dan about going to kill John Painter and him forgiving me. I told him about being in jail and asking Jesus for salvation. Dan asked me a few questions and seemed satisfied with my answers.

Marty told Dan about my experience in Granny's church and how it confused and frustrated me.

"Why did you go down front to give the money instead of just putting it in the collection plate? Did you want to make a big deal out of it?"

"No, I heard him talk about proving your faith and I wanted to prove it. I didn't put it in the offering plate because they passed the plates before the sermon."

"Would you have put the money in the plate if the offering had been after the sermon?"

"I don't know. I really wanted to give them the money."

"Owen, only God can judge your intentions. What you do with your money is your business."

"Would you have taken the money if I did that in your church?"

"Probably not. But not for the same reason the other pastor gave. I would have asked to sit down with you in private and talk about your intentions. The invitation is not the time to draw attention to yourself."

"This is all new to me. I don't know how I'm supposed to do this stuff."

"It's OK. It will come as you grow in your relationship with the Lord."

"What about what the other preacher said, about this being 'the devil's money?'"

"Personally, I think that was a lousy thing to say. I think our God is bigger than that. I think that when he redeemed you, he redeemed that money as well. I don't think it is the devil's money. I think it is your money."

As we sat talking, it dawned on me that it was not the devil's money. But the preacher was wrong; it wasn't my money either. If God redeemed me and I now belonged to Him, then the redeemed money now belonged to Him, too.

## Chapter Thirty-eight

# Peace

"How do you plead?"

"Guilty, your honor."

"Being that this is your first offense, I'm sentencing you to one hundred hours of community service. See the court clerk for details."

I figure I got off easy. True, this was my first time to be arrested, but they didn't know that I had more on my mind than drunk driving. I deserved a whole lot more.

I spoke to the court clerk and was given a list of places where I could complete my sentence. It included some highway trash crews, a crew to paint playground equipment, a crew to move books in the city libraries and a crew to restripe the parking lot at the fairgrounds. To be honest, all of these assignments sounded like punishment. Each of them was better than extended jail time, though.

I was just about to choose the playground equipment crew when I realized there was a second sheet attached that included some other community service opportunities. I read down the list and immediately decided on the one I had to choose - the John 3:16 Mission.

I didn't know a thing about the place or what they did, but I really didn't care. Even if I had to wash the feet of homeless people, this was the place for me. I told the clerk my decision. She marked it down in my case folder. She handed me a card with the address and told me I had six months to complete the hours.

My night of insanity a week ago brought me to the lowest point in my life, but allowed me to have a fresh start, a new life. I didn't go back to Granny's church but went instead with Marty and Tracy to Woodland Hills Bible Church. I went to Marty and Tracy's Sunday School class; it was a lot better than all the old women in Granny's class. I felt a little out of place because most everyone were married couples. Marty stuck close to me like a mother hen, making sure I had enough coffee and a Sunday School lesson book. The teacher, Bob, was a guy about my age. Everyone was friendly and made me feel welcome. I actually liked being there.

Marty and Tracy walked with me into their sanctuary. It was a pretty building with a tall cathedral ceiling. It had stained glass windows, but they weren't intricately decorated. They made a formless mosaic. At the front, they had a big piano, a little band and a group of singers. I knew some of the songs we sang, but others I didn't.

I didn't make the mistake of trying to give them a million dollars. Pastor Dan told the visitors that they didn't have to put anything in the offering plate but asked for a completed visitor's card. I thought that was pretty cool. They all knew I was a millionaire.

Pastor Dan was a good preacher. I hung on his every word. I felt like my soul was starving to death and he was spoon feeding me. It was wonderful. I found myself smiling. It was more than just having fun – I felt like I belonged there.

When the service was over and the last prayer had been said, I didn't want to leave. I heard Marty's boys tell Tracy they were hungry, so I moved out into the aisle. Other people shook my hand and told me they were glad I had visited and invited me to come back anytime I wanted. And I wanted to, every chance I got.

We drove over to Marty's house for lunch. They asked me how I liked their church. I told them that I never experienced church like that before. Tracy fixed a delicious lunch, and we sat around and talked about the sermon, the Sunday School lesson and the music. I could hardly believe that I wanted to talk about these things; they always bored me before.

I told Marty about my court date and my sentence. He thought it was pretty cool that I choose John 3:16 Mission. He asked me what I would be doing there. I told him I had no idea, but that I didn't really care because it would be good for me.

My statement took me back. It really would be good for me to serve others. My whole life had been devoted to serving ME. Every thought, every effort and every action up to this point had been about me. When I honestly consider my life, it has been nothing but a selfish quest for pleasure. All the porn, the booze and the women were used to fill up that empty hole in my heart. Up until I God forgave me; I had never felt whole.

I wasted so much of my life. So many years could have been spent serving the Lord, but I was my own god. It was the religion of Owen-ism. I was the deity that demanded devotion but was never satisfied. I was a false god. I was worshipping myself. I was wrong.

I spent the whole afternoon with the Westbrook family. We watched a little football between snores. Marty and I were closer than we had ever been. We shared the common bond of togetherness in the Lord. It would only grow stronger.

I drove back over to The Rigsby. I had been so proud of it. Now, its empty rooms mocked the folly of my greed. I couldn't bring myself to recognize that I didn't need a fourteen thousand square foot oil mansion. I didn't know what to do with it. With the failing economy, I'd never be able to recoup my investment. I sat in my TV room and thought about it for a while. I fell asleep in my chair.

Monday morning arrived with the excitement of my community service. I imagine there aren't too many people who look forward to the actual work required in community service. I got in my truck and headed over to the John 3:16 Mission.

I would have never taken the Ferrari. It was still in the repair shop anyway. My trip home from John Painter's house was more reckless than I had remembered. I only thought I nearly smacked the concrete wall of the bridge. The long scrapes proved otherwise. I had to send it back to Arlington to get it repaired; no shop in Tulsa would touch it. My insurance man told me that most likely my claim would be denied, since I was driving drunk. The guys in Arlington told me it would cost around eighty-five thousand, including the new paint job, tires and wheels.

I reported to the Mission with my court documents in hand. They were warm and showed me where I could go to the bathroom, take a break and even get a snack. There was a choice of chores to be done. I halfway expected one of them to be washing people's feet. I chose to mop floors.

It was only ten in the morning and most of the building was empty. I worked alone for the first hour. By eleven, a man approached me and asked where the dining hall was. I had already mopped it, so I pointed him in its direction. Several other men arrived about the time I finished my job. The staff told me to wash my hands, put on some gloves and serve food in the lunch line. I spent the next hour or so, putting a spoonful of corn and a spoonful of spinach on plates and passing it to the next person.

The column of men that moved along the serving line was pretty much what I expected to see. Many lacked basic hygiene, some lacked teeth and most smiled and thanked each individual person who served them. I was extremely nervous and didn't want to make eye contact. I don't know what I was afraid of; they were just people just like me. Sure, some were drug addicts, and some brought their current circumstances upon themselves, but some were regular people who were homeless because of a variety of reasons.

The men ate their lunches with minimal conversation. I saw several of the volunteers and staff members sit down and have lunch with the people and engaged them in conversation. I watched as they treated them like real people, not like bums. I discovered I had a previously unknown prejudice against the poor. I didn't like finding that out about myself.

Gathering all the courage I could muster, I took my lunch tray and sat down next to a scruffy looking man who appeared to be in his sixties. I was shocked to learn that he was about my age. He was a veteran of the first Gulf War and had returned but never got plugged into the Veteran's Administration. His name was Spencer Ellis. He told me to call him Spence. I introduced myself, only telling him my name was Owen. I didn't want any unexpected guests at The Rigsby.

There was something wrong with Spence. To me, it appeared that part of him was still fighting in Iraq. He blinked a lot and winced each time someone banged their cup on the table. He told me that he killed lots of Iraqis and was going to have to go to Hell because of it. It broke my heart. I started to tell him about my experience with God, but as soon as I mentioned God, he stood, picked up his tray and moved to another seat.

I was dumbfounded. I figured that anyone would want to know how to be forgiven. One of the volunteers had been watching and came to sit in Spence's vacated seat. He asked me to tell him my story. He seemed genuinely excited as I told him how I was saved in the drunk tank. He gave me a broad smile when I told him I was there doing my community service. He encouraged me to continue to be friendly to the men and to be faithful to tell my story.

One by one, the men finished and placed their trays at the wash window. The staff asked me if I'd like to help wash dishes. I was taken back by their politeness. I reckoned they'd be ordering me to do this or that, but instead, they asked me if I'd like to help. I soon realized that universal respect was the way they worked. I liked it.

I spent the rest of the day doing odd jobs. I mopped the dining hall again and helped prepare for the evening meal. I spent ten hours at the Mission my first day. I drove home with a sense of fulfillment. Yes, I was doing it because I had to complete one hundred hours of community service, but it was something I needed to do.

I worked five days a week for the next three weeks, racking up 136 hours. The staff actually came and told me my obligation was completed when I hit 100 hours. They handed me a copy of the paper they were sending into the court. They thanked me for my diligent service to the Mission. I thanked them for the opportunity and told them I wasn't done, that I would be a regular volunteer.

I don't think any of them knew that I was a millionaire. I arranged to donate large sums of money anonymously to the Mission. It is something that I feel good about and it is a reputable charity that actually does what it says it is going to do.

In a moment of quiet reflection, I realized that I had forgiven John Painter. But he didn't know that yet. I didn't want him to think I still wanted to kill him, but I needed to see him and talk with him. This would be the most difficult meeting of my entire life, but perhaps the most meaningful encounter with any other human being.

I hired Pete Langford again, but this time to make contact with him and invite him to a meeting at the Santa Barbara. Pete indicated he didn't really do that kind of errand, but I found his price and he agreed. He told John Painter that I wished him no harm and wanted to meet him again, but this time in public place. He convinced him that my intentions were honorable, and Painter agreed to meet me at The Prado.

Waiting for John Painter to arrive, I was sweating worse than a ditch digger on a hot July afternoon. I drank nearly a whole pitcher of ice water. My hands were shaking, and my stomach was churning.

I saw him being led in by the Santa Barbara's maître d'. I stood and offered him a seat. He was dressed in a pair of slacks and long-sleeved shirt. He was reasonably well groomed, but he appeared wary of me.

"Mr. Painter," I said as I sat. "I'm sure you're wondering why I wanted to meet with you."

"Look," he started. I don't want no trouble."

"I don't want to give you any trouble. I need to tell you something."

"What?"

"That night, when I went to your house, I intended to kill you."

"I know. I could see it in your eyes."

"I've been mad at you my whole life. In fact, I've hated you for thirty years."

"I don't blame you for that, Mr. Rigsby. I surely don't. I want to say again how very sorry..."

"You've already asked for forgiveness, Mr. Painter. And that's what I'm offering tonight. Mr. Painter, I forgive you for killing my father," I said as tears began to fill my eyes. "I forgive you. Now, I must ask that you forgive me."

"As I told you that night, I forgive you," he said, with tears rolling down his cheeks.

"You need to know something," I said. "I got arrested for drunk driving after I left your house and spent the night in jail. It was the best thing that ever happened to me. And you played a huge part in it. That night, you told me about how you found forgiveness in prison and was born again. Those words burned in my heart all the next morning. Because you forgave me, I was forced to deal with my own selfishness and found forgiveness in Jesus, too, in the drunk tank."

"Well, praise the Lord," he said, through the tears. "I'm so glad you told me. Have you been baptized yet?"

"No, not yet. I've been thinking about it, though."

"I hope you don't think this is crazy, but I'd really like to be there when you're baptized. It'd mean a lot to me."

We sat and talked together for the next two hours. I bought him supper — one of the big steaks that I enjoy so much. He couldn't eat it all. He told me about the problems that had driven him to drink in the first place. His wife cheated on him with his best friend, then divorced him. He turned to alcohol and women to soothe his hurt. His story sounded all too familiar.

We parted not as adversaries, but as brothers in Christ, both broken men regenerated by the power of God. I'm not sure what the future holds for either of us, but I can tell you it doesn't include revenge. We can both sleep now, resting in the peace that comes from reconciliation with both God and your fellow man.

I no longer say that I am "a simple man with simple needs." I am a complicated, messed up man with only one profound need — forgiveness. What liquor, women and money could not do; God did out of His great love.

CPSIA information can be obtained
at www.ICGtesting.com
Printed in the USA
JSHW042037251022
32087JS00001B/4

9 781955 581844